INVISIBLE TERROR collection

FORBIDDEN DOORS

INVISIBLE TERROR collection

The Haunting

The Guardian

The Encounter

Bill Myers

ZONDERVAN®

ZONDERVAN.com/
AUTHORTRACKER
follow your favorite authors

We want to hear from you. Please send your comments about this book to us in care of zreview@zondervan.com. Thank you.

ZONDERVAN®

Invisible Terror Collection

The Haunting

The Guardian

The Encounter

Requests for information should be addressed to:
Zondervan, *Grand Rapids, Michigan 49530*

ISBN 978-0-310-71535-1

Interior design by Christine Orejuela-Winkelman

Printed in the United States of America

08 09 10 11 12 13 14 • 21 20 19 18 17 16 15 14 13 12 11 10 9 8 7 6 5 4 3 2 1

The Haunting

Therefore put on the full armor of God, so that when the day of evil comes, you may be able to stand your ground, and after you have done everything, to stand. Stand firm then, with the belt of truth buckled around your waist, with the breastplate of righteousness in place, and with your feet fitted with the readiness that comes from the gospel of peace. In addition to all this, take up the shield of faith, with which you can extinguish all the flaming arrows of the evil one. Take the helmet of salvation and the sword of the Spirit, which is the word of God.

Ephesians 6:13–17

1

1:36 a.m. WEDNESDAY

The cloaked figure stood outside the house. Slowly, reluctantly, she started to climb the porch stairs. At the top she reached for the doorbell, then hesitated.

"No," she whispered, her voice hoarse and pleading. "It is too late, it is— "

Suddenly she convulsed, doubling over as though someone had punched her in the gut. She leaned against the wall, gasping. Carefully, almost defiantly, she rose. She was a handsome woman, in her late fifties. Strands of salt-and-pepper hair poked out from under her hood. There was a distinct air of sophistication about her, though her face was filled with pain ... and fear.

Another convulsion hit. Harder, more painful.

She rose again. More slowly, less steadily. This time she would obey.

She stretched her thin, trembling hand toward the doorbell and pressed it. There was no response. She tried again. Nothing. The doorbell didn't work. Not surprising in this neighborhood.

She opened the screen door, which groaned in protest, then rapped on the door.

Knock-knock-knock-knock.

Rebecca was the first to hear it. She stirred slightly in bed, thinking it was still part of a dream.

The knocking repeated itself, louder, more urgent.

Her eyes opened.

Knock-knock-knock-knock.

She threw off her covers, then staggered out of bed and into the hallway. Scotty's door was shut. No surprise there. He was the world's soundest sleeper (that's the beauty of not having a care in the world). She glanced toward Mom's room, then remembered. Her mother was off at a funeral of some third aunt twice removed.

"I'll only be gone three days," she'd assured them. "I've asked that nice Susan Murdock from church to check in on you. You think you'll be okay for three days?"

Seventeen-year-old Becka and her fifteen-year-old brother figured they'd be okay for three weeks, let alone three days. They tried their best to convince Mom that they didn't need some semistranger from church checking up on them. Of course, it hadn't worked.

"Well, I'll have her drop by, just in case," Mom had said.

Becka reached the stairs and started down, hanging on to the banister for support. The cast had only been off her leg a few days, and she was still a little shaky. Then there was Muttly, her pup. His bouncing and leaping around her feet didn't help.

"Muttly, get down," she whispered. "Get down."

Knock-knock-knock-knock.

Becka reached the bottom of the stairs and crossed to the front door. She snapped on the porch light and looked through the peephole. An older, frail woman stood there. Becka hesitated. The visitor certainly looked harmless enough. And there was something very sad and frightened in her eyes.

Knock-knock-knock—

Becka unbolted the door and opened it. It stuck slightly, and she had to give it an extra yank. But even then she only opened it a crack.

"Rebecca Williams?"

"Yes."

"I am sorry to bother you at this time of evening, but there is someone . . ." She trailed off, pulling her cloak tighter as if fighting off a chill. "There is someone who needs your help."

Becka fidgeted, eyeing the woman carefully.

"Please," the woman insisted. "If I may come in for just a moment? It is most urgent."

Becka's mind raced. The woman hardly looked like a robber or a mugger. If worse came to worst, Becka could always scream and bring Scotty running downstairs. Besides, she couldn't shake the image of those eyes: tired, sad, frightened. It was against her better judgment, but—

Becka opened the door. The woman nodded a grateful thank-you and stepped into the entry hall. "You won't regret this, I assure you. My name is—" She broke off at the sound of a harsh little growl.

Becka looked down. Muttly had his hackles up and was doing his best imitation of being ferocious. "Muttly!" she scolded. "Stop that!"

The puppy growled again until Becka reached down and gave him a little thwack on the nose. He looked up at her and whined feebly.

"I'm sorry," Becka said as she turned back to the woman. "That's not like him at all. He's usually so friendly."

"It does not surprise me," the woman answered, keeping a wary eye on the animal. "I am afraid he senses it too."

"Senses it?" Becka asked. Normally she would have invited the stranger to have a seat, but at 1:30 in the morning the woman had a little more explaining to do. "What exactly does my dog sense?"

The woman pulled back her hood and shook out her hair.

It fell past her shoulders, long and beautiful. She extended her hand. "My name is Priscilla Bantini. We have not met officially, but we have many friends in common. I am the owner of the Ascension Bookshop."

Becka sucked in her breath. The Ascension Lady! The woman who owned the New Age bookstore, who made the charms for her friends ... who sponsored the kids in the Society. Becka swallowed hard. She wasn't sure how to respond.

The woman watched her carefully. "I know what you must think; however, I assure you I had nothing to do with the pranks the children have been playing on you."

Pranks! Becka thought. *I almost get hit by a train, and then I'm kidnapped by satanists. Some pranks!*

The woman continued. "Someone desperately needs our help. They have been calling upon me, begging for my assistance, but I have neither the strength nor the power."

"I'm sorry ..." Becka shook her head. "What are you talking about?"

"Someone needs help."

"What's that got to do with me?"

"You have the strength and the power they need."

Becka blinked. "What?"

The woman spoke calmly and evenly. "As a Christian, as a disciple of Christ, you have both the strength and the power to help this ... person."

Becka closed her eyes a moment. She'd heard the Ascension Lady was weird—but she didn't know she was a total fruitcake. "You're going to have to run that past me again," she said.

"There is a spirit—the soul of a deceased human—that is trapped in a mansion across town. It desperately wants to be free, to reach its resting place, but it cannot do so on its own. It needs your help."

Becka scowled. "I'm not sure what you're—"

"I know you disapprove of the source of my power, but this poor creature needs to be set free. Together you and I can—"

"What creature are you talking about?"

"The one inhabiting the Hawthorne mansion across town. It is the spirit of a human, a victim of a tragic murder, that is trapped there by negative energy. It desperately wants to be free." The woman's voice grew more urgent, her eyes more pleading. "The anniversary of its death will be here in just three days, and it is begging me, pleading with me to seek your help."

Becka shook her head. "I still don't understand. How am I supposed to be able to help?"

"According to my charts, the anniversary of the murder is in conjunction with a unique alignment of planets. This Friday, April twenty-one, is when the spirit can make its escape. This is when we can join forces—bringing it forth in a séance and helping it reach its eternal resting—"

Suddenly a voice boomed, "*What are you doing here?*"

Becka and the woman spun around to see Scott, Becka's younger brother, towering above them on the stairway. Although he was only a ninth grader, his height and position above them gave him a commanding presence.

Priscilla cleared her throat. "You must be Scott Williams. My name is—"

"I know exactly who you are." He started down the steps toward her.

Priscilla forced a smile. "Yes, well, I was just telling your sister that—"

"No one invited you here."

Becka looked on, shocked at her brother's manners. "Scott."

He continued down the stairs toward the woman, and there was no missing his anger. "Haven't you caused us enough trouble?"

Priscilla backed half a step toward the door. "I am not here to cause trouble. I am here to help. According to my astrological charts—"

"I don't give a rip about your astrological charts." He reached the bottom of the steps, but he didn't stop. He walked directly, purposefully, toward her.

"Scotty!" Rebecca exclaimed.

He turned toward Becka. "This woman brings in that channeler creep, nearly gets you killed, helps those cruds who snatched you, and you expect me to be polite?" Before Becka could answer, Scott turned back to Priscilla. "Get out of here."

The Ascension Lady reached behind her, fumbling for the door handle.

"Scotty—"

"Get out."

The woman pulled the door open and backed outside. "I apologize for the intrusion. I was expecting more Christian love, but I can certainly understand." She stumbled over the threshold as she backed out onto the porch.

Scott continued toward her. "Get off our property before I throw you off."

"I did not come for myself."

Scott reached for the door.

"As I told Becka, the spirit of a deceased human desperately needs our—"

He slammed the door shut.

Becka stood in the silence, staring at her little brother. She was both shocked and a bit in awe. Then, for the first time, she noticed he was trembling.

He turned to her. "They won't hurt you again," he said, his voice quivering. "I promise you, sis. I won't let them hurt you again."

2:45 a.m.

An hour later Scott lay in his bed, staring at the ceiling. No way would he be able to get back to sleep. Not after tonight. He was too steamed. How *dare* the Ascension Lady show up at their door. How dare she ask for a favor. After all her people had done to them? No way!

As for that cheap line she threw in about "Christian love" ... give me a break!

Normally Scott was pretty much a happy-go-lucky guy. "Live and let live," "Be everybody's bud"—those were his mottoes. And if things ever got too tense, there were always his wisecracks. But there were no jokes tonight. And for good reason.

He turned on his side, his thoughts still broiling. They had moved to this town three months ago, after Dad had died. And for three months, he and Mom and Becka had been constantly hassled by the Society and all their hocus-pocus.

Why? Why did those creeps have to keep bothering them? Weren't he and Mom and Becka the good guys? Why were they always the ones put on the defensive?

He knew Becka wouldn't fall for the woman's line about helping some deceased spirit. Becka's heart might be soft, but her brain wasn't. Still, there had to be some way to stop these guys from their constant harassment. Better yet, there had to be some way to get even.

To get even ... His eyes lit up with interest. Now there was an idea.

But even as he thought it, a still, small voice whispered that he might be stepping out-of-bounds—that getting even wasn't exactly the right plan of attack.

Scott ignored the voice. Enough was enough, and he and Becka had had enough. Again the thought of evening the score tugged at him. He toyed with contacting Z, his mysterious friend in the computer chat room. Maybe Z would know of some weakness in the Society that Scotty could use against them. But he already knew what Z's response would be. He'd heard it before.

He'd even used it before: "These people are not your enemy; they're only prisoners of your enemy."

Yeah, right. Well, prisoners or not, Scott was going to find a way to protect his sister. And it being the middle of Spring Break, he'd have plenty of time to think of something.

11:50 a.m.

Becka turned from the front seat of the car to her friends. "You sure this is the right house?"

"Oh yeah." Julie, one of her best pals — a super jock with perfect clothes and a figure to match — grinned at her. "Everyone in town knows this place, right, guys?"

The others agreed: Ryan, the driver with the killer smile; Krissi, the airhead beauty; and Krissi's part-time boyfriend and full-time intellectual, Philip.

When Rebecca had called Julie to tell her about the visit from the Ascension Lady and the invitation to participate in a séance, Julie thought it would be fun to grab the rest of the guys and go for a drive. So here they were, driving up a steep hill and slowly approaching the Hawthorne mansion.

Becka looked out her window. For a haunted house, it was a little disappointing. She'd expected something covered in weeds, unpainted, and overflowing with cobwebs and banging shutters. Granted, the place was two-and-a-half stories high and had pitched roofs sloping every which direction, but instead of looking like a home for the Addams Family, it looked more like it belonged to the Brady Bunch.

As if reading her thoughts, Julie explained. "They pay a gardener and housekeeper to keep it spruced up, just in case someone ever wants to buy it."

"It's been vacant all these years?" Becka asked.

Philip answered. "My dad's a real estate agent. They get offers all the time, but they always fall through."

Krissi giggled, “Right after they spend a few minutes alone in there.”

“You’re going to help, aren’t you?” Julie asked. “You know, take part in that séance?”

“You’re going to a séance?” Krissi asked nervously.

Philip joined in. “Hey, maybe we can all go.”

After all Rebecca had been through, attending a séance was not at the top of her “Things I Gotta Do” list. Ryan, on the other hand, was silent and noncommittal.

“Pull over here,” Philip said, pointing to the curb. “Let Becka get out and take a look.”

Ryan brought his white vintage Mustang to a stop directly across the street from the mansion. Everyone piled out except Krissi.

“Aren’t you coming?” Philip asked.

“I’m not feeling so great. I think I’ll sit this one out.”

“Come on,” Philip insisted. The others joined in until Krissi finally gave in. “All right, all right,” she whined as she crawled out of the car, “but if we die, you’re all going to live to regret it.”

No one was quite sure what she meant, but that was nothing unusual when it came to Krissi.

As they crossed the street, Ryan fell in beside Becka. Although he wasn’t officially her boyfriend, he was definitely a boy and he was definitely a friend—maybe her best. She liked everything about Ryan Riordan. But it wasn’t just his thick, black hair, his sparkling blue eyes, or that heartbreaker smile of his. It was the fact that he was always there for her. And if she needed proof, all she had to do was look at the scar on his forehead—a memento from their last encounter with the Society.

The group had just crossed the street and was standing on the walk in front of the house when Julie came to a stop. “Listen … do you hear that?”

Everyone grew quiet. It was faint, but there was no missing

the low, quiet whistling — like wind blowing through a screen window, but deeper. It almost sounded like moaning.

"Guys ..." Krissi sounded uneasy. "I don't think this is such a — "

"Shhh!" Philip scowled.

Julie took a step or two closer. "It's coming from over there." She pointed at the massive brick chimney that ran the height of the house.

"Maybe it's just the wind," Krissi offered feebly. "You know, blowing down the chimney or something."

Becka looked at the oak trees towering over their heads. There wasn't a single leaf stirring. She glanced back at the house — and then she saw it. In the second-story window. "Look!"

But by the time they'd turned, it was gone.

"What was it?" Ryan asked.

"A person. At least, I think it was. I only saw her for a second."

"Probably just the housekeeper," Julie said, not sounding all that convinced.

"I don't think so. It looked like — like a child. A little girl with long black hair."

The group exchanged nervous glances. Becka frowned. "Why? What's that mean?"

"Guys ..." It was Krissi again. She was leaning on Philip, slightly stooped. "I don't feel so good."

"What's going on?" Becka repeated. She looked at Ryan, but he gave no answer.

Krissi was clutching her stomach now, breathing deeply. Julie crossed to her. "You going to be okay? Kris, are you — "

Krissi shook her head and suddenly convulsed, once, twice — until she dropped her head and vomited.

Becka stood, staring.

Krissi caught her breath, then retched again.

"Come on," Ryan said when Krissi had finally finished. "Let's get out of here."

Krissi looked up and nodded in gratitude as Julie handed her a tissue to wipe her mouth. With Philip on one side and Julie on the other, they helped Krissi back to the car. Ryan turned and followed.

"Ryan ..." Becka tugged at his arm as they walked. "There's a little girl up there—I'm sure of it. Don't we want to see if she needs help?" They arrived at the car, and Julie and Philip helped Krissi into the back.

"Ryan?" Becka repeated. "What's wrong? What's going on?"

He opened the passenger door for her, then finally answered. He was clearly unnerved. "You know the person that was murdered there? The one who's supposed to be haunting the place?"

"Yeah?"

"It's a little girl."

2

2:04 p.m.

"Just tell me how you can be so sure," Ryan said as the surf washed up and swirled around their bare feet. The water was chilly, but it was still a great afternoon for walking on the beach ... especially for Becka ... especially with Ryan. Muttly ran ahead, barking and attacking the foam bubbles with all of his puppy fury.

Ryan continued. "People have been saying that house is haunted for years, and now you come along and say it's just a hoax?"

Becka shook her head. "That's not what I'm saying. I believe there's something there. Absolutely. I just don't think it's the ghost of some little girl."

"But you saw her," Ryan insisted. "You above all people should believe— "

"I saw something, yes. Maybe it was only a reflection. I don't know, maybe it was just the housekeeper."

Ryan snorted. "Come on, Beck. That was no housekeeper."

Becka knew he was right. She also knew it was time to shoot straight with him. But how to begin? She watched Muttly.

The foam he'd been chasing was suddenly being sucked out to sea. Unfortunately, that didn't stop the little guy from pursuing it. He ran after the foam, barking for all he was worth, until he looked up and saw a giant wall of water towering above him. He tried to turn, but it was too late. The water crashed down on him, twirling and tumbling him like a stuffed toy, until it finally threw him back up on the beach. He coughed and snorted, looking around all confused.

Becka tried not to laugh. "Ohhh, poor Muttly." She slapped her leg. "Come here, boy, come on." The dog leaped to his feet and bounded toward her as if nothing had happened. She knelt down and patted him a few times until he spotted another clump of foam and raced off for another attack.

Becka rose and took a deep breath. "Ryan ... you've been reading the Bible we gave you, right?"

He nodded. "Pretty good stuff."

"Have you run across the part that says if we're away from the body then we're at home with the Lord?"

Ryan frowned. "Meaning?"

"Meaning that once we die, we go straight to be with the Lord. No stopovers at haunted houses. No guest appearances at séances or with Ouija boards. Just death. Then God and judgment."

"So what you're saying is ...?"

"That could not have been a little girl's spirit."

"Beck—" there was the slightest trace of impatience in his voice—"how can you deny what you saw with your own eyes?"

"I can only go by what the Bible says."

Ryan picked up a stone to skip. It was obvious he didn't want this to become their first argument. "Look, the Bible makes a lot of sense—especially what it says about Jesus and stuff. But ... I mean, it doesn't have to be a hundred percent right about everything."

"Why not?"

"Why not?" Ryan paused, trying to put his thoughts into words. "Well ... it was a long time ago."

"But if we can't believe what it says about everything, how can we believe what it says about anything?"

He opened his mouth to answer, but nothing came.

Becka reached for his hand, making it clear that she wasn't trying to preach. A while back he had started to read the New Testament. Every once in a while they talked about God and Jesus, but it was never a forced thing. Usually Ryan would just have a question, and Becka would do her best to come up with an answer.

But now ... now they were entering an area in which she definitely had more experience. You don't grow up in the remote Amazon jungles around natives practicing voodoo and witchcraft without learning something about the darker side of the supernatural. Then of course there were the more recent attacks from the Society. Both she and Scott had learned a lot. Becka took a deep breath and tried again. "Ryan ... I believe what I saw in the window was not a person."

Ryan nodded. "Agreed."

"But it was not some departed spirit, either."

"Then what?"

"My best guess? It was a demon."

Ryan threw her a look.

She shrugged. "That's exactly what we ran into when Scott was fighting the Society's Ouija board. He thought it was our dad talking to him, but it was nothing more than some demon pretending to be him. My dad's in heaven with God."

Ryan looked out over the water. He didn't agree, but he didn't disagree, either. "And ... what exactly do you mean by 'demon'?"

"Angels that got thrown out of heaven when they followed Satan."

Ryan looked at her like she had to be joking.

She wasn't.

They walked in silence a long moment, neither sure what the other was thinking. Finally Ryan spoke. "But … if you saw a little girl in the window, and it was the same little girl others have been seeing for years, and if a little girl was murdered in that house …"

"But how do we know?" Becka asked. Ryan looked at her and she continued. "Isn't it just like what you were saying about the Bible? If it happened so long ago, how do we know anybody was even murdered there?"

"That's completely different."

"Why?"

"Why?" Ryan repeated. "Well, because … because it is, that's why."

Becka grinned. She had him and he knew it. He frowned, then slowed to a stop. "There is one way, though … one way to find out."

She searched his face. "How's that?"

"Come on." He turned and pulled her toward the car as he called over his shoulder, "Let's go, Muttly! Come on, fella." The dog gave a couple of yaps, then raced after them.

"Ryan, where are we going? … Ryan?"

He gave her a smile. "It's time you and I do a little ghost hunting."

2:30 p.m.

Darryl, Scott's nerdy friend, approached Cornelius's perch and began teasing the parrot with his finger. Cornelius bobbed up and down, giving an occasional *CRUAWK* or *SQUAWK* of irritation. Darryl paid little attention. "So you really want to get even with the Society?" his voice squeaked. Darryl's voice always squeaked. Today it sounded like part squealing tires and part fingernails on a blackboard.

"Absolutely," Scott said as he plopped on his bed and began cracking sunflower seeds between his teeth. "I'm tired of being their punching bag. I don't know what the Ascension Lady is up to with her séance stuff, but it's time for a little 'eye for an eye.'"

Darryl gave a loud sniff and continued teasing Cornelius. "How're you going to do it?"

Scott cracked another sunflower seed. "Uh, Darryl, I wouldn't be doing that to Cornelius if I were you. He packs a pretty mean bite."

Darryl shrugged and repeated the question. "How're you going to get even?"

"I've been giving it a lot of thought. The surest revenge is to go for the leader."

"You mean Brooke?"

Scott shook his head. "She's pretty much out of the picture since the kidnapping. I'm talking the Ascension Lady."

Darryl's eyes widened in surprise. "Priscilla Bantini?"

Scott nodded.

Darryl gave a nervous sniff. "I don't know. She's pretty heavy-duty."

"So much the better." Scott cracked another seed.

"But ... I mean, she knows stuff."

"You're saying she's psychic?"

"For starters, yeah. How can you pull off something on someone who knows everything?"

"I'm not sure." He reached for another handful of seeds. "The trick is to find a weakness."

"Good luck." Darryl pushed up his glasses. "Between her psychic abilities, her magic potions, and her astrology charts, she's got everything pretty well covered."

"Astrology charts?" Scott stopped cracking the seeds. "She's an astrology nut?"

"The biggest. She claims it's her 'insight to the future.'"

"So what does she use? Books and charts and stuff?"

Darryl turned back to Cornelius and resumed teasing the bird. "It's all done on computer."

"On computer, huh?" Scott's mind started turning.

"What are you thinking?"

"Your cousin, the computer hack ..."

"Hubert?"

"You think he might want to help us out again?"

"Depends." He looked back to Scott. "What's up?"

Scott rose to his feet and crossed over to his own computer at the desk. "I'm not sure. Let me check with Z first, see what he knows about astrology."

"You're going to talk to Z? Now?" There was no missing the interest in Darryl's voice. Z was a mystery. The man (or woman—they really didn't know) had become Scott's private source of information on the occult. Z knew everything. And not just about the occult. Sometimes he knew about their own personal lives, things only family would know—which often gave Scott and Becka the willies. But Z would never reveal his identity. They'd even tried to track him down once, but with little success.

Z was always one step ahead.

Darryl pushed up his glasses and gave another obnoxious sniff. "Doesn't he, like, you know, just talk to you at night?"

Scott snapped on the computer. "Usually ... but I can still leave a message."

Darryl nodded, then suddenly let out a bloodcurdling scream as he grabbed his finger. "OWWWW!"

"*SQUAWK*. MAKE MY DAY, PUNK, MAKE MY DAY!"

Scott looked up from the computer and chuckled. "I told you not to tease my bird."

Darryl glared at Cornelius as the bird continued bobbing up and down, a particularly satisfied gleam in his beady black eyes.

"MAKE MY DAY, MAKE MY DAY, MAKE MY DAY."

3:23 p.m.

When Ryan had suggested ghost hunting, the last place in the world Becka thought they'd wind up was in the public library. But here they were, inside the dimly lit microfilm-viewing room. Before them were a dozen boxes of microfilm envelopes, with one packet of envelopes for each year that the *Crescent Bay Gazette* had been in publication.

"Here's the last of them," the librarian said with a grin as he hauled in the final two boxes and placed them atop the others. "All one hundred and forty three years. If there's anything about your little girl or her murder, it'll be right here."

Becka and Ryan stared blankly at the boxes. "But where?" Ryan asked. "Where do we start?"

"Well, son," the old man chuckled, "that's your job now, isn't it?" With that he turned and shuffled out of the room. He stuck his head back in to say, "We close at six," then gave them a wink and shut the door behind him.

At first Becka and Ryan were overwhelmed. But soon they started to make headway. Well, sort of …

Becka remembered the Ascension Lady wanting the séance the day after tomorrow; that was Friday, the twenty-first. "She'd said the twenty-first was some sort of window," Becka explained. "The anniversary of the girl's murder."

Ryan nodded. "Then that's the date to check."

Becka moaned. "But that's one hundred and forty-three issues."

Ryan flashed her his famous grin. "Guess we'd better get started, then."

Reluctantly she reached down and turned on the bulky microfilm machine in front of her. The screen glowed and a little fan inside began to whir. Ryan followed suit with his own machine.

"Let's start with last year and work backward," Becka suggested.

The hours dragged on as they went through year after year. Some of the history was interesting, but for the most part it was a continual stream of boring who-did-what-to-whom or who-built-this-and-bought-that.

Because of the date, there were frequent articles on the Easter season and various church services. This got Becka to thinking about their previous conversation. "Hey, Ryan, how come you believe all this stuff happened—" she nodded at the pile of microfilm—"but you don't believe the Bible?"

Ryan threw her a glance. "Run that past me again."

"Why do you accept all this stuff as history, but not the Bible?"

"Well, this stuff was accurately reported. It was witnessed by the people who lived here."

"And the Bible?"

"It's thousands of years old."

"And?"

"Well, there's nobody around to prove it."

Becka thought this over as she continued going through the microfilm. Ryan had a point. And yet, no one was alive today who could prove George Washington was the first president. Or that Columbus had sailed to America. Before she could put these thoughts into words, Ryan let out a groan.

"What's wrong?" She looked over to his machine. He was on the last microfilm. "There's nothing here; we missed it." He leaned back in his chair and rubbed his eyes. "We've gone through every April twenty-first issue, and there's nothing, not a thing."

Rebecca closed her eyes. She hadn't realized how tired she was.

"So," Ryan continued, "for all these years that murder has only been a rumor? No one was really killed at the mansion?" He looked at her and raised an eyebrow. "That means your theory about no ghosts might be correct."

Becka nodded, grateful that she'd been proven right. But the victory was short-lived. Soon Ryan was tapping his finger on his jaw, the way he always did when he thought. "Unless ..." She watched. He continued, "If the murder took place on the twenty-first ... Oh, man ..."

"What?" Becka asked. "What's wrong?"

"It wouldn't be in the papers on April twenty-first. That's the night it happened. If it was a murder, it would be in the paper the next day or the day after that."

It was Becka's turn to groan. Her eyes were tired and her neck was stiff. But he was right. "Does that mean we have to start all over again?"

"Not if you don't want to." She caught the twinkle in his eye. "If you want to concede and admit you were wrong, that's okay with me."

"No way, bucko." She grinned. "If you can hang on, I can hang on."

"What a man." He smirked. "What a man."

She gave him a look, and they started all over again from the top—this time checking out April twenty-second and twenty-third.

In less than an hour, Becka found it. The article was dated April 23, 1939, and the headline read, "Man Arrested for Murder of Maid's Daughter."

"Take a look," she said. Ryan joined her, and they read the article together:

> Mr. Daniel Hawthorne was arrested Friday evening and charged with the murder of his housekeeper's daughter, Juanita Garcia, age eight. Juanita's mother, Mrs. Maria

Garcia, had been employed by Hawthorne for nine months. Both mother and daughter were citizens of Mexico. Friday evening, around 10:00 p.m., neighbors heard what was described as the screaming of a little girl and telephoned the police. Juanita was found on the second-story bedroom floor, lying in a pool of blood. She had been stabbed countless times. Police Chief Warren believes the girl underwent extreme suffering before her demise. Hawthorne has denied all charges despite the fact that when police arrested him, his face and neck were scratched, his clothing was torn, and he was covered in blood. Hawthorne offered no explanation for his condition.

The more Becka read, the lower her heart sank. Not only over the little girl's fate, but also because of her own defeat. And maybe the Bible's. Granted, just because a girl was murdered in that house didn't automatically mean the place was haunted by her ghost. But there was something else gnawing at Becka.

Ryan noticed her expression. "Beck, you okay?"

She continued staring at the screen. "That girl, Juanita, was from Mexico."

Ryan nodded. "Yeah. So?"

"The little girl I saw up in the window ... she had dark hair and skin. She could have easily been Mexican."

3

11:54 p.m.

Once again Scott had a difficult time getting to sleep. His mind churned with anger—and with thoughts of revenge. He ran scene after scene through his head, thinking of ways to get even, to make the Ascension Lady look like a fool.

He rolled over and looked at his radio clock. It was hard to make out the exact time through his dirty socks, but he knew it was late. A thought came to mind. He threw off the covers and padded across to his computer. He snapped it on, typed in a few command strokes, and entered the chat room. He moved and clicked the mouse only to discover that Z had left a message.

To: New Kid
From: Z
Topic: Astrology
Good to hear from you. Most occult experts think astrology is foolishness. Even your Bible mocks those who believe it: "All the counsel you have received has only worn you out! Let your astrologers come forward, those stargazers who make predictions month by month, let

them save you from what is coming upon you. Surely they are like stubble; the fire will burn them up. They cannot even save themselves from the power of the flame. Here are no coals to warm anyone; here is no fire to sit by" (Isaiah 47:13–14).

FACTS:

• Astrology is the belief that lives are controlled by the position of the stars. The theory has several holes. First, it was conceived and based on the idea that the stars rotated around the earth. (Most of us have discovered that's not true.) Second, there are different versions of astrology with many directly opposing each other. Some believe there are 8 signs of the zodiac; others believe 12, 14, or even 24. Third, it is difficult to find any two astrologers who will give the same advice to the same person on the same day.

Even with these holes and a lack of any supporting scientific evidence, people still believe.

• God is opposed to practicing astrology for many reasons:

1. It takes away our freedom of choice. After all, "It was in the stars—what could I do?"
2. It's turning to sources other than God for your hope, future, and well-being.
3. It's a form of manipulation. Since we're all open to suggestions if somebody or something tells us we will be doing a certain thing, we may just find ourselves starting to do it.

As far as supernatural powers, astrology is like any other superstition: It has no power unless people allow it to direct their lives. For this reason, although it is one of the silliest forms of the occult, it can still harm those who insist upon believing it.

Z

Scott read the final line again: "It can still harm those who insist upon believing it." A smile slowly crept across his lips. "It can still harm those who insist upon believing it." He reached over and shut off the machine.

Somewhere in the back of his head that still, small voice was whispering, *It's wrong. Stop seeking revenge.* But as he crossed back to bed and crawled under the covers, he was able to push that voice aside and replace it with another:

It can harm those who insist upon believing it.

12:10 a.m. THURSDAY

Rebecca's mind reeled with the new information on the little girl. Maybe Ryan was right; maybe the Bible couldn't always be trusted. Maybe with the big picture, yes. But after all those years, maybe some of the details had been tweaked or changed.

She slept restlessly, tossing and turning, dreaming of pretty little Mexican girls with long black hair and pleading eyes. Then she heard knocking. Reluctantly she pried open her eyes.

Knock-knock-knock-knock.

For the second night in a row, Becka threw off her covers, staggered into the hall, and stumbled down the steps. By the time she reached the door, the knocking had stopped. She snapped on the porch light and checked through the peephole. Nobody.

She unlocked the door and stepped outside. The air was cold and the fog was thick, but nobody was in sight. With a sigh she stepped back in. Then, just before closing the door, she noticed a small black case on the doormat. Frowning, she bent down and picked up a videocassette. An envelope was taped to the top.

Becka took one last look up and down the street, then closed the door. As usual she had to give it an extra push before it would shut. She fumbled to snap on the light in the entry hall, then squinted under the glaring brightness. She opened the envelope and pulled out a letter.

Dear Rebecca,

The alignment is less than 48 hours away. I understand your fears and doubts. But please, please remember the child desperately needs our help. This video documents research by a group of parapsychologists who investigated the house back in 1993. Please look it over and get back to me. We have so little time remaining.

Priscilla

Becka stared at the letter, feeling a chill—along with her growing doubts.

10:15 a.m.

Scott and Darryl crossed town, entered a dilapidated two-story house that hadn't seen paint since Columbus took up sailing, waded up a stairway covered in thousands of electronic gizmos and gadgets (not to mention empty pizza boxes), and finally entered the room where Darryl's cousin, Hubert, worked his computer magic. To say Hubert was an eccentric hermit might be rude. To say that the guy ate, drank, slept, and breathed computers (while never bothering to shower) would at least be accurate.

Scott and Darryl had used Hubert's computer genius once before to track down Z. Of course, they'd failed, but that wasn't Hubert's fault. Hubert was good. Very good. Z was just better. A lot better.

"So ..." Hubert wiped his nose with the back of his hand. He didn't bother looking up. He was too busy soldering something from the mountain of electro-junk before him. "You want this Priscilla person to pull up a bunch of bogus zodiac info on her computer in hopes that she'll follow it, right?" He gave a loud sniff and pushed up his glasses, which looked identical to Darryl's except for the masking tape holding them together.

"Yeah." Darryl gave a sniff back to him. "Can you do it?"

As if to answer Darryl's sniff, Hubert gave another sniff (it was easy to tell these two were related). "No sweat. I build you a Remote Data Acquisition Device, you break into her place, hardwire it directly to her CPU's database, make sure she calls up all necessary data onto her monitor, then you break back into her place, remove the R-DAD, and return it to me."

Scott and Darryl traded uneasy looks.

Darryl cleared his throat and asked hopefully, "And then you'll be able to make her do what we want, right?"

"No way." Hubert took another swipe at his nose. "Next I'll need to rewrite her existing program, give it to you, you'll have to break back in the place for a third time, load it into her computer, and exit without being detected."

Scott's heart sank. "Isn't there, you know, any easier way?"

"Easier?" Hubert scoffed. "You want easier!?"

"Well, yeah . . ."

"You didn't say you wanted it easy." Hubert sighed his best why-am-I-surrounded-by-morons sigh. Then, still without looking up, he produced a single computer disk. He handed it to Scott and said, "Just stick this into her computer."

Scott and Darryl stood dumbfounded. "That's it?"

"Of course that's it." Hubert gave a louder-than-normal sniff. "It will provide me access to her main database and mass storage through her modem, where I can ascertain the specific astrological program and download it to my system. Most likely it will be a program from which I can surreptitiously procure the source code, which is no doubt written in language C+, thereby allowing me to reconfigure her program to produce any response you desire."

"Oh," Darryl said, exchanging blank looks with Scott.

"Of course." Scott nodded.

There was a long pause. Darryl and Hubert both gave loud sniffs.

"So," Scott asked, "how soon can we do this?"

"Load her computer tonight, then come back here while I work on the program. By tomorrow morning, she'll do whatever we say." Hubert gave one loud and extremely long sniff, making it clear that their meeting was over.

Moments later Scott and Darryl were scampering down Hubert's rickety porch steps toward their bikes.

"That cousin of yours sure has a brain," Scott said.

"Yeah," Darryl said, drawing in a deep breath of fresh air and obviously enjoying it. "Too bad we can't convince him to try a shower."

Scott grinned as he climbed on his bike. "Once he changes Priscilla's chart, you're sure she'll follow it?"

"Hey," Darryl sniffed, "if it's on her astrological chart, she'll do it. I've listened to her talk about this stuff. Believe me, she'll do whatever it says."

Scott began to smile. He liked that idea. A lot.

They rode off. "So when do you want to do it?" Darryl asked.

"Do what?"

"Load this disk," Darryl said, patting the shirt pocket that held the disk.

"How 'bout tonight? Can you get us in?"

"A piece of cake. What time?"

"I don't know. How does midnight sound?"

"Perfect." Darryl grinned. "The Bookshop tonight, at midnight."

5:48 p.m.

Julie paused her ancient VCR, and the group stared at the freeze-frame picture on the screen. Becka had taken the videocassette over to Julie's house, and after viewing it, they had decided to invite Ryan, Krissi, and Philip over for a "second opinion."

"There," Julie said, pointing to the screen, which showed a long hallway full of doors. Several cameras and measuring devices were scattered up and down the hall. "This is where it gets interesting."

Julie pushed the Pause button again, and the video started. Everyone watched in silence. For several seconds nothing happened. Then, ever so gradually, some of the papers and charts on the hallway floor began to stir.

"Did someone open a window?" Ryan asked.

No one answered. The wind grew more intense. Some of the instruments mounted in the hallway began to shudder. Suddenly one with aluminum cloth stretched between brackets blew over and fell with a crash.

Krissi gave a start.

"Hang on," Julie said. "It's not over yet. Keep your eye on the farthest door, the one at the end of the hall."

More seconds passed. The wind increased until suddenly the door flew open. The entire group jumped. As they watched, a small shadowy figure from inside the room darted past the doorway and out of sight.

"What was that?" Ryan demanded.

Julie pressed Slow Motion Rewind. The figure reappeared, moving backward. When it was in the center of the door's opening, she pressed Pause.

"Wow," Philip said as he dropped to his knees and got a better look.

"What is it?" Krissi chirped a little nervously.

"That's what we want to know," Julie said. "It's so far away and so blurry, it's hard to tell."

Everyone continued staring. "It looks like a little girl," Philip finally said. He moved closer to the screen and pointed. "See, here's her hair, long and dark, it's blowing all over the place, and this, this could be an arm ..."

An eerie silence stole over the group.

Finally Ryan turned to Rebecca. "Is this who you saw in the window yesterday?"

Becka looked at the ground.

Ryan continued—not mean, just perplexed. "And you still don't think it's a ghost?"

When Becka answered, her voice was just above a mumble. "I'm ... I'm not sure. It looks just like the girl, but Scotty and I—" she glanced up and held Ryan's gaze—"we've been fooled before."

"I think we should all go there and investigate," Philip said.

Becka answered quietly. "I don't think that's such a good idea."

"Why not?" he insisted. "You might be in danger if you go with the Ascension Lady. I say we go ahead of time and check out the place."

Becka swallowed, struggling to find the right words.

Ryan reached out and touched her shoulder. They'd had enough talks about the supernatural for Ryan to know what was on her mind. "Beck's afraid because we're not Christians. She's afraid we might get hurt."

A strange sort of silence filled the room. Finally Julie spoke. "Is that true? Is that what you think?"

Becka searched for the words. She didn't want to sound high-and-mighty or judgmental to her friends, yet they deserved to hear the truth. "The Bible says there's no such things as ghosts. Only demons."

"And angels," Krissi interrupted, trying to sound cheery. "Don't forget angels."

"Angels don't go around haunting houses," Julie corrected.

Becka hesitated, then continued. "So, if I'm right, that little girl is not a ghost, but ... a demon."

Philip asked the next question. "And you're worried about us, because . . . ?"

Here it comes, Becka thought. *There's no getting around it.* "Because Jesus gave those who believe in him authority over demons." There—she'd said it. She took a breath and waited.

"And the rest of us?" Philip persisted.

"I . . ." Becka looked down. "I'm not sure of the details."

After a moment, Krissi blurted, "Hey, I'm a Christian." The group turned to her in vague surprise. "Sure, I go to church every Christmas, sometimes Easter too."

Everyone chuckled. "I think there's more to it than just that," Ryan said kindly. "From what I've been reading in the Bible, it's not just a church thing; it's what you believe inside . . . and what you do with it."

Becka looked at Ryan. He gave her a wink.

"I say we investigate anyway," Philip insisted. "Take our chances."

"And if we're wrong?" Julie asked with an arched eyebrow. "If it's more than just a ghost?"

"Then we got our own personal Ghostbuster." Philip gave Becka a playful nudge. "Right, Beck?"

She smiled feebly.

"When?" Julie asked. "I mean, if the Ascension Lady wants a séance tomorrow night, then we should probably do it— "

"Tonight," Philip finished for her. "Let's grab something to eat and hit the place about eight."

"Sounds good to me." Julie grinned.

Ryan also nodded, but more slowly as he kept a careful eye on Becka.

"I don't know, guys," Krissi whined, her hand going to her stomach. "Not after yesterday."

"Come on, babe." Philip grinned encouragingly. "I'll be right beside you. It should be fun."

"Yeah," Julie agreed, "it'll be fun."

Becka's eyes drifted back to the frozen image on the TV screen. Somehow, *fun* wasn't exactly the word she had in mind.

"Beck?" She turned to see Ryan at her side. He spoke quietly. "You going to be all right?"

She nodded.

"How 'bout Scotty?" he asked. "It might not hurt to have him along."

Becka broke into a grateful smile. Of course he was right. It wouldn't hurt to have her little brother along. It wouldn't hurt one bit.

Or so she thought …

4

7:10 p.m.

Hey, check this out," Scott said as he pulled his Bible closer. "Remember when Jesus cast those demons out of that guy and into the herd of pigs?"

Becka looked up from her Bible and notes, which she had spread out on the kitchen table. "Yeah, so?"

"Do you know why Jesus sent them into the pigs?"

She shrugged.

"Because—" Scott looked down and read: " 'They begged him repeatedly not to order them to go into the Abyss.' "

"The abyss? That's hell, isn't it? The 'bottomless pit'?"

Scott nodded. "And from what this says, it's so bad even the demons don't want to hang out there. Cool, huh?"

Cool wasn't exactly the word Rebecca had in mind. She glanced at her watch. "Look, we've got less than an hour before we go to the mansion. Let's stick to the subject and keep getting ready, all right?"

"This *is* the subject," he said defensively. "Well ... sort of."

She gave him a look, then turned back to her notes. Ever since their first encounter with the Society, she and Scott had started paying a lot more attention to spiritual warfare—jotting down verses from the Bible, sharing information. Now, before they went to the mansion, they'd agreed to review what they'd learned and to spend some time praying.

"Okay," Becka said, then cleared her throat. "First, we know about the armor of God."

"Check," Scott said. "The shield of faith, the sword of the spirit, the helmet of ... whatever. We've been through all that already."

Becka hesitated. She wasn't too thrilled by Scott's careless attitude, but she continued. "Second, we know Christ gives us authority over Satan."

Scott leaned back, put his hands on top of his head, and quoted: " 'I have given you authority to trample on snakes and scorpions and to overcome all the power of the enemy; nothing will harm you,' and 'Whatever you bind on earth will be bound in heaven.' "

Becka was impressed. She looked back at her notes. "Here's one on Satan: 'There is no truth in him. When he lies, he speaks his native language, for he is a liar and the father of lies.' "

"Meaning?"

"Meaning we shouldn't believe what Satan or his little demon creeps say."

Scott nodded.

"Here's another: 'If two of you on earth agree about anything you ask for, it will be done for you by my Father in heaven.' "

"Okay, all right," Scott said, nodding again. "Let's get down to the agreeing part." He closed his Bible with a thump. "Let's do some praying and get going."

Becka glanced at her notes. There were a dozen more verses ... but because of time—and Scott's impatience—they would have to wait. Reluctantly she closed her Bible. Something didn't feel right. She couldn't figure out what, exactly, but it made her nervous.

Very nervous.

"Dear Lord . . . ," Scott started, his eyes closed. Becka bowed her head and joined him.

8:03 p.m.

"How're we getting in?" Ryan whispered.

"Don't these old places have coal chutes or something?" Julie asked, shining her flashlight along the back of the house. "You know, some sort of slide thing that goes into the cellar?" The group huddled together in the thick, dripping fog near the back kitchen entrance of the mansion. They were well out of sight of the street.

"We could always break a window," Krissi suggested.

Scott smirked. "Only if we want the neighbors to call the cops."

"So what do we do?" Julie demanded.

"How 'bout using the door?"

They turned to see Philip effortlessly push open the back kitchen door.

"How'd you pull that off?" Julie asked.

Philip held up a single key. "My dad's the realtor, remember?"

The others snapped on their flashlights and stepped through the door into the darkness. Julie led the way, followed by Krissi, Philip, and Ryan. Rebecca and Scott were the last to enter. Scott was scowling hard and rubbing the back of his neck.

"You okay?" Becka asked.

He nodded. "I've got the world's biggest headache."

"From what?"

"I don't know. It came on real sudden, soon as we crossed the street."

"You want to go back, stay in the car?"

"Forget it." He tried to smile and make one of his jokes. "I'm in the mood for kicking a few demons' behinds, aren't you?"

It was Becka's turn to force a smile. Scott wasn't just bragging—though he was pretty good at that—he was also speaking from experience. He'd faced demons several times before and come out the winner.

Each time, she and Scott had fought, and each time, thanks to prayer and God's power, they had won. Barely. But barely was close enough.

But tonight ... tonight something was wrong. She was growing more and more sure of that. Besides the uneasy feeling she couldn't seem to shake, there was also the fact that Scott was feeling sick. Scott hardly ever got sick. And, as far as she knew, he never had headaches. So what was going on? For the time being she said nothing more. But she would keep a careful eye on him.

Once inside, things went pretty much as expected. After the initial goofing off—grabbing and scaring each other—they settled down to exploring the ground floor.

First there was the kitchen. It was massive: double ovens, pantry, lots of counter space, cupboards. *Mom would go nuts here,* Becka thought.

Next came the dining room, then the music room, then the glass-enclosed conservatory, and finally the giant entry hall.

"Wow," Philip exclaimed as they shone their lights on the rich mahogany paneling, the towering gilded mirrors, and a floor that was completely covered by thick gray slate.

Everyone was impressed. Everyone but Scott. He was standing off to the side, hunched over and holding his head.

"Hey, Scotty," Ryan asked, "what's wrong?"

Scott lowered his hands and tried to smile, but it was more of a grimace. "I don't know. My head ... it's like a herd of elephants tap-dancing inside."

Becka and Ryan exchanged looks.

Krissi was shivering. "I'm cold. Couldn't someone turn up the heat?"

"Uh, I don't think so," Philip chuckled.

"Look at this." Julie was slightly ahead of the group, shining her light up at a giant crystal chandelier. It was directly over her head and breathtakingly beautiful. But it wasn't the beauty she was referring to. It was the movement of the crystals. They had started to gently clink against each other.

"Must be wind," Ryan offered, but he didn't sound too convinced. He turned back to Scott and Becka. "You were the last ones in. Did you guys shut the door?"

"Yeah," Becka answered softly, "we shut it."

The clinking grew louder as the chandelier started to sway almost imperceptibly.

"Well, now." Julie tried to sound glib. "I think maybe we should be moving on. Don't you?"

The group voiced agreement and continued forward, keeping a wary eye on the chandelier and going out of their way to avoid walking directly under it.

They arrived at the stairway. It was massive, sweeping up and above their heads. They stood a moment, looking in awe. Finally, Julie asked the inevitable. "Okay, troops ... who's going first?"

Everyone exchanged glances, but no one answered. Philip looked over his shoulder and smiled mischievously. "Becka? Scott? This is your guys' department, right?" There were a couple of nervous snickers. Philip kept looking at them, waiting for an answer. "Well?"

Scott finally stepped forward, doing one of his hokey superhero imitations. "You're right, earthling. Step aside. This is no job for mere mortals." The group chuckled as Philip happily obliged.

Becka was a little more reluctant, but she also moved forward to join her brother. She hated it when he played Mr. Macho—especially when it involved her life (or death). "What about your head?" she whispered.

"Hey—" he forced another smile—"we're the good guys, remember?"

"Scotty—"

"Come on." He motioned for her. "Let's show your friends some ol'-fashioned ghostbustin'."

"Scotty ..."

Without a word, he started for the stairs. Becka stared after him a moment, then gave a heavy sigh and followed.

The banister was made of dark wood with intricately carved designs. Elaborate stained-glass windows towered to the right, along with rich curtains trimmed in gold braid. The group had only traveled three or four steps before they noticed the breeze. It was faint at first but seemed to increase with every step they took.

To relieve the tension, someone began whistling the theme from *The Twilight Zone*. "Knock it off," Julie ordered. They did.

"Philip ..." Krissi was somewhere in the back whining again. "Philip, I'm cold."

But instead of answering her, Philip said, "Listen! Do you hear that?"

It was a low whistling, the same one they'd heard from the chimney the day before. As the wind grew stronger, the sound grew louder. Becka threw a nervous glance at Scott. He was squinting and grimacing, trying his best to hold back what appeared to be intolerable pain. Beads of sweat were forming on his forehead. "Scott," she whispered, "Scott, are you okay?"

"We've beaten these things before," he answered. "If we've got the faith, there's no reason we can't beat them now."

Becka had no answer. He was right—but something was wrong. Terribly wrong.

They were halfway up the stairway. The breeze increased. The whistling grew louder, its low drone sounding more and more human.

"I'm so cold." Krissi shivered. "Isn't anybody cold?"

"It's just your nerves," Julie said.

Philip shook his head. "I don't think so."

"Me neither," Ryan said. "Check it out." He held the flashlight up to his mouth and blew. They could all see his breath.

"Let's go back!" Krissi shuddered. "We've seen enough."

"We're practically there," Philip insisted. "Let's go on."

Becka and Scott resumed the climb. The wind blew harder, tugging at their clothes and hair. Becka looked back to her brother. He was also shivering. Violently. But it wasn't from the cold; she knew that. It was from something else. Maybe the pain. She leaned over to him. "Scotty, we don't have to go any further if— "

"Be quiet," he hissed through gritted teeth.

She pulled back a little surprised. "What?"

"The Bible says we've got authority, so we've got authority. If you don't have the faith, fine. But don't pull me down with you."

Becka could only stare. This wasn't like him. Not at all.

The eerie droning grew louder, sounding more and more like a muffled cry—as if someone was trying to scream but was being smothered.

At last they reached the landing, Becka and Scott first, followed by the others. They stood silently on top. To their right was a dust-covered window; to the left was the hallway. All eyes moved down the hall to the last door, the one they had seen on the videotape.

The cry broke into a shriek—a bloodcurdling, heart-stopping shriek. Long and continuous.

"Let's get out of here!" someone shouted.

They turned to race back down the stairs when, suddenly, the door at the end of the hall flew open, crashing loudly into the wall. The group froze. But it wasn't the wind that had thrown open the door. It was a shadow. A dark shadowy creature, looking very much like the little girl. It exploded out of the room and flew down the hall at them.

Krissi screamed. Others joined in as they scrambled for the

stairs. Everyone but Scott. Instead of running, Scott spun around to confront the shadow. From past experiences, he knew what to do. He raised his hand and, despite the throbbing in his head, he shouted, "In the name of Jesus Christ of Nazareth, I command you to—"

He said no more. The shadow smashed into him, directly into the center of his chest. He gasped and reeled backward until he hit the wall beside the window and slowly slid to the floor.

"Scotty!" Becka raced to him.

Others stood staring, dumbfounded.

"Scotty!" Becka dropped to his side. "Scotty, are you all right?" The shadow girl was gone, but the wind was still shrieking, and she had to shout to be heard. "Scotty!"

His eyes fluttered, then opened. He looked dazed and confused. "What ... what happened?"

That's what Becka wanted to know. She brushed the hair out of his eyes, searching his face for clues. She reached for his arm to help him up. "Come on, let's get you out of—"

He looked down at his chest, and suddenly his eyes widened in horror. "Get them off!" he shouted. He started slapping and hitting his chest. "Get them off!"

"What?"

"Get them off!"

"Get what off?"

"The flies!" He began to writhe and kick, all the time beating and slapping at his chest. "Get them off! Get them off!"

Becka was at a loss. "Scotty, there are no—"

"Get them off!" He was screaming. "Get them off!"

"Scotty!"

"Get them off! There's millions of them!"

She reached for his hands, trying to stop him, but he knocked her aside, continuing to slap and hit and shout and writhe.

Ryan joined their side. "It's okay, Scotty."

"Get them off!" Scott was starting to cry, tears streaming down his face.

"It's okay. We'll get them—just come with me." Ryan slipped his arm under Scott's shoulder and raised him to his feet.

"Get them off! Get them off!"

"It's okay. We're going to get you out of here."

Becka rose to follow Ryan, but as she turned she felt something cold and damp brush against her skin. She spun around to the window beside where Scott had hit the wall. In the dust a design had started to form ... all by itself. Becka felt herself growing colder.

But she would not turn away. As she watched, she began to realize it wasn't a design that was forming. It was letters. Words. Someone or something was writing on the dust of the windowpane. The letters formed slowly, but they did not stop until the message was finished. It read:

¡Ayúdame! ¡Por favor, Rebecca, ayúdame!

Becka's Spanish was rusty, but not that rusty. She knew what it said: *Help me! Please, Rebecca, help me!*

10:58 p.m.

The group had barely entered the car before Scott tried to cover his fear with a *Ghostbusters* joke. "I think I've been slimed," he said, gingerly testing his bruised ribs. But the humor fell flat. Maybe it was because his voice still had a slight tremble. Or maybe it was because of the tension that filled each member of the group.

Without a word, Ryan fired up the Mustang, and they started for home.

"I don't get it." Krissi finally broke the silence. "You kept shouting about flies."

"That's 'cause there were thousands of them, they were all over me — I was crawling with them."

"And yet we didn't see a thing," Julie said. "How weird."

"When did they leave?" Philip asked. "When did they all disappear?"

Scott looked down at his arms and chest just to make sure they had. "I don't know," he answered more quietly. "I guess — I guess by the time we got outside ... definitely by the time we got off the property."

More silence as all of the kids fell into their own thoughts ... and fears.

Rebecca's mind reeled. First, because of Scott's defeat. Weren't they supposed to have authority through Christ over this sort of stuff? And second, because of the writing on the window.

It had been in Spanish. Juanita's language.

Becka looked around the car, wondering if she should tell the others. No, that type of information would only support their theory that this was not some sort of demon, but that it was actually the little girl's ghost.

As they pulled up to the front of Becka and Scott's house, Ryan finally spoke. His voice was earnest. "I don't think you should be a part of that séance tomorrow, Beck." Rebecca looked at him. He took a deep breath and slowly let it out. "But if you decide to go ... then we should all go along with you."

More silence. Slowly each member of the group started to nod. Philip cleared his throat and said what each was thinking.

"Ryan's right. That ghost thing definitely has it in for you two. And if we're there with you ..." He hesitated.

"There's safety in numbers," Ryan finished.

"Oh, really," Scott quipped, still massaging his chest. "I hadn't noticed."

Becka looked at them. They were friends. Good friends. And she appreciated them now more than ever. "Thanks, guys." She tried to smile. "I'll let you know."

She opened the car door. After they said good night and the car pulled away, Scott and Becka headed for the front porch. Becka opened the screen door. It gave its customary groan. And then she saw it—the front door was not completely shut. The thing always stuck, and if you didn't give it an extra pull, it always stayed ajar.

"Scotty ..." Her voice grew thin and wavery as she pointed to the door.

Scott saw it too.

"I'm sure I closed it," Becka said in a half-whisper. "I always give it an extra yank."

Scott swallowed. "Me too."

They traded looks. Steeling himself with determination, Scott reached for the knob. He turned it and gave a push. It squeaked as it unstuck.

There was no other sound.

Scott entered the darkened living room, slowly, cautiously. Becka was right behind. He headed toward the nearest lamp. It was eight feet away, but it could have been eight miles. Why hadn't they left a light on before they'd gone? Then again, that had always been Mom's department. Across the room, over by the kitchen, Becka noticed the tiny red light blinking on the telephone answering machine. There were two messages.

She watched the outline of Scott's body bumping into furniture and stumbling over clothes and stuff they'd left in the middle of the room (another disadvantage of not having Mom around). He made progress toward the lamp, but far too slowly.

Then, from the hallway, Becka heard a faint snarl. At first she thought it was her imagination. She strained, listening harder. There it was again.

"Scott ..."

Before he could answer, there was sudden, animal-like clawing. Whatever it was, it had decided to make its move. It raced down the hallway, digging into the carpet, heading directly for them.

"Get that light!" Becka screamed. She could see nothing in the dark, but heard the thing tear into the room and bear down toward her. She hunched over, bracing for impact.

Suddenly the room was flooded with light as Scott clicked on the lamp to reveal—

"Muttly!" they cried in unison.

The animal leaped at Becka's legs and began bouncing and jumping all over her feet. It had been hours since he'd had any company, and the puppy was all squirming body and wagging tail. Becka stooped down and patted him. "Hello, boy, good dog, easy now, easy ..."

Scott had already started for the kitchen. "Check it out," he said, pointing to the table. "It's a note." He snapped on the kitchen light, and Becka moved in for a better look. It was a note with a key on it.

Dear Becka and Scott: Just swung by to see how everything's going. Here's the key your mom left. Hope you can make it to youth group tomorrow. Call if you need anything. Love, Susan

There was a notable sigh from both brother and sister. Susan was the youth worker from church. She must have dropped off the key, then left without knowing she had to yank the door shut.

"I guess you might say we're a little wound up," Scott said wearily.

Becka agreed.

Scott crossed to the fridge (as he always did when he got home), and Becka headed for the answering machine (as she always did when she got home). She pressed Play.

"Hi, guys, it's Mom. Beck, I had the weirdest dream about you last night. Kinda spooky. I'll have to tell you when I get back. Aunt Bernice's funeral is tomorrow. I should make it home by noon, Saturday. Don't forget the leftover casserole in the fridge, and Beck, please, *please* make sure Scotty's wearing clean T-shirts. Love you guys. Bye." *BEEP.*

Scott gave a sniff under his arms. "It's good for a few more days," he called. He stuck his head back into the fridge and resumed his search-and-devour mission.

The second message began.

"Hello ... this is Priscilla Bantini—from the Bookshop."

Becka froze.

"Juanita, or her spirit, told me what happened tonight. She wants me to say how sorry she is. You snuck up on her and frightened her, that's all. Please call me at your earliest convenience." *BEEP.*

"Frightened *her!*" Scott exclaimed. "*We* frightened *her??*"

"I don't get it," Becka sighed as she shed her jacket. It was time to say what had been rattling in her head the past twenty-four hours. "Maybe Ryan is right; maybe we can't trust the Bible in every instance."

"Whoa, hold the phone," Scott said as he pulled his head out of the fridge. "What are you talking about?"

Becka flung her jacket across the room to the growing pile of clothes on the sofa. "Figure it out. We're Christians, right?"

"Right."

"We're supposed to have authority over demons, right?"

"Right."

"Well, no offense, little brother, but you weren't exactly the conquering hero this evening."

Scott said nothing as he closed the refrigerator and crossed to the table. In his hands were a carton of milk, a jar of dill pickles, and some dijon mustard. Not exactly a gourmet meal, but it was the best he could come up with on such short notice. He pulled a pickle from the jar and dipped it into the mustard. Becka watched, trying not to retch as he crammed half of it into his mouth. She could tell he was as troubled as she was; he just expressed it differently ... by becoming a human garbage disposal.

She turned and headed for the stairs. But just before she arrived, she heard a very quiet and very heartfelt "I'm sorry, Beck."

She slowed to a stop and looked at him.

He continued softly, slowly, "I let you down... I let us both down. I'm sorry."

Becka's heart went out to him. "It's not your fault." She shrugged. "Things just aren't making sense anymore." He continued to look down, and she went on, "The Bible says there are no ghosts, yet we run into ghosts. It says to put on God's armor, to use his shield and sword to beat demons. We do and we get clobbered."

"But we've won before," Scott said, looking up at her.

Becka nodded. "Not this time. This time ... everything's going haywire." She paused a moment as they both thought through the evening. "Listen," she finally said, "you don't mind if I use the computer to talk to Z, do you?"

"I don't know that you'll get him," Scott answered as he wolfed down the second half of his mustard-covered pickle. "I doubt he'll be online, but you're welcome to try."

Becka nodded and started up the stairs. Everything was unraveling: her confidence, her little brother's strength, her faith in the Bible. Then, of course, there was tomorrow night ... the infamous séance. Should she go? Was tonight a warning that they should prepare harder?

Or was it an omen of an even darker encounter, a showdown that would lead to even greater defeat?

5

11:33 p.m.

It had taken Becka twenty minutes to log on to the computer chat room. It would have taken two minutes, but Rebecca's computer skills were as bad as Scott's eating habits. After five or six attempts, she finally got online. And to her surprise, Z was there waiting.

Good evening, Rebecca. This is our first time alone, isn't it?

Rebecca swallowed back her nervousness and typed:

Hi.

How was your evening?

She caught her breath. Did Z know about their visit to the house? Or was he just fishing? She thought about asking, then decided to skirt the issue and move on.

I know this isn't your area of expertise, but is there a way, I mean, what real proof do we have that the Bible is 100% true 100% of the time?

There was a pause. A moment later the following verse appeared:

"All Scripture is inspired by God ..." 2 Timothy 3:16 (New Living Translation).

You mean people got all worked up and inspired by God so they started writing a bunch of—

No. In the original language *inspired* means "God-breathed." So all Scripture is breathed by God.

Becka thought a moment, then typed:

But just because the Bible says it's true ... Just because something says it's true, doesn't mean it's true.

There is other evidence. Jesus believed the Bible was accurate. He quoted from it frequently. In fact, when he fought Satan in the wilderness, that was all he used. Think about it—a battle between the most evil force in the universe and the Savior of the universe. They could choose any weapons they wanted, but instead of swords or guns or nuclear bombs, they used what both knew to be the most powerful force in the universe ... God's Holy Word.

Becka nodded. He had a good point. She typed back:

Everybody says it was written so long ago ...

That is correct. But in all of history there is no other book that has been proven to be so completely reliable. Again and again historians and archaeologists uncover other historical writings and ancient artifacts that prove the Bible's accuracy.

Becka stared at the screen. She was relieved. Yet, how could the Bible be so accurate when everything she had experienced in the past twenty-four hours seemed to prove it was so wrong? She looked up as the final set of words appeared:

It is late. I must sign off, but you must promise me one thing.

What's that?

Whatever your decision may be regarding tomorrow night, promise me you will be very careful. There is far more danger than meets the eye.
Z

Becka's mouth dropped open. Quickly she reached for the keyboard and typed:

Z? How do you know these things, Z?

But there was no answer. Only the last set of words:

Be very careful. There is far more danger than meets the eye.

12:11 a.m. FRIDAY

Scott hadn't bothered to tell Rebecca about the little breaking-and-entering routine he and Darryl had cooked up for that night. He figured she had enough on her mind. Come to think of it, so did he. But a promise was a promise. And revenge was sweet no matter what time of day ... or night.

"Give me a boost," Darryl's screechy voice whispered.

Scott laced his fingers together and held open his palms. Darryl stepped into them, and Scott hoisted him up to the tiny bathroom window at the back of the Ascension Bookshop.

Darryl had gone into the bookstore a few hours earlier, when it was still open, snuck into the bathroom, and unlocked the window. "I saw this on an old *MacGyver* episode," he squeaked, "or was it *Matlock?* Come to think of it, maybe it wasn't either. Maybe it was—"

"Just push open the window and get inside," Scott whispered.

"I can't reach it. Let me stand on your shoulders."

Before Scott could protest, Darryl scrambled out of Scott's hands, up his chest, and onto his shoulders—leaving plenty of greasy tread marks along the way.

"Oh, man," Scott whined as he looked down at his T-shirt.

"I still can't reach it. Let me stand on your head."

"Do what?!"

"I'm too short to reach the window. Let me stand on your head." Again Darryl's little feet scrambled, and again Scott wound up with tread marks—this time across both ears and his forehead.

Suddenly a voice demanded, "Whad—whad're you doin' down here?"

The boys froze. Because of Darryl's weight on his head, Scott couldn't turn, but he shifted his eyes as far to the right as they would go. It was Mr. Leery, the town drunk, staggering home after another long night of tipping brews. Mr. Leery continued his stumbling approach until he was staring directly up at Darryl, who was towering a good five feet above him.

"S'not right, you boyz bein' here."

Scott's mind raced. Mr. Leery was right, of course. Standing in a back alley and breaking into a bookstore at midnight was not exactly the role of a model citizen. So what was this old man going to do? Blow the whistle on them? Call the police? And what was Mom going to think when she came home and had to bail her son out of jail?

"Great," Scott moaned silently, "just great."

Mr. Leery wagged his head from side to side. "S'not at all right. You—you shudn't be here," he repeated as he continued staring up at the giant before him. "The Lakerz are playin' tonight — you should be with the res' of yer team, gettin' thoze rebounds and makin' them fanzy bazkets ... they need you, boy."

Mr. Leery threw a look up to Darryl. The little guy nodded down at the man but said nothing.

Mr. Leery nodded back, pleased that he'd made his point. "Go — go get sooted up then," he ordered and held out his hand, waiting for a high five.

Darryl reached out and obliged. Of course Mr. Leery didn't quite connect with his hand, but it was close enough. The old-timer turned and staggered away, pleased that he'd done his part to help the L.A. Lakers toward another championship.

Scott stared after him. He knew his mouth was hanging open, but he didn't much care.

As soon as the man staggered out of sight, Darryl burst out laughing.

"Come on," Scott ordered, "you're killing my head."

Darryl resumed twisting and turning atop Scott's skull (grinding in any grease he hadn't already wiped off on Scott's face and T-shirt) until he finally pushed open the bathroom window and squirmed inside.

"How long will it take?" Scott whispered up to the window.

"Just long enough to get her computer up and load in the program. Ten minutes max."

Scott breathed a sigh and threw another cautious glance up the alley. He looked down at his stained T-shirt and began rubbing the top of his head. This revenge business sure could be painful. He glanced at his watch. They still had to run over to Hubert's and get him to reprogram the astrological charts. But with any luck, they'd have the Ascension Lady making a major fool of herself by morning.

12:54 a.m.

Earthquake!

The thought exploded in Becka's mind and sent her bolting upright in bed. Having moved to California, she figured she'd eventually experience some rocking and rolling from Mother Nature. She just hadn't planned on experiencing it quite this soon. But here it was.

Or was it?

Her room was lit by only an outside streetlamp that shone through the window, but even then she could tell that nothing else in the room was moving. Not her bookshelves, not the lamp on her nightstand, not even the water in the fishbowl on her dresser. Only her bed.

She laid her hand on the mattress. It wasn't her imagination — the bed really was vibrating. Not a lot, but enough.

Next she noticed the cold. Saw it, really. White puffs of breath coming from her mouth ... exactly as they had in the mansion. She threw a look to the window. It was closed. Even if it had been open, it was spring outside. And spring in this part of the country did not mean this type of cold.

The shaking increased. Soon the headboard started banging against the wall. But there was another sound too. A buzzing — faint at first, then it grew louder and louder with the shaking. Becka pulled the blankets up around her. Part of her wanted to leap out of the bed and run for her life. And part of her was too frightened to move. For the moment, the "too frightened" part was winning.

She shivered. But it wasn't from the cold or even from the fear. It was something else. She couldn't put her finger on it, but there was something even icier, even more frightening, in the room. Something she'd felt before ...

Her heart pounded. It was the same cold dampness that had brushed against her in the hallway of the mansion. And now it was touching her face.

The shaking of the bed turned to violent lungings. The buzzing sounded like a thousand flies circling her head, like a chain saw roaring. She opened her mouth to yell to her brother in the next room, but no sound came. The cold dampness had wrapped itself around her throat and was quickly tightening its grip. She tried breathing, but her air was being shut off. It was strangling her, suffocating her.

It was trying to kill her.

She reached to her neck, clawing at it, trying to peel whatever it was away. But there was nothing to grab. Just icy dampness. Her lungs pleaded for air. She twisted and struggled, trying to draw in the slightest breath. No air would come.

The bed was bouncing out of control, its headboard crashing into the wall with every leap. Becka's lungs burned, screaming for air. The outside edges of her vision started to grow white. She was going to pass out; she knew the signs. She had to do something, and it had to be fast. Mustering all of her strength into one final act of defiance, she lunged forward and—

Becka bolted awake in bed.

It had been a dream! She sat on her bed, gasping for breath, filling her lungs with precious oxygen and her mind with blessed reality. Strange. Everything had seemed so true, so real. It was definitely not your average nightmare. But she was awake now. She was safe.

Yet, even as she sat there, catching her breath, forcing herself to relax, she noticed something that sent another chill through her body. Small white puffs of breath were coming from her mouth. The same chill she had felt in her dream was there, in her room. The same cold dampness. And this time it was for real. She looked at her window and sucked in her breath. A thick layer of frost had formed ... on the inside.

"Scott!" she called. "Scotty!" There was no response.

She threw off the covers. She was getting out of there. She was not falling victim to this thing a second time.

Her feet barely touched the floor before she stopped. The skin on her arm prickled as something icy touched it. The sensation traveled up her arm and across her body, making her give an involuntary shudder. Then it was gone. Almost. Whatever it was, it was still in the room.

She'd had enough. This was her bedroom—she wasn't about to be driven out of her own room. She cleared her throat and demanded, "What ... who are you?" There was no answer, but she would not be put off that easily. "I said, who are you?" Still no answer.

Then, remembering all that she and Scotty had learned about spiritual warfare, Becka tried again. "In the name of Jesus Christ, I order you to reveal yourself."

Becka watched and waited in speechless anticipation. Soon the air began to ripple. In the middle of the room an image wavered and slowly formed. At first it appeared to be a darker version of the darkness that already filled the room. A shadow within a shadow. But gradually it took shape. Features slowly formed. Becka gasped. Although it was still transparent, there was no mistaking who it was. Little Juanita.

Becka tried to swallow, but her mouth was as dry as cotton. "What ... what do you want?" she demanded.

The girl turned to her, cocking her head as if she didn't quite understand.

"What do you want?"

The image shimmered and grew more solid. Now it was possible to clearly see the girl's face. She was puzzled, confused, and very, very frightened. Remembering the writing on the window, Becka tried again, this time in Spanish, "*¿Quién es? ¿Qué quieres?*"

Before the girl could answer, another image suddenly rippled in the air and formed to her left. It seemed to be a handsome woman with long, beautiful hair. She wore an expensive black nightgown. Becka had only seen her once but recognized her immediately. It was Priscilla, the Ascension Lady.

Priscilla looked to Becka with her tired, sad eyes and smiled. Then, turning her attention toward the girl, she knelt down and reached out her arms. It was an offer of help, of comfort. At first the girl resisted, afraid to come near. But the Ascension Lady waited patiently, making it clear that she was there to help.

At last Juanita took a tentative step toward her. The Ascension Lady smiled broadly. Encouraged, the girl stepped closer. Then closer again. The Ascension Lady continued to smile, waiting.

Another step, and then another. Now the little girl was standing directly in front of the woman. Becka watched as, with great tenderness, the Ascension Lady reached out and wrapped her arms around the helpless child.

There was no missing the gentle affection. The woman looked over to Becka and smiled.

But the smile suddenly froze. Her expression turned from joy to surprise … and then to horror. There was a tearing sound, as if something was ripped. The woman screamed, her voice shrill and agonizing as she grabbed her stomach and fell back from the girl.

The little girl turned to Becka, confused, afraid, and looking very helpless. But in her hands were shredded pieces of the woman's nightgown.

The Ascension Lady was writhing on the floor, screaming, holding her stomach in agony. Juanita looked down at her with deep pity … and confusion. Then, without warning, she leaped on the woman and began beating her with powerful blows and clawing at her with suddenly razor-sharp fingernails. The woman screamed and tried to protect herself, but she was no match for the child's superhuman strength and animal-like claws.

Somehow, for a brief second, the Ascension Lady managed to pull herself free from the girl. That's when her eyes found Becka's. They were full of anguished pleading. "Help me," she gasped, reaching for Becka. "Help — " Before she could finish, the girl leaped on her again, and again she tore into the woman.

Becka managed to shake herself from her horror. "Stop it!" she screamed. "You're hurting her!"

The girl did not hear.

"I order you to stop!"

Instead, Juanita reached out and, to Becka's astonishment, picked up the woman, lifting her as easily as though she were a stuffed doll. She raised the Ascension Lady effortlessly over her head, then flung her across the room. Priscilla hit the back wall hard and slid to the floor in a daze. The girl looked puzzled over what she had done, as though confused at her own powers.

Becka took a step closer and shouted. "You're hurting her! I command you to stop!"

Juanita paid no attention. She began searching the room, looking for something. Then she found it. The lamp on Becka's nightstand. In a flash she leaped to it. She grabbed it, ripped off its shade, and bounded back to the Ascension Lady.

For a moment she stood over the groaning woman, looking down at her with pity and compassion. Then slowly, sadly, she raised the lamp high over her head.

Becka understood what was coming. Whether the child knew what she was doing or not, she had to be stopped. Becka was certain that if she didn't do something, the girl would smash the lamp into the semiconscious woman. She stepped closer and angrily shouted, "Stop it! I command you to stop it and leave my room!"

The little girl turned to her. This time her confusion was mixed with hurt. But hurt feelings or not, she had to be stopped. "In the name of Jesus Christ of Nazareth ..." Becka faltered. The little girl had started to cry. Becka watched a moment, unsure what to do. Tears streamed down the sad little face, but Becka forced herself to continue. "In the name of Jesus Christ of Nazareth, I command you to go. Leave!"

The child was sobbing now. Helplessly. Uncontrollably.

Becka bit her lip. What was going on? Was she doing the right thing?

With the lamp still poised over the Ascension Lady, Juanita looked at Becka. Her face was stained with tears; her bottom lip trembled with emotion. Her eyes seemed to plead with Becka, as though she hoped she would give her permission to finish the job.

Becka shook her head. "No. I command you to leave! Leave my room, now!"

Juanita's expression dropped even lower. She turned as if to leave, then suddenly raised the lamp and brought it crashing down on the woman's chest.

"Nooo!" Becka screamed. "I command you to leave! Leave my room! *Now—!*"

Rebecca shot up in bed, wide awake. Another dream! A dream within a dream.

She quickly reached for the lamp on her nightstand. It was time to flood the room with light, with reality.

But the lamp was not there.

She threw off the covers and raced to the wall switch by the door. She snapped it on and squinted as the overhead light glared into the room, replacing the darkness with bright, cleansing light. The brightness hurt her eyes, but it was a small price to pay.

Until the light revealed something across the room, near the corner. It was hard to make it out at first, since it had been broken and the shade ripped off. But after a second, Becka realized she was staring at the shattered lamp from her nightstand.

6

4:32 a.m.

"Hi, Scotty."

Scott gave a start as he entered his bedroom and fumbled to turn on the light. He saw Becka sitting at his desk in the dark. "What are you doing here?" he asked in surprise.

"My room was getting a little crowded for sleeping."

"What?"

"Never mind. Where have you been? It's 4:30 in the morning."

Scott was exhausted. It had been quite a night ... and morning. First there was that little field trip through the Hawthorne mansion, then the visit to the Bookshop. And finally, for the past few hours he'd been working with Hubert as they dreamed up false info for the Ascension Lady's astrology charts.

"Where have I been?" he echoed. "Let's just say your friend at the bookstore will have a brand-new look the next time you see her."

"My friend ... the Ascension Lady? You've done something to the Ascension Lady?"

"Not me." He smirked. "She'll be doing it to herself. It's all in the stars … and her computer." He pulled off his jacket and tossed it on the growing pile of clothes in the corner.

"What did you do?" she asked.

He waved her off. "It's a long story, but the lady will definitely be sporting a new 'do the next time you see her." He gave a long, noisy yawn. "Right now I'm bushed." He started peeling off his T-shirt.

Becka had been sitting there for almost an hour trying to think what she should say when he came back. Should she tell him more about her growing doubts? What about the experience in her room? What about her decision to visit the Ascension Lady to try and warn her?

It looked as though she had just wasted her time. Scotty, with his usual male egocentrism, wasn't interested in anything but his own accomplishments … and, of course, sleep. She got up and started for the door.

He gave another yawn. "What were you saying about your room?"

"Forget it," she answered. She would say nothing more. At least for now. If he was lucky, maybe she'd leave a note on the table, letting him know she'd be at the Bookshop. But as far as anything else, it looked like she'd have to work things out on her own.

"Hey, Beck?"

She stopped in the doorway and turned.

"So what's the deal? Are you going to that séance tomorrow?"

She took a deep breath and slowly let it out. "I don't know, Scotty."

2:10 p.m.

Becka stood outside the Ascension Bookshop. The sign on the door read Closed for Lunch. She peered through the posters and stickers plastered over the window and saw someone rummaging around inside.

"I hope I'm doing the right thing," she sighed as she reached out and rapped on the door. She waited, folding her arms against the cold ... not the cold of the morning, or even the cold of fear. But the cold of gnawing uncertainty.

She ran through it all again. Was the little girl a demon or Juanita's ghost? The Bible said there are no ghosts. Okay, fine. If that was true, then why was the girl Becka had seen the same age as Juanita? Why did she look like Juanita would have looked? Why did she speak Spanish like Juanita surely must have done?

Then there was the question about a Christian's "spiritual authority" ... all that stuff in the Bible about beating the devil. Why wasn't it working for Scotty? Why wasn't it working for her?

Finally, there was the love question. Granted, Juanita wasn't exactly the most likable being, but even in her dream Becka was pretty sure the kid was acting more out of fear and confusion than meanness. And the Ascension Lady was the only one trying to help. Not Becka, not Scott. Only the Ascension Lady was reaching out in love.

That's how Becka saw it, anyway. And that's why she was there. She had to warn the Ascension Lady. No matter how much the woman wanted to help Juanita, who knew what would happen to her if she went through with tonight's séance?

Becka heard the bolt unlock. Then the door to the Bookshop swung open. But it was not the Ascension Lady who greeted her. Or was it?

Instead of the long salt-and-pepper hair, this woman had a closely shaved buzz. And it was tinted red. But that was nothing compared to her breath. A wave of garlic stung Becka's nose, making her eyes instantly water.

The woman broke into a smile. It was the Ascension Lady's smile. And those were her eyes—those same sad, frightened eyes. "Rebecca, please come in." She opened the door wider, and Becka stepped inside.

The Bookshop was not at all what she had expected. Instead of dark, foreboding shelves covered in spiderwebs, and a handful of witches standing around stirring cauldrons, this place was bright and cheery. Sunshine poured through overhead skylights. The floor was covered in aqua blue carpeting, the shelves were white and inviting, and the books they held looked friendly and colorful.

"Sorry about my breath," the Ascension Lady laughed as she shut the door. "It's all part of my new identity."

"Identity?" Becka said, trying to blink back the tears.

The woman nodded. "After our rendezvous last night, I realized I had better change my identity."

"Rendezvous?"

"Yes, our little get-together in your room."

Becka's heart skipped a beat. "You were there? You saw what happened?"

"Of course I was there. Didn't you see me?"

Becka was stunned. "But I thought … I mean …"

"You thought it was a dream?"

Becka nodded.

The Ascension Lady smiled. "I was astral projecting—leaving my body while I slept. It's not an uncommon practice, not for those of us involved in the deeper secrets of New Age. In a sense, I suppose you could say I was dreaming too. But not really."

"So … you saw what happened?"

"Oh yes—" the Ascension Lady smiled and rubbed her abdomen—"and felt it."

Becka could only stare.

The woman crossed toward the counter. "It was all symbolic, of course. But it made clear to me the drastic actions that had to be taken for tonight."

"Was cutting your hair part of that drastic action?"

The woman ran her fingers over her shaved head. There was a trace of sadness to her voice. "It really wasn't my decision." She picked up a clove of garlic on the counter and popped it into her mouth, between her gum and teeth. She winced as it burned, yet she continued to suck and chew. "But it all made sense after this morning's forecast."

"Forecast?"

"My astrological forecast. Great things are going to happen to me tonight, but I must keep my identity hidden. In fact, the charts have never been more specific—they even said I should shave my hair, and dye it—I shaved my eyebrows too; did you notice?"

As Becka stared, a faint bell sounded in her head. Scott had said something about the Ascension Lady sporting "a new 'do."

"And, of course, these garlic cloves—" the woman fanned her mouth, indicating how much they burned—"they are to help me alter my normal olfactory signature."

"Your what?"

"My scent. That way I won't be recognized by my scent either."

Becka continued to stare, wondering if the woman had any idea how foolish she looked, or sounded ... or smelled.

"In all my years I've never encountered an astrological forecast like this one. But when I read it on the computer this morning, I knew something was happening."

Becka closed her eyes. Computer, astrological forecast, shaved head. She knew what was "happening." Or who. Scott. This woman's absurd looks and crazy actions were all Scott's doing.

Rebecca cleared her throat and tried to change the subject.

"So you're, uh, you're still going tonight, even after all that happened in my room?"

"Juanita's just confused," the Ascension Lady explained. "She just misunderstood my actions. But with a new identity we'll be able to start over, and I'll be able to reach her." The woman turned and looked directly into Becka's eyes. There was no missing her sincerity. "She needs us, Rebecca. You know that now. You have seen it yourself."

Becka glanced away.

The Ascension Lady approached. Her voice was full of understanding and compassion. "I know you're frightened. I know you're starting to have doubts about your beliefs."

Becka bit her lip. It was as if the woman had read her mind.

The Ascension Lady reached out and gently touched Rebecca's arm. Becka's eyes met the older woman's gaze.

"It's alright to feel as you do. Supernatural experiences often help expand our too-limited views of God."

Becka tensed. What was she saying? That her doubts were right? That the Bible couldn't be trusted? That God wasn't who he said he was? No! This was wrong! And yet …

"Please," the woman continued, "I know it is unnerving, but search the Christ within you, and see if he would not have you reach out to this little girl in his love."

Becka continued to look into the woman's eyes.

"Join with me. We are not enemies. We are coworkers. We are on the same side. The side of love."

The woman was making more and more sense. "But what …" Becka cleared her throat, trying to find her voice. "But what about Juanita's powers? Aren't you afraid of them?"

The Ascension Lady laughed gently. "Of course I am. I am terrified. That is why I need you at my side. We both saw how you were able to help me last night. She may attack again, only more violently."

"And you'll go, even if I don't?"

"I must. She needs me. She needs us."

"Becka?" A voice spoke from the door.

Becka turned to see Ryan. He looked puzzled and concerned.

"Ryan," she exclaimed, "how'd you know I was here?"

"I called your brother. He read your note." Ryan continued checking out the situation and the woman. "Listen, we need to talk. There's something at the library you need to see."

For a moment Becka was torn. For a moment she actually didn't want to leave the Ascension Lady.

"Now," he said firmly.

"Oh ... yeah, sure." She started toward the door.

"Rebecca?"

Becka turned.

"I will be starting at eight. Your friends are also invited."

Becka looked at her and nodded.

3:34 p.m.

"I still don't get why you were there," Ryan said as he slipped a microfilm into the machine and snapped on the switch. The light came on and the fan whirred quietly. "You're the one who said she was evil."

"I ... I might have been wrong," Becka answered. "She's only trying to help. When you think about it, aren't we really both fighting on the same side? For the little girl?"

Ryan looked up at her from the machine. His expression made it clear that he had his doubts. Come to think of it, so did she.

Without a word he directed his attention back to the screen, and then started to adjust the microfilm as he said, "The more I've been thinking about what you said about the Bible, the more this whole thing's been bugging me."

Becka looked on, waiting.

"I mean, you're right. Either the Bible's true or it isn't. So I got here early this morning and started going through the newspapers again." At last he had the microfilm lined up. "Take a look at this."

Becka leaned over and read the headline: "Hawthorne Hill: Site of Holy Rituals."

She glanced to Ryan, who nodded for her to continue reading. It was a 1988 interview with an older Native American from the area. He spoke of having hunted and fished in various locations that were now parts of the city. A few paragraphs later he spoke of Hawthorne Hill, the location of the mansion:

> "It had always been a sacred place. Our grandfathers, our great-grandfathers, and their fathers before them practiced their magic on that hill. It was a place of strong power. Spirits frequently appeared. Even as children we knew this was no place to play."

Becka came to a stop. She did not have to read further.

Ryan spoke quietly. "There were things happening on that hill long before Juanita was ever murdered there. Probably centuries before."

Becka nodded.

Ryan continued, "So what we saw in that house …"

Becka finished the phrase for him: "… may not have been the girl's ghost, but one of those evil spirits."

Ryan looked at her a long moment and then slowly nodded.

7

5:45 p.m.

Becka looked out the car window at the passing houses. "I just wish there was somebody I could run all this stuff past. With Mom gone and Scotty playing Rambo, there's nobody."

"What about Z?" Ryan asked as he eased the Mustang around another corner.

Becka glanced at her watch. "Z usually doesn't come online till nine. The séance will already be going."

Ryan gave a heavy sigh. "I still don't think you should go."

Becka glanced at him. Her heart fluttered, moved by his constant concern for her. Who else would spend all Friday morning in the library trying to prove her right and himself wrong . . . just to make sure she would be safe? Ryan was a treasure. One she hoped never to lose.

She looked back out the window. "If I don't go, will that stop Julie and the others from showing up?"

"No way, they're making it a major event."

"And it sure won't stop the Ascension Lady. If I don't show, who knows what will happen to her."

"But she's your enemy."

Becka looked back to him. "She's trying to do right; she's just all mixed up. Besides, even if she was my enemy—"

"I know, I know," Ryan interrupted. "'Love your enemies.'" He threw her a mischievous grin. "I've been doing my reading."

Becka laughed. "But do you believe it?" Her comment carried a double meaning. She wasn't just asking if he believed in a Bible verse. For several weeks he'd been flirting with making a commitment to Christ, and for several weeks he'd been reading the Bible, trying to decide.

He looked over to her and quietly answered. "I'm almost there, Beck. Just give me a little more time."

Becka nodded. She wouldn't rush him. Even if she could stand for a little more Christian company ... especially tonight.

"I've got it!" Ryan suddenly said. "Susan, from the church. The one who helped rescue you from those satanist guys."

Relief flooded Becka. "Of course! Why didn't I think of it? Mom even asked her to check in on us."

Without a word Ryan threw the car into a U-turn and they were off.

7:07 p.m.

"But if this thing is a demon, shouldn't Beck and her brother have been able to, you know, make it obey them? I mean, isn't that what the Bible says?" Ryan was pacing back and forth in Susan's tiny office. He seemed more agitated than Becka.

Susan leaned forward on her desk, listening. As usual she was working late. She was a college student and a newlywed. She and her husband, Todd, worked part-time as youth pastors for the Community Christian Church.

She had listened with interest to Becka and Ryan's story. When Becka expressed her confusion over the ghost seeming to be real, Susan had nodded.

"I can see why you've started to believe in this thing. But don't forget that demons have knowledge of all that has happened. It wouldn't be too hard for them to masquerade as the little girl who was killed there."

"And they could speak Spanish?" Ryan had asked.

"They could speak whatever they wanted," Susan had agreed. "If Spanish is called for, that's what they will use."

Now Susan nodded again at Ryan's insight. "Yes," she agreed, "in theory, as believers, Becka and Scott should have authority over the demons."

"So what gives?" Ryan's voice had an edge of impatience. "Becka has a special guest appearance in her bedroom, Scotty's attacked by flies, and— "

"Wait a minute ... did you say flies?"

"Yeah, thousands of them. Why?"

"One of his names ... one of the names God gave Satan was Beelzebub."

"Be-elle-za-what?" Ryan asked.

"Beelzebub. It's like one of God's jokes on him. It means 'Lord of Flies.' "

Becka felt the old familiar chill run across her shoulders. It took a moment to find her voice. "So what you're saying is we might be dealing with more than just a demon?"

Ryan stopped pacing and looked at the women. "You're not talking about—I mean, are you saying it might be *Satan?*"

Susan shrugged. "Hard telling. Lots of times demons will claim that very thing to try and freak you out. But from what you've described, with the history of occult activities on that hill, whatever they are doing is definitely big-time."

"They?" Becka repeated. "You said *they.*"

"You're probably dealing with a cluster of them, yes."

"But why do they always appear as Juanita's ghost?"

"Ghosts, angels of light, spirit guides—demons come in all sorts of disguises."

"Still, the Bible says we have authority over them, and my brother tried and got trounced. Why?"

"A good question." Susan reached over to her shelf and pulled out a Bible. She began leafing through the pages. "Christians shouldn't go out looking for fights with the devil. After all, his job is to kill and destroy. But when they meet him, they will win if they are using God's power."

She found her place. "Ah, here we go, Ephesians 6:12: 'For our struggle is not against flesh and blood, but against the rulers, against the authorities, against the powers of this dark world and against the spiritual forces of evil in the heavenly realms.'"

Becka nodded. "I know. Believe me, Scotty and I are very familiar with those verses."

Susan continued. "There's more: 'Therefore put on the full armor of God, so that when the day of evil comes, you may be able to stand your ground, and after you have done everything, to stand.'"

Again Becka nodded. "But Scotty wasn't exactly standing up. When Juanita—or whatever it was—got through with him, he was lying flat on his back, thinking he was covered with flies."

Susan nodded, still looking at the pages. "Hmmm, there are some conditions. The armor of God is not just some flowery phrase. There are very specific pieces of protection that we need to put on before going into battle."

"Like what?" Ryan asked.

Susan found her place and continued reading: "'Stand firm then, with the belt of truth buckled around your waist, with the breastplate of righteousness in place, and with your feet fitted with the readiness that comes from the gospel of peace. In addition to all this, take up the shield of faith, with which you can extinguish all the flaming arrows of the evil one. Take the helmet of salvation and the sword of the Spirit, which is the word of God.'"

"Man! That's a lot," Ryan said.

"And prayer," Susan continued, reading: "'Pray in the Spirit on all occasions.'"

"Okay," Becka said, "let's go down the list just to make sure. We've got our sword." She pointed to Susan's Bible. "I'm learning to believe in the Bible, more so than ever. What's the 'helmet of salvation'?"

"The knowledge of your salvation through Christ. When you know you're secure in him, that stops Satan from playing with your head, from fooling you into thinking you're not saved so you don't think you have power."

"Got that," Becka said. "I know I'm saved."

"And if we aren't?" Ryan asked, clearing his throat and shifting a little uncomfortably.

Susan looked at him. "It's your choice, Ryan, but I wouldn't wait too long with all that's coming down."

Ryan nodded. "I hear you."

"What else is in that armor?" Becka asked.

"The shield of faith."

"Faith, I've got that."

"Shoes to spread the gospel." Susan looked up. "You're ready to tell people about Jesus, aren't you?"

"I can vouch for her on that," Ryan chuckled. Becka grinned back at him.

"That just leaves two things. The belt of truth—you're not lying or deceiving anybody?"

Becka shook her head.

"And finally the breastplate of God's approval."

"Meaning?"

"Meaning you're being as righteous as you can … and if you mess up, you're asking Jesus to forgive you."

Ryan chuckled again. "Beck and her brother are the squeakiest-clean kids I know."

"You don't have to be perfect," Susan corrected. "You just

have to be certain you're trying to be, and that you ask Jesus to forgive you."

Becka started to nod, then caught herself.

Susan was the first to notice. "What's up, Becka?"

"It's just ... I mean, playing a practical joke on somebody, that's not like sinning, is it?"

Susan smiled. "I think God has a sense of humor. Just as long as nobody's getting hurt or it isn't done out of anger."

"Uh-oh."

Both heads turned to Becka. She took a breath. "Scotty, he's been playing this elaborate joke on the Ascension Lady, getting her to shave off her hair and stuff."

Ryan started to laugh. "That was Scotty's doing?"

Becka nodded, then turned to Susan. "Is that a problem?"

"It's pretty funny," Susan agreed, nodding, "but it's pretty mean too."

"He was looking for a way to get even, to get some kind of revenge for all the stuff she's done to us."

A frown crossed Susan's forehead. "Revenge?"

"Yeah."

"So he hasn't forgiven her."

"No way."

"Is that a problem?" Ryan asked.

"Unforgiveness? Yeah, Ryan, that's a big problem. The Bible says we have to forgive, that seeking revenge is wrong." Susan turned back to Becka. "I don't suppose he's asked God to forgive him?"

Becka shook her head. "I doubt it. I think he's having too much fun."

Susan took off her glasses and rubbed her eyes. "I think we've found it — the missing piece in his armor." She stopped, then quickly looked back to Becka. "He's not going to that séance, is he?"

"He knows everyone else is going to be there ... and he'll definitely want to see his handiwork on the Ascension Lady."

Susan tried to keep her voice calm and even but didn't quite succeed. "He could get hurt, Becka. If he goes in there unprotected, he could get hurt very badly."

Becka looked at her watch. "It starts in less than an hour. Can I use your phone?"

Susan nodded and handed it to her. Becka dialed and waited. A moment later she sighed in frustration as Scott's recorded message came on: "Hi, I'm not. You are. I will be. So leave a message so when I am, I can ... I think."

After the beep she spoke quickly into the phone. "Scotty, if you're there, pick up. Scotty. Scotty!" No answer. "Listen," she said, glancing at her watch again. "It's 7:20. Don't go anywhere. Do you hear me? Wait till Ryan and I get there. We're on our way. We've got to talk. Don't go." She hung up.

Susan was on her feet, opening her door for them. "Do you think he's left already?"

"I don't know," Becka said as she and Ryan headed out into the hall. "Thanks, Susan."

Susan followed them a step or two. "Be very, very careful."

Becka gave a half-wave as she pushed open the outside door and headed into the parking lot.

As the door slammed, Susan leaned against the wall. Then she went back into her office, crossed to her desk, and sat a moment. As a Christian, Becka had no business going to a séance. And yet, she had to go to rescue her brother—maybe even the Ascension Lady ...

Susan shook her head, then lowered it into her hands and started to pray.

7:33 p.m.

Becka yanked the front door to her house shut and let the screen slam as she raced back to Ryan's Mustang. She held a wadded piece of paper in her hand.

"Not there?" Ryan called.

She shook her head. "We've got to get to the mansion."

Ryan nodded and fired up the Mustang. "What's the note say?"

She smoothed it out and read: " 'Beck: Julie called. They'll meet you there. I'm grabbing a bite to eat with Darryl. Should be fun.' "

Ryan tromped on the accelerator, and they sped off.

8

7:53 p.m.

BANG!

The Mustang careened to the left. Ryan hit the brakes and fought the wheel, trying to keep the car on the road.

"What is it?" Becka cried.

"A tire!" Ryan shouted as he slowed the car and carefully nursed it toward the side of the road with the sickening *RUTT-RUTT-RUTT-RUTT* sound of a flat.

"Do we have a spare?"

"Yeah." The car rolled to a stop, and Ryan opened his door. "It's going to take some time, though."

Becka threw open her own door. "Can I help? What can I do?"

Ryan crossed to the back and opened the trunk. "Give me a hand unloading all this junk."

Becka joined him and groaned. The trunk was full of crushed pop cans, a baseball mitt, various pieces of a tennis racket, a partially deflated soccer ball, dirty sweatshirts, torn jerseys, old high-tops, new high-tops, greasy two-by-fours, wrenches, ratchets, and other car junk—along with anything else Ryan had ever used since birth or planned to use until death.

"I know it's in there somewhere," he said.

She gave him a look. He shrugged. They started unloading.

8:04 p.m.

"It is after eight," the Ascension Lady said. "It is imperative that we be punctual."

"If we could just wait a couple more minutes," Julie said. "I know Becka wanted to be here." She turned to Scott. "She did say she was coming, right?"

Scott tried to focus on Julie. The pounding in his head had returned—so bad he'd barely heard. "Yeah," he mumbled, "sure."

"You don't look so good," Krissi said, adjusting her hair for the hundredth time. "Are you okay?"

"I'll be fine," Scott answered hoarsely. He had come for two reasons. The first was out of good old-fashioned curiosity. Second, he wanted to have a few laughs over the Ascension Lady's new look. Unfortunately, by the time he had joined the others in the mansion's dining room, his head hurt so badly he couldn't laugh. He couldn't even smile.

The Ascension Lady eyed him carefully. She knew something was up; she just couldn't put her finger on it. She turned back to Julie. "I agree with you. I, too, would like to wait for Rebecca. But Juanita has told me her murder occurred at ten at night. The corridor between our two worlds will be open only at that time. If we are to help, I am afraid we must start now."

There were no chairs or tables in the room, so she motioned toward the floor. "Please." She set her camping lantern on the hard wooden floor, dimmed its light, and eased herself down beside it, cross-legged.

Krissi, Julie, Philip, and Darryl exchanged glances. It had been a surprise to see the woman with a dye job and her newly shaved head and eyebrows. Then of course there was her garlic breath. "Well, at least there's no chance of vampires," Julie had giggled. But now … now they were about to participate in something they were completely unsure of. Something Becka had warned them about. And something that Becka wasn't even there to protect them from.

Philip was the first to sit. The others followed his lead, a little more reluctantly. But Scott held back. Something inside was telling him this was wrong, very wrong. And more than that — it was dangerous.

"What's the matter?" Darryl squeaked good-naturedly. "You forget your flyswatter?"

The others chuckled nervously.

"I am sorry — " The Ascension Lady was puzzled over the joke. "I do not understand."

Philip explained. "Last night, when we were here, Scott had a little run-in with flies here."

"Flies?" The woman turned to Scott. "You had an experience with flies in this house?"

Scott shook his head. "It was just my imagination, something I thought I saw. No biggie."

The Ascension Lady looked at him very carefully. It was obvious she knew something he didn't. And it was obvious that it made her nervous. "We must be careful," she said, still looking at him. Then more quietly, she continued, "If you do not wish to join us, that is understandable."

"No," Scott said, sensing a challenge, "I'll join you. Why wouldn't I?" As he sat down in the circle directly beside the woman, part of him was already kicking himself for being such a hotshot. *She gave you an excuse. Why didn't you take it and get out of here?* But there was another part, the part that knew he had fought this sort of stuff before and won. The part that hoped last night's experience was just an exception and that the authority he had would still beat the bad guys.

If only his head would stop pounding.

"Now—" the Ascension Lady held out her hands—"if you would all join hands with one another to create an unbroken circle."

They took each other's hands.

"We shall start by emptying our minds. Think of nothing ... no worries, no cares ... let your minds be free and empty."

"No problem for you there, huh, Krissi?" Darryl cracked.

The others snickered.

"Quiet now." The Ascension Lady frowned. "You must let your minds be clear ... let the peace of the universe prevail."

They settled down. After a moment, Philip cleared his throat. "I, uh, I don't think I can do this." All eyes turned to him. As the intellectual of the group, he was having a harder time shutting down. "I don't know if I can just think of nothing."

The woman seemed to understand. "You must try," she said. "By emptying your mind, you will make it easier to hear from the beyond. You will make it easier for Juanita to communicate."

8:24 p.m.

The Mustang raced up the hill toward the Hawthorne mansion. It squealed to a stop directly behind Philip's car. Changing the tire had taken longer than Ryan had expected, and both his hands and Becka's were smudged with grease and grit. But at last they were here.

"Look!" Ryan pointed through the windshield up to the second-story window, the same window where Becka had first seen Juanita. There were fleeting, shadowy movements inside—fighting silhouettes—one larger, one smaller. A man and a girl. Ryan threw open his door. "We've got to stop them!"

"Who?"

He leaped out of the car. "Juanita ... or whatever ... and whoever it is trying to kill her."

Becka was out of the car too. "Ryan, no!" Her voice brought him to a stop. "That's not Juanita; it can't be. You said so yourself."

"But—" he pointed toward the window—"can't you see them?"

She looked back up to the window. He was right—there was obviously something going on up there. And it definitely looked like a big man and a little girl. But they'd been fooled before. "No." She shook her head. "I see what I see ..." She hesitated, then continued, "But I know what I know."

Ryan looked at her.

"We've been down this road before, Ryan. There are no ghosts. Only demons counterfeiting as ghosts."

He looked back up at the window. The fighting continued.

"It's not real ... it can't be." She forced herself to look away, to look directly at him. "If we go in, we have to remember that. We have to go by what we believe. We believe the truth, God's truth. The rest of that stuff—" she motioned toward the window—"that's all lies."

Ryan turned to her. "So we're back down to faith, huh?"

She smiled and reached out her hand. He looked at it, then slowly took it. It was a pact, an agreement. He would do his best to believe. So would she. They turned to face the house. "Let's do it" was all he said. They started across the lawn toward the front porch.

As they reached the massive stone steps, Ryan threw one final look up to the window. The shadows were gone.

They climbed the steps and crossed to a heavy wooden door. Leaded glass panes ran down both sides of the entrance, revealing a faint glow of light inside.

Becka knocked, but there was no answer. "They've already

started," she concluded. She grabbed the handle and gave the door a little push. It groaned quietly and opened.

Immediately they were hit by the smell.

"Whew!" Ryan said, fanning the air.

"It smells like rotten eggs," Becka said as she coughed.

"It's sulfur."

Becka turned to him.

He nodded. "I'd recognize it anywhere. It happens in chemistry class sometimes when things backfire. Yes sir, that's definitely sulfur."

"Wonderful," Becka muttered.

"Why, what's up?"

"In the Bible, sulfur's another name for brimstone."

"Brimstone?" Ryan repeated.

Becka nodded. "As in fire and brimstone."

"You mean like hell?"

"Yeah, like hell."

8:32 p.m.

Susan raised her head from her desk. She was exhausted. She had been praying nonstop for Becka and Ryan ever since they left her office. And still she felt something was wrong. She knew she had to keep interceding.

She reached for the phone and started dialing. Todd would be home. She needed help; she needed someone to join her. The battle was not over yet—in many ways it hadn't even begun.

8:34 p.m.

Becka and Ryan paused outside the entry hall a moment, each making sure the other was determined to go ahead—each unsure if they really wanted to. Gathering all of her strength,

Becka finished opening the door and stepped inside. Ryan followed. It was the same entry hall they had visited the night before. The same gray slate tile, the same towering stairway, and the same crystal chandelier.

"Over there," Ryan whispered. He pointed to a room a couple of doors down, through a distant archway. They could see the faint glow of a lantern reflecting off beige walls. A voice was quietly murmuring.

They started forward. The voice became clearer, and they recognized it as the Ascension Lady's.

"Empty your minds ... see if she would use you as a vehicle by which to communicate. Juanita, we are here for you. We understand your need, and we have come to help ..."

As Becka and Ryan approached the room, the group came into view. Julie, Philip, Krissi, little Darryl, Scott, and the Ascension Lady—all sitting in a circle holding hands with their eyes closed. The only light was from the camping lantern.

"I sense a presence," the Ascension Lady said. "Juanita, is that you?"

Scott was the first to sneak a peek at Becka and Ryan as they arrived at the archway. The others followed suit. Everyone but Krissi. She and the Ascension Lady seemed to be oblivious to the newcomers. They were the only ones really getting into it.

"Is that you?" the Ascension Lady repeated. "Juanita, do you have something to say?"

Becka motioned for Scott to join her. He hesitated. She motioned again. Finally he pulled Darryl's hand over and replaced it in the Ascension Lady's. "Do not break the circle," the woman warned, her voice sounding farther and farther away. "Do not disturb the flow."

Scott silently rose to his feet and stole behind the woman. "I feel movement," she droned. "There is a definite stirring in the spirit world."

Julie and Philip barely held back their snickers. Krissi, on the other hand, was totally gone. "Me too," she whispered in excitement. "I feel it too."

Scott followed Becka out of the room and behind the arch.

"You look terrible," she whispered.

He nodded wearily. "I feel it. But I'm not giving in. Not this time. This time we're going to fight to the end."

"No, Scott." Becka frowned.

"What?"

"You're not ready. You're not protected."

"What are you talking about?"

"The Ascension Lady ... what you did to her hair, her breath."

Despite the pain, Scott managed a grin. "Pretty cool, huh?"

Becka shook her head. "No. That's the problem." He looked at her but didn't understand. "Remember with that Ouija board, when they were supposedly calling up Dad—remember that section we'd read in the Bible about the armor of God? The shield and sword and stuff?"

Scott nodded, then winced. The pain in his head was getting worse.

"Are you okay?"

He took a breath, trying to fight off the throbbing. "Yeah ..."

She kept a careful eye on him and continued. "Remember all the parts of armor we're supposed to wear?"

Again he nodded.

"Well, we talked to Susan, and you're missing a piece. The breastplate of righteousness."

"The what?"

"Your pranks against the Ascension Lady, your unforgiveness toward her ... God sees those things as unrighteous."

Scott stared at her incredulously. "After all the junk she's pulled, you think a little practical joke is wrong?"

"It's not the joke, Scott. It's you. Inside. We're supposed to forgive—you know that."

The throbbing increased. Scott took another breath, trying to hold the pain at bay. "After all they've done to us, you're telling me we can't ..."

She nodded. "If you're in it for revenge, if you haven't asked God to forgive you for your wrong attitude, that's exactly what I'm—"

She was suddenly interrupted by a terrified scream. It was Krissi. They rushed around the arch and into the room. Krissi was holding her right hand directly in front of her. It was trembling. "My hand," she cried, "what's happening to my hand?"

"Do not fight it." The Ascension Lady was also staring at it. "Do not fight it, sweetheart, do not fight it."

"What's happening?!"

"Let it have its way." The Ascension Lady dug into her coat pocket.

Krissi continued staring. "What's happening? What's happening?"

The woman pulled a tablet and pencil from her pocket. "Don't fight it," she repeated. "It's Juanita, she's wanting to communicate."

The group watched, wide-eyed, as the woman took Krissi's shaking hand and shoved a pencil into it. Then, placing the pad in Krissi's other hand, she commanded, "Write."

"What?"

"Let her write through you. She's using your hand to communicate with us."

"Please," Krissi was starting to whimper, "I don't want this—"

"Let yourself go. I promise you, you will be safe. Just let your hand go; let her write."

Krissi threw a frightened look at Philip. For a moment he was unsure. Finally he nodded. "It'll be okay, Kriss, we're right here with you. Go ahead and do what she says."

Keeping her eyes glued to Philip for support, Krissi lowered her right hand to the pad. As soon as the pencil made contact, the writing began. It was wild and erratic, but she was definitely writing letters.

Julie moved for a better look. "It's Spanish! She's writing in Spanish."

"But . . ." Krissi stared at her hand in unbelief. "I don't know Spanish!"

"Let her have her way," the Ascension Lady kept coaching. "Just relax and don't fight it."

The letters formed quickly and sloppily until an entire sentence was finished. And then the writing stopped. Just like that. Krissi released the pencil and began rubbing her hand.

"What's it say?" Julie demanded. "Does anyone know Spanish?"

Becka stepped farther into the room. "I do."

The Ascension Lady looked up and saw her for the first time. "I knew you would come." She smiled.

"What's it say, Becka?" Krissi asked anxiously. "What did I write?" She turned the tablet around so Rebecca could see.

Becka felt that old familiar chill. It read: *"Ustedes son míos."*

"What's that mean?" Krissi asked. "Translate it for us."

Becka fought to keep her voice from shaking. "'You are mine.'"

Everyone grew silent. Everyone but Krissi. "'You are mine'? That's stupid. What's that supposed to mean, 'You are mine'?" The group turned to the Ascension Lady. But even in the dim light it was possible to see that most of the color had drained from her face.

"Are you all right?" Julie asked.

The woman stared straight ahead as though she saw something no one else could see. Suddenly she cried out in alarm.

"Stay away! Stay away!"

"Priscilla? Ms. Bantini?" Julie reached out to touch her, but the woman paid no attention to her. Her eyes were wide with horror.

"No!" she shouted. "Not the children! Get away! Get away!"

She threw up her arms just as the camping lantern exploded, sending shards of glass in all directions, plunging the room into darkness and chaos. Everyone shouted and screamed—but none so loudly as the Ascension Lady. "Stay away! I am here to help! Stay away!"

"Turn on a flashlight," Philip shouted. "Someone turn on your flashlight."

"Mine's dead," Darryl yelled.

"Mine too," Julie cried.

"No, please! Get away! Get away ..."

The floor began to shake. Instantly. Hard and violent.

"It's an earthquake!" Ryan yelled.

But this was no earthquake. It was more like a roller coaster gone berserk. The floor rolled and pitched in every direction. Everyone screamed. Unable to stand, unable to crawl, they were bounced and tossed across the room like rubber balls, smashing into walls, hitting doorframes, screaming against the terror and chaos.

"Nooooo!" The Ascension Lady wailed. Her voice rose above their heads. "Put me down! Put me down!"

9

8:57 p.m.

"Let me go! Oh, please, put me down!"

The woman's voice seemed to be rising higher and higher. Something was lifting her above their heads! The floor continued to buck and pitch, and a howling wind filled the room. Just when it seemed the noise had reached its peak, the Ascension Lady was hurled through the arches, toward the entry hall, and up the stairs.

"NOOOOoooo!"

The shaking stopped. So did the wind. There was only silence ... and the quiet groaning and sobbing of kids.

Then smoke seeped into the room — a freezing, impenetrable fog that filled the darkness. With the smoke came an even stronger smell of sulfur. It was overwhelming, burning the back of Becka's throat, making her eyes water. The voices around her grew louder — coughing, groaning, weeping.

"Help me ... please ..." The cry was weak, but Becka immediately recognized the whine. It was Krissi. She sounded as though she were just a few feet to the right.

"Krissi, Krissi, are you all right?"

"My face ... what happened ... to my face?"

Becka rose to her knees and crawled blindly in the fog and darkness toward the voice. "Krissi, what's wrong?" She reached the girl's leg, then felt her way up her body toward her head.

"My face ... Becka ..."

"It's okay, Krissi. I'm right here, I'm right here."

At last Becka felt the girl's shoulders. The fog was so thick she had to bring her eyes in very close to see. Krissi had both hands covering her face. Becka pried them away. And then she gasped.

The beauty queen's face was shriveled like a piece of old dried-up fruit. The sagging eyes and drooping mouth belonged on a two-hundred-year-old hag, not a seventeen-year-old beauty.

Krissi saw the horror in Becka's eyes, and her hands instinctively shot back to her face. Carefully her fingers traced the wrinkles. "Becka ... help me ..." Tears spilled down Krissi's cheeks as her fingers explored every crevice, every fold. "What's happening?"

Becka felt a wave of revulsion sweep over her, but Krissi was her friend. She pulled the hideous face into her arms. "It's okay, Krissi. It's okay."

"My face ..." She was crying now. "Dear God ... not my face ... please ... please, make it stop, Becka. Make it stop."

As Becka held Krissi, her mind raced. What was happening? Was this for real? Or was it another demonic counterfeit? What could she do?

"Beck?"

Her ears perked up. "Scotty," she called. "Scotty, over here."

She could hear him crawling toward her. When he arrived he looked more haggard than ever. "What happened?" he gasped. "What's going on?"

"I don't know. I've never heard of anything like this."

"Are we ..." He hesitated. "Are we in hell?"

The thought sent Becka reeling. She fought it back instantly.

"No, we can't be. We're Christians. This is demonic. It's an illusion."

Scott grabbed his head and winced. "Aughhh!"

Becka watched helplessly as he battled the pain. It lasted for several seconds. Finally he looked up to her. "That was a beaut."

"Scott, listen to me. You've got to protect yourself. You've got to get rid of your unforgiveness." He looked at her blankly. She grew more frustrated. "I can't fight this myself! You've got to forgive the Ascension Lady and help me!"

Before he could answer, there was another cry, weak and pathetic. "Help me, help me ..."

"It's Philip," Scott said.

"Please ... help me ..."

He spun around and disappeared into the fog.

"Scotty! Wait!"

He didn't. "I'm right here, Philip," Scott called. "Where are you? What's wrong?"

The voice was full of fear. "I ... I ..."

Scott followed the sound. A moment later he found Philip curled up in a little ball, eyes wide in fear. "Philip, what's wrong?"

"I ... I ... Scotty, I don't know anything. My mind ... it's, it's ... going."

"No, man," Scott answered. "It's a trick. They can't do this sort of thing."

"But I—I'm stupid! I don't ..." He paused a moment as if trying to remember something. Suddenly he blurted, "I can't even remember my name. Help me!"

"It's a trick. They're messing with your mind—"

"Please! Help me, help me ..."

"Becka!" Scott called.

"Right here," she answered. She emerged through the fog, half dragging, half carrying Krissi.

As Krissi grew close enough for Philip to see, he gasped, "Who are you?"

Krissi began sobbing uncontrollably.

"Look," Becka ordered, "you two, stay put! Stay right here. Scott and I, we'll find the others."

"No! Please, don't leave me here," Philip begged. "I wouldn't know ... I don't know where I am. I don't know how to get out."

"Right now, none of us do," Scott answered.

"Becka ...," another voice wailed. "Becka ..."

Rebecca recognized it instantly. It was Julie — straight ahead, near the center of the room. She eased Krissi against Philip. "Stay here. I'll be right — "

And Darryl's voice, off to the left. "My eyes, I can't see ... my eyes ..."

"I'll get him," Scott said. "You take care of Julie."

Becka nodded and made her way through the cold, choking vapor. "Julie," she called, "Julie, where are you?"

"Here ..." The always-assured Julie sounded very, very frightened. "I'm over here."

At last Rebecca spotted her through the fog. She lay on her back with her head raised. "My body ... I can't — " Panic filled her voice. "Becka, I'm paralyzed. I can't move!"

The thought filled Becka with fear and rage. Julie was a gifted athlete. She was going to State in track. She lived and breathed sports. And there she was, lying on the floor, twisted in a heap. "Stop this!" Becka shouted to no one in particular. "I demand that you stop this! Stop these lies!"

As if in response, the floor started to rumble and shake again. But Becka would not back down. "In the name of Jesus Christ, I demand that you stop this! Now! Stop it this instant!"

The rumbling subsided. Slowly, until it had completely

died. As it faded, the fog also began to dissolve. Not completely, but enough that Becka could make out the others scattered around the room.

There were Philip and Krissi huddled together on the floor. Beyond them she could see Scott helping Darryl to his feet. And beside her was Julie—too strong to cry, but unable to move and wild-eyed with fear.

But where was Ryan? And what had happened to the Ascension Lady?

Becka knew what she had to do. As frightening as it was downstairs, she knew the source of the evil was upstairs. In the room at the end of the hall. The room where they had seen the shadows fighting. The room that had been videotaped ...

If they were going to put an end to this, they were going to have to confront whatever was in that room. And the only place to confront it was at its source.

Becka fought off a shiver. "Okay," she said as she slowly rose to her feet. "Somebody give me a hand with Julie."

"Where ... where are we going?" Philip asked timidly.

"We're going to stop this once and for all. We're going to get everyone back to normal." She sounded firm and in control on the outside. She just wished she felt that way inside.

It took all of Scott and Rebecca's encouragement and insistence, but the beleaguered troop finally rose to their feet and started forward. Becka nervously took the lead, followed by Julie, who was supported by Scott and Philip, and Darryl, who was led by Krissi.

Becka's face was firm with determination. This had to stop. Now.

9:10 p.m.

"You look terrible," Todd said as he entered the church office.

Susan glanced up from her desk and instinctively straightened her hair. It was a mess. Though she and Todd had been married several months, she still always wanted to look her best around him.

"I brought Chinese," he said, referring to the large white sacks of food in his hands. The smell was wondrous, reminding Susan that she'd completely forgotten about dinner. He set the bags on the desk, gave her a kiss, and pulled up a seat. "So tell me what's going on."

"Rebecca Williams, her brother, and a bunch of friends are over at the Hawthorne mansion."

"What are they doing there?"

"They're with Priscilla Bantini, the owner of the Ascension Bookshop. She's holding a séance."

Todd whistled softly. "We'd better get over there."

Susan shook her head. "No, I don't think so. I can't explain it, but I think … I think we're supposed to stay here. I think we'll be of more help staying here and fighting for them in prayer."

Todd looked at her a long moment. He really loved this lady. There was a quality about her, something so virtuous and connected to God that it made her more appealing than he'd ever dreamed a woman could be.

He smiled and pushed up his sleeves. "Then we'd better get down to business."

She nodded. They took one another's hands and bowed their heads. Susan glanced wistfully at the food sitting on her desk. It was going to be a while before they got to it.

9:25 p.m.

Rebecca and the group made their way into the entry hall. Just like before, there was the tinkling of crystal as the chandelier over their heads began swaying. And everyone went out of their way to avoid walking underneath it.

Now they stood before the massive stairway that loomed above them. As they paused, looking up, Scott joined Becka. "What do you think?"

"I think we don't have a choice."

Scott nodded silently.

"What was that?"

"I didn't hear— "

Becka held up her hand for quiet. There it was again. A faint whimpering. It came from under the stairway. "Who's there?" she called.

It stopped for a moment, then continued. Becka threw a look at Scott, then cautiously moved to investigate. "Who is it?" As she worked her way along the base of the stairs, she strained to see through the darkness. At last a shape came into view. It was the shape of a young man—one she knew very well—huddled against the wall.

"Ryan?"

The shape pulled itself closer to the wall, burying its face into its knees.

"Ryan?" She knelt and touched him. He looked up; his cheeks were stained with tears. It made her skin crawl. In all the time she had known him, she had never seen him cry. "Ryan ... Ryan, what's wrong?"

His voice was thick. "They're dead!"

"What?"

"Mom, my sister, my little brother— " he swallowed back the rising emotion— "they're all ... dead."

Becka's heart broke as she reached out for him. "No, Ryan, it's not true, it's a lie!" She pulled him close. He buried his face deep into her arms like a little boy. She held him tightly and could feel his body trembling with silent sobs. "It's all lies, Ryan, it's not true. None of it is true."

He looked up at her. Becka's throat ached with emotion as she stared down into those deep blue eyes. Eyes that usually sparkled with such life but that were now filled with agony.

"I saw them," he choked. "I saw the crash." His lip started to tremble, but he fought to continue. "I was standing right there in the road, Beck. They swerved to miss me—I saw them hit ... I saw them hit the truck."

"No, Ryan, it wasn't true, it was— "

"I saw!" He was shaking again, fighting back another sob. "I saw them go through the windshield ... I saw my sister ... her little head— " He broke off.

Becka's arms tightened around him. Tears burned her eyes as she stroked the back of his head, trying in vain to console him. At last she turned his face toward hers and looked directly into his swollen, red eyes. "Listen to me, Ryan. It's not true. It's a lie."

"But I saw it ... I heard them screaming."

She shook her head. Tears spilled onto her own cheeks. "They're lies. That accident never happened."

He searched her face, trying to understand. She continued. "You can't go by what you see."

"But the screams— "

"You have to believe. Remember? We can't go by what we see or what we hear. We have to trust God, to believe what he says. His truth, Ryan, remember?"

New tears sprang to Ryan's eyes, only now they were tears of helplessness. "I can't," he croaked. "It's ... too hard."

Becka swiped at her eyes. "I know. I know. But *he* can give you the faith. If you ask him, he'll give you the faith."

His eyes started to falter, to look away.

She gripped him tighter. "Ryan, God will help you believe!" She was practically shouting. "He'll help you believe, but you've got to ask, you've got to ask him!"

Her intensity drew his attention back to her. Then, ever so slowly, he began to nod. "Yes ...," he whispered.

Before Becka could respond, there was a sudden tumbling and crashing on the stairs above them. They scurried to their feet and ran to the base of the steps. Becka was the first to see him.

"Scotty!"

Her brother lay sprawled out at the bottom of the steps. He and the others had started to climb on their own, but he'd slipped and fallen. Yet it wasn't the falling that horrified Becka—it was her brother's neck. She had never seen a head twisted in such a strange position. Instantly, she knew the reason. His neck was broken.

"Scotty! Scotty, *no!!*" She dropped to his side. He did not respond. His eyes were closed and he was not breathing. "Scotty, Scotty, wake up! Scotty! Oh, God—no ... please, please, not Scotty!" She threw her head back and cried. "Please, Jesus! Please."

Tears fell from her lashes onto his lifeless body. "I warned you!" she yelled. "I said you weren't protected. Dear God, please, please ..."

"Becka—" Ryan knelt beside her. "This—this isn't true. It can't be."

"What are you talking about?" she wailed. "Look for yourself."

"No, no, it's just what you told me. This isn't real; this couldn't have happened."

"Look at him!" she shouted.

"It's not real, Beck." Ryan's voice was growing steadier. "It's another lie. He believes in Jesus; he's protected."

"No, that's just it—he wasn't protected. He wasn't wearing his—"

"God wouldn't let something like this happen, not the God I've been reading about. He wouldn't let this happen to one of his own. Not by that—" he motioned toward the top of the stairs—"that thing."

"But—"

"Believe … Becka. You said it yourself, you've got to believe. Don't go by what you see; go by what you know. God wouldn't let something like this happen. Not here, not like this."

She continued staring at her little brother. Next to Mom, this was her greatest love, the only family she had left.

"Believe," Ryan repeated. "It's another lie … it's not true, it's a lie."

Becka blinked. Slowly her eyes rose to meet Ryan's. Was it possible? Was this just another counterfeit?

She looked back down to the body. No! This could not be her brother. Whatever it was, it was not Scotty. Scotty was not dead. He couldn't be dead. Scotty was alive, Scotty was—

"Beck. Hey, Beck."

It was her brother's voice. But it wasn't coming from the body. It was coming from …

She looked about, baffled.

"Up here." She turned to the landing at the top of the stairs. There was Scotty, standing with the others. She gasped and looked back to the body in front of her.

It was gone.

"Beck, are you okay?" She looked back up. He was leaning against the rail, bracing himself against the pain in his head. He motioned for her. "There's something up here you'd better see. Hurry."

She threw a look at Ryan. He gave a half-smile. Together they rose and raced up the stairs.

10

9:50 p.m.

When Becka arrived she threw her arms around her little brother. "Oh, Scotty, Scotty, you're all right!"

"Hey, easy." He glanced at the others, a little embarrassed. Still he let her hold him a minute because she seemed to need it. Come to think of it, he did too. Finally he pried her away.

"Scotty," she spoke quickly, "you've got to forgive the Ascension Lady. If you don't you could get hurt. This isn't a game. Not this time. You've got to believe me on this, you've got to forgive her, you've got—"

"Hey, I know, I know—"

"You don't understand, you've got to—"

"I *know,* Beck." She stopped to look at him, and he nodded. "I know." He motioned toward the open door at the end of the hallway. She slowly turned, then drew her hands to her mouth.

There, through the doorway, in the middle of the room, danced the Ascension Lady. Her arms and legs flew in all directions; there was no flow, no sense of rhythm ... just maniacal bouncing and jerking. It was as if she had become a marionette whose arms and legs were attached to invisible strings yanked by an insane puppeteer. The only control she had was over her face. It was full of bewildered horror.

"She needs us, Beck," Scott said quietly. "She needs our help. God's help."

Without taking her eyes from the doorway, Rebecca nodded.

Scott went on. "She and I may have our differences, but that ... no person should have to go through that." He motioned to their friends huddled together. "Or any of this."

Rebecca turned to him. "So you forgive her?"

"You think I'd be willing to go in there and face that ... *whatever* it is, to help her if I didn't?"

Becka nodded. "But your headache, what about your headache?"

He shrugged. "It's starting to go away, but it's sure taking its time about it."

Becka looked back to the room. "We have to go in there, don't we?"

"If we're going to help her. Yeah."

Becka swallowed. "Just you and me?"

Scott looked back to the pathetic group huddled a few feet away—Philip with his near-blank expression helping to hold up the paralyzed Julie, Krissi with her ravaged face, Darryl unable to see.

"I think so, kiddo," Scott said, meeting his sister's eyes. "Just you and me."

"And me," Ryan stated as he stepped forward. "I'll go in there with you."

Becka and Scott exchanged looks. Finally Becka shook her head. "I appreciate the offer, Ryan, but, uh—"

"You think just because I'm not Christian I can't face that." He sounded hurt and a little defensive.

Scott tried to explain. "It's nothing against you, Ryan. It's just—if you go in there and you're not protected, if you don't have the authority of Christ ... who knows what will happen. It just isn't smart."

"But you guys going in there by yourselves is?"

Becka knew he was trying to help, to protect her—and she loved him all the more for trying. "No." She shook her head. "That's the whole point. Scotty and I are not going in there by ourselves. We'll have help. We have God."

Ryan stared at her and slowly understood. He didn't like it, not one bit—but he understood. "Well ... I'm right here. If anything goes wrong, if you need me, I'm right here."

Becka smiled. Then she rose up on her toes and kissed him softly on the cheek. "Thanks." They held each other's gaze a moment. Finally Becka turned back to face the room.

The wind had picked up again and was blowing against their faces.

"Well?" Scott asked.

Becka nodded. No more needed to be said. She held out her hand and he took it. They started forward. With each step they grew more and more nervous. Yet there was another part of them that grew more and more confident. They'd done this before. Well, sort of. And they'd definitely read about it. But was that enough?

"Know any good hymns?" Becka asked.

"That might not be a bad idea."

They continued to approach. "I'm waiting," she said.

After a moment Scott started to sing. "Jesus loves me, this I know ..."

Becka threw him a look.

"Hey, it's the best I can do on such short notice." He continued, "For the Bible tells me so ..."

Becka took a deep breath and joined in. Her voice was weak and unsteady, and she felt more than a little foolish, but something was better than nothing.

"Little ones to him belong. They are weak, but he is strong."

They arrived at the door. The Ascension Lady looked helplessly at them. She was past exhaustion, and yet she continued the crazed dance. Wind whipped and howled around her so fiercely that Becka and Scott had to squint against it.

"Yes, Jesus loves me. Yes, Jesus loves me. Yes, Jesus loves me, the Bible tells me—"

Suddenly a voice began to chuckle, to reverberate throughout the room. But it wasn't one voice, it was several. They grew louder and louder. Mocking. Shrieking.

Becka covered her ears. "Stop it," she cried. "I command you to stop!"

The laughter decreased, but only slightly.

"Now!" Scott insisted. "We command you to stop, now!"

The laughter faded into the howling wind.

"And the Ascension Lady!" Scott shouted. "Release her! Now!"

There was no response. In fact, she seemed to leap and bounce even more violently.

"Now!" Becka shouted. "In the name of Jesus Christ, let her go, now!"

Instantly the woman crumpled to the ground in a heap.

Becka and Scott raced to her side. She groaned and stirred. But the ordeal had been too much, and she lapsed into unconsciousness.

Scott scanned the room. Other than the wind it was completely empty. "Where is she?"

"Who? Juanita?"

"Yeah, or whatever it is."

Becka looked about, shaking her head. Scott rose and took a step forward. "Where are you?" he shouted.

No response.

"We demand that you reveal yourself!"

At first neither of them saw a thing.

"In the name of Christ the Lord, we demand that you reveal yourself!" he repeated.

Slowly, faint outlines began to waver and shimmer all across the floor, filling the entire room.

"Are you seeing what I'm seeing?" Scott asked.

Becka nodded. "There's hundreds of them."

"No." He shook his head. "It's another trick." Raising his voice, he shouted, "In the name of Jesus Christ of Nazareth, I command you to stop your lies! I demand to see the truth."

But the images grew brighter, more solid. They averaged between two and three feet high. Their bodies were misshapen, some hunchbacked, some twisted and gnarled, most were covered with fur or hair. Their faces were equally grotesque: bulging eyes, pig snouts, gaping fangs, a few even had horns. Becka was struck by how much they looked like the pictures she'd seen of gargoyles on top of ancient buildings in Europe.

"We demand the truth," Scott repeated. "We demand to see you for who you are!"

The images grew even more solid.

"Scotty ... maybe they are telling the truth. Maybe there is more than one."

The creatures stared at them, snarling, growling, snapping their teeth. Many began taking tentative, threatening steps toward them.

"Now what?" Scott asked.

Becka rose to her feet. The creatures continued closing in. But when Becka brushed the blowing hair from her eyes, the quick motion set the entire group scurrying backward.

Scott looked at Becka and raised his eyebrows.

When the creatures were convinced the threat had passed, they started toward them again. Suddenly, Scott made a quick movement of his own. Once again, they scurried backwards.

Scott shook his head, marveling. "It's a bluff. They want us to think they have power, but it's all a bluff. They're scared to death of us."

He turned on a group to his left. "Boo!"

The things jumped and fell over each other in their attempt to back up. Scott couldn't help laughing.

Becka saw no humor. "Scotty, this isn't a time to fool around."

He spun to the right. "Booga-booga!" Again they scurried backwards, but not quite as far or as fast. And their recovery was a lot quicker. They resumed closing in.

"Scotty ..."

He paid no attention. This time he leaped forward. "ROAR-rrr ..." But he stopped short as his foot tripped over the nearest creature, a hairy troll-like animal. Before Scott could catch himself, he stumbled forward, nearly caught his balance, then lost it again, falling headlong into the swarming mass of fur and claws.

They covered him instantly.

He screamed, but his voice was quickly muffled.

"Scotty!" Becka lunged for him, directly into the midst of the ghouls. She kicked them aside, slapping and hitting the ones trying to crawl up her legs. But there were too many. When she knocked one down, a dozen took its place. But she wouldn't stop.

The creatures latched onto her legs and started to swarm over her. Raw panic filled her mind.

"Scotty!" she screamed.

More and more reached up from the floor, grabbing her legs, trying to pull her down. She kicked and stomped. They tugged harder. She stumbled, began to lose her balance.

"Scot—"

She fought hard and kicked with all her might, but nothing helped.

They had her.

She tripped once, twice, then fell, plunging into the mass of swarming creatures. They were all over her, smothering her, choking her, yet she managed to scream out, "In the name of Jesus, stop! I command you to stop!"

Instantly, there was only floor. No ghouls, no gargoyles, no furry monsters. Just hard oaken floor. The creatures ... the demons were gone.

She groaned and rolled onto her side. Scott was lying next to her. "Scotty." She reached out and shook him. "Scotty, wake up. We've got to get out of here."

He stirred slightly but remained unconscious. With great effort Becka forced herself to sit up.

And then she saw it—and her blood ran cold as a horrified scream froze in her throat.

11

10:00 p.m.

Susan and Todd had been interceding so intensely that they had no idea of the time that had passed. As they sat together, their prayers came in different forms. Sometimes they just offered earnest pleadings: "Dear God, please, please ..." Other times, they worshiped quietly: "We love you, Lord; we adore you." They also sang gentle songs and read sections of the Bible—and they took authority over Satan and bound and rebuked him.

But now, suddenly, they felt a strange peace. Instantly, they both knew everything would be all right, that it was all under control. Not because they knew what was happening at the mansion ... but because of the presence ...

As they sat together, their eyes closed, they both knew there was something—some*one*—filling the small office. Neither Susan nor Todd heard a thing, nor did they open their eyes. They didn't have to. They just knew. And as the presence of God continued to flood the room, the peace continued to pour into their hearts. There was a power all around them. An indescribable power. Love. All-consuming love.

"Thank you, Jesus," Susan whispered. "Thank you, thank you ..."

Todd nodded in agreement as tears slipped from his closed eyes.

Neither one knew how long they sat like that. It could have been a minute; it could have been hours. Time no longer seemed to exist. As the presence remained, a thought slowly took shape in Todd and Susan's minds. A command. They were to continue praying. Only now it was for something specific.

Susan was the first to put it into words: "Dear Lord, we ask you raise up others to pray. Right now. We pray that you would raise up other believers to intercede for our friends, to help them fight their battle ..."

10:03 p.m.

"Pull over."

"What?"

"Stop the car!" Mom Williams shouted across the seat to the driver. "We have to pull over."

"Now?" the driver, her oldest sister, asked.

"It's my kids. Something's wrong with Becka and Scotty. We've got to pray for them."

Mom's sister gave her a wary look. The afternoon funeral for their aunt had taken its toll on everyone's emotions. But Claire was the last person she thought would crack under the strain. After all, wasn't she the strong Christian in the family?

Mom saw the look on her sister's face and tried to explain. "Please, Sharon, don't ask me how I know. I just ... I just know."

"We'll be home in ten minutes. Can't it wait?"

Mom thought for a moment, then slowly shook her head. "No." She peered out the windshield. "No, it can't. Look, there's a McDonald's up ahead. Pull into the parking lot and pray with me."

Sharon hesitated.

"Please, you've got to trust me on this."

Grudgingly, Sharon nodded and pulled into the parking lot. She'd barely turned off the ignition when her sister had reached out and taken her hands. A moment later, the two women had their heads bowed and were praying.

10:10 p.m.

At the far end of the room — across from where Becka sat, exhausted, her hand resting protectively on Scott's unconscious form — the shadowy form of a little girl was taking shape. She was made up of the creatures. They had reappeared and were scurrying over to her, leaping into her, creating her very being, her substance. As each one entered her shadow, it became a part of her body, making her just a little larger.

Becka looked on in astonishment as the girl's height rose four, five, six feet. And still the creatures poured in. By the time the final ghoul had entered, the girl towered nearly ten feet tall, filling the bedroom from floor to ceiling.

Once her form was complete, she turned to Becka, who instantly recognized the face. It was Juanita. Instinctively, Becka pulled herself closer to Scott, hoping somehow his presence would help.

It did not.

Juanita slowly raised her hand and pointed her finger directly at Rebecca. She spoke. Her voice thundered, low and guttural.

"You!"

Becka started to tremble. She was cowering in fear and she hated herself for it, but she had been through too much, seen too many things. She was exhausted.

The shadow smiled maliciously, then started to approach. It pointed to the Ascension Lady's body lying on the floor, then swept its hand to include Scott's still form.

"This is your doing."

Becka could not respond. She drew even closer to Scott.

"All this suffering—everyone suffers because of you."

Becka shook her head, trying not to listen. But the voice was powerful and persuasive, as were the creature's eyes. As she watched it approach, Becka found it more and more difficult to resist or look away.

"It is your pride, your narrow-mindedness that has created this."

Becka tried to block the voice from her mind, but it had gotten inside. And the closer Juanita approached, the more it seemed to make sense.

"You think there is only one way. Your way! Such arrogance has led to this suffering."

Becka closed her eyes. Was this thing right? Was it really her fault? What would have happened if she'd listened to the Ascension Lady and helped from the beginning? She should have been open-minded, she should have been more willing to compromise …

Her eyes started to burn with tears. It *was* her fault. When you got down to it, all of this was her doing.

"There are many ways to the light. Your stubbornness has blocked them all."

Becka started to cry. Deep, heart-wrenching sobs shook her. The thing moved closer. Becka didn't have to open her eyes to feel it towering above her. But she no longer cared … she no longer had the energy or the will to fight. Whatever happened next was what she deserved. It was time to quit. Time to stop hurting others and give in.

The closer the thing bent toward her, the more she could feel her will and determination drain away. All she wanted was to sleep. To stop fighting, to give in, to let the thing take control.

"You will no longer resist. You will learn other ways. You will—"

"She will not!" It was Ryan. His voice sounded far, far away, but Becka still heard it. "There are no other ways! Jesus said, 'I am the way and the truth and the life. No one comes to the Father except through me!'"

The thing cried in surprise and staggered backward.

Becka felt her strength returning. Her eyes fluttered, then opened. Ryan stood inside the room. The shadow thing looked angry and confused, but when it spotted Ryan, its confusion gave way to mocking laughter.

"And who are you to oppose us?"

Ryan swallowed hard and shouted. "I am Ryan Riordan."

"You have no authority."

The boy was nervous, but he held his ground. "Of course I do. I am a Christian."

Becka's heart leaped to her throat. Was it possible?

"That gives you no authority."

Ryan hesitated, unsure. He threw a frightened look at Rebecca.

She looked on, still stunned. Then slowly a thought took shape. Maybe it was true. Maybe Ryan couldn't face this thing. Any more than she could … not on their own. But with the two of them together, joining forces … joined in faith … What was it the Bible said? "If two of you on earth agree about anything you ask for, it will be done for you by my Father in heaven. For where two or three come together in my name, there am I with them."

She took a deep breath, then shouted, "You're a liar!"

The thing spun back to her. "HE HAS NO AUTHORITY."

Becka racked her brain, trying to remember more of the Bible verses she'd been learning. Another sprang to her mind, and she shouted, "'I have given you authority ... Whatever you bind on earth will be bound in heaven.'"

The shadow cried and fell backward as if it had been hit.

Becka and Ryan exchanged looks across the room. They understood instantly. *This* was the sword they had talked about: the power of the Word of God. Ryan took a step closer and shouted: "'I am the way and the truth and the life. No one comes to the Father except through me.'"

Again the creature roared, part in anger, part in anguish. Rebecca threw a look to Ryan, puzzled that he'd chosen the same verse as before.

He shrugged. "It's the only one I know."

She almost smiled. With courage growing, she finally rose to her feet. They were finally on the offensive. Another verse came to mind. "'Resist the devil, and he will flee from you.'"

More agonized shouts. The shadow thing started to back up toward the distant corner. "THIS IS OUR DOMAIN. WE HAVE BEEN GRANTED IT."

"You're a liar," Becka shouted. "Everything you say is a lie. 'There is no truth in him ... He is a liar and the father of lies!'"

The creature roared.

"Stop it!" Becka cried. "Stop it this instant."

The shadow fell silent.

Still trembling, Becka forced herself to approach. "I demand that you stop these—"

"You have no authority."

"'The Lord rebuke you!'"

The creature shrieked, this time writhing as if someone had thrown acid on it. With growing confidence, Becka continued her approach. Ryan followed suit.

"I order you to stop these lies!"

"I am not—"

Becka raised her hand for silence, and the creature obeyed.

"I order you to stop these lies. No more games, no more counterfeits."

"I will not. I will—"

"In the name of Jesus Christ, I command you to go!"

The creature glared in rage.

"Now!"

Suddenly a brilliant light exploded from the thing's very center. It was so intense that Becka and Ryan had to look away. It sparkled and crackled throughout the creature's body. The thing screamed in agony and the room roared with thunder that reverberated through the entire house. But as the light faded, so did the creature. In less than a second it was gone. Its tormented shrieks and thundering took a bit longer to fade as they echoed about the room, but they, too, finally disappeared.

Rebecca and Ryan looked around. Everything had returned to normal. No wind, no howling. Most importantly, no Juanita. It was over.

Julie stuck her head through the doorway. To Becka's relief she looked perfectly normal.

"Is everything okay?" she asked.

Becka nodded. Julie stepped inside, followed by the others. Each looked worn and rumpled, but the illusions were gone. Everyone was back to their original selves. Even the Ascension Lady had regained consciousness and was sitting up, although she still looked pretty dazed and confused.

Ryan eased a step toward the corner where Juanita had last been. "Is she gone? She is, isn't she?"

"No."

Becka turned around to see Scott rising to his feet. "She ... they're still here," he said. "I can feel them. They're just playing possum."

Becka shuddered. Would this never end? She watched as her brother crossed to her. He reached down, took her hand, gave it a squeeze, then lowered it gently to her side. Without a word, he turned and walked toward the corner.

"Scotty?"

He did not answer.

"Scotty!"

When he reached the corner, he turned back to Becka and tried to flash her that lopsided grin of his. He didn't quite pull it off.

Becka watched as he turned back to the corner. He took a deep breath, hesitated, then said in a loud, controlled voice: "By the power and authority of Jesus Christ of Nazareth, I cast all of you out of this house and into the abyss!"

Nothing happened. There was no response. The room was as silent as ever. Scott cleared his throat and took another breath. "I command you to obey me … now!"

A faint breeze began to stir.

Everyone exchanged looks.

The breeze increased, blowing their hair. Soon it was tugging at their clothes, whipping their jackets. The moaning returned, growing louder and louder as the wind turned into a full-fledged gale. The moans evolved to wailing, then shrieks. The group bent down, some hanging onto one another — anything to keep their balance.

Scott was the first to see it. A slit of light in the corner directly before him. It was no longer than a foot and only a couple inches wide. The wind raced into it. Faster and faster the air roared past Scott and into the hole, until Scott himself started to be pulled in.

"Scotty!"

His footing slipped once, twice. He was losing his balance, being sucked into the opening. He tried to fight it, to pull back, but the force was too great.

Becka raced to his side, grabbing his arm, pulling for all she was worth. Ryan joined her and pulled the other arm. Together they hung on, refusing to let go. It seemed to last forever, though it was probably only a few seconds. Finally the wind died and, as the last of it disappeared, rushing into the opening, the slit of light vanished as well.

The wind was gone. Everything was still. Only the heavy breathing of Becka, Scott, and Ryan broke the silence.

Scott looked to Becka, then to Ryan, who was flipping the hair out of his eyes. They traded grins. It was over. For real this time. They were sure of it. Becka was the first to hold out her arms. The two guys instantly responded, and they fell into a three-way hug, each holding the others for all they were worth.

The others joined in—Julie, Philip, Krissi, Darryl ... even the Ascension Lady. She had stood off to the side, watching, until they motioned for her to join them. Everyone held everyone else in a massive group hug. It had been quite a night. It had been quite a seventy-two hours!

Of course, it wasn't entirely over. Both Becka and Scott knew there would be plenty of questions to be asked and explanations to be made. But one thing was certain: The Bible could be trusted. Always.

It said there were not ghosts, only Satan and his fallen angels.

It was right.

It said Christians had authority through Christ to beat them.

Right again.

All they had to do was take that authority, use the sword of God's Word, and wear God's armor—*all* of it, including the breastplate of righteousness.

Becka and Scott weren't fools. They knew they didn't have to be perfect to face the enemy—they just had to be headed in that direction. And when they messed up, they had to make sure they admitted it and asked Christ to forgive them.

All of these were important lessons they'd learned. Lessons that would help them in upcoming battles. Not that they'd go looking for fights with Satan and his groupies. They knew better than that. But they knew if and when they were called to help, they would go into battle, willing to fight and, with God's help, to win. That was a part of being warriors for the Lord.

Only now there were not just two warriors. Becka looked at Ryan and gave him an extra-hard hug. He flashed her that killer smile, the one that always made her stomach do flip-flops, and she smiled back.

Now there were three.

The Guardian

Satan himself masquerades as an angel of light.

2 Corinthians 11:14

1

"Well, that was a lot of fun," Scott said as he threw open the door to the old Hawthorne mansion and stepped outside. "Wha'dya want to do tomorrow night? Duke it out with Satan? Drop by and visit hell?"

The group groaned.

"I feel like I've already been there," Philip said, rubbing his neck.

The others agreed as they headed out of the darkened house and into the brisk early morning air. They still couldn't quite take it all in. What had started off as a simple séance in a deserted mansion had ended up as a major showdown between good and evil.

"I still don't get it," Krissi, the group's full-time beauty and part-time airhead, exclaimed. "I mean, so much stuff was going on; it was like a crazy, mixed-up dream, all jumbled and everything."

Rebecca took a deep breath of the cool air and slowly let it out. *No way was that a dream*, she thought.

Ryan had been watching her expression, and he reached out and gently pulled her toward him. It had not been a dream for him, either. Or for Scott. The three of them had just fought the battle of their lives. Everyone else had been distracted by illusions and hallucinations, but these three had fought with everything they had. And then some.

It had been close—too close at times—but God had used the three of them to literally beat back the forces of hell.

As they headed down the sidewalk to their cars, Priscilla, the only adult in the group, turned to Rebecca. She hadn't spoken since they left the upstairs room. Now her voice was hoarse with emotion. "Becka ...," she faltered. "Without your help ... if you hadn't shown up ..." She looked down to the ground and shook her head, unable to finish.

Becka nodded. Nothing more had to be said. As a channeler of the spirits, Priscilla had been in the most danger. True, Krissi, Philip, Darryl, and Julie had also been attacked, but their fight was more on an emotional level. The evil had actually entered Priscilla's body, so her battle had been more physical. And more violent.

Julie tossed her thick blonde hair to the side and motioned toward the eastern sky. "Hey, check it out." The horizon was already showing signs of pink and orange. "Can you believe we were in that place all night?"

"It felt longer than that," Darryl said, sniffing loudly.

"Anybody for breakfast?" Scott asked. "I'm starved."

"You're *always* starved," Ryan joked.

"Hey, we deserve it," Scott said, doing a mock karate kick and a couple punches in the air. "We beat them bad boys bad. If you ask me, it's time for a little victory celebration."

Becka winced. She loved her brother. She just wished he would do something about that ego of his. She sighed. Then again, he was a guy, so what could she expect?

"You kids go ahead," Priscilla said. She pressed the remote alarm on her key chain, and her car gave a little *beep-bop.* "I'm really exhausted."

The group nodded in understanding. Priscilla, better known

as the Ascension Lady because of the New Age bookshop she owned, climbed into her white BMW. She turned the ignition and gave a little wave as she pulled off. The group waved back and watched her disappear down over the hill.

Then slowly, one by one, their gazes drifted back to the mansion. There it stood on the hilltop, absolutely quiet, absolutely still. No more shadows fighting in the window, no more screams echoing down the hallway. Everything was normal, just as it should be. Just as it would always remain.

Still, there were the memories …

"Well," Philip finally broke the silence, "I think I'd better call it a night too." He held a hand out to Krissi and she took it.

"Sounds good to me," she said.

"What about the eats?" Scott asked.

Philip shook his head. "Some other time. Maybe we can get together tomorrow or something."

The others agreed, and Philip and Krissi started across the street toward his car. Halfway there, he turned back to Julie and called, "You riding with us?"

"Yeah," Julie answered, "I'll be right there." She turned to Becka, then reached out to take both of her hands. There was a moment of silence as the two friends held each other's gaze. "I don't know what all happened in there," Julie said quietly, "but I think we'd better talk. The sooner the better."

Becka held her look.

Julie continued, "I know we've teased you about your faith and everything, but part of me really takes that stuff seriously. And if what I saw in there really happened …" She hesitated, then shrugged. "Well, I just think it's something we need to talk about."

Becka nodded, hiding her excitement. This was something she had wanted to do for months. "Sure." She shrugged. "Anytime."

Julie gave her a quick hug, then turned and headed for the car.

Philip and Krissi had already climbed inside and cranked up the radio nice and loud. It was an oldies station. There was something about the old-time music blasting into the early morning that seemed reassuring. As though it reminded everyone that the world was still turning, that life still went on.

Ryan pulled Becka closer, and she looked into his blue eyes. Even though strands of jet-black hair hung in them, there was no missing their gentle sparkle — or that killer smile that always made her knees just the slightest bit weak.

"You did okay," he said, grinning.

"Yeah," she answered softly. "We both did."

The grin grew. They turned toward his car, a white vintage Mustang. Scott and Darryl stood beside it, stomping off the cold and waiting. "Yes sir," Scott was saying, "a three-egg omelet and a stack of cakes will do me just fine."

"And a side of onion rings," Darryl added.

"Onion rings?"

Becka started to comment, but the words never came. She wasn't sure if she saw it first or heard it, but an older gray car appeared out of nowhere. It roared over the top of the hill with only its parking lights on.

Becka spun to Julie, who hadn't quite finished crossing the street. The music from Philip's car was so loud she didn't hear the other vehicle.

"Look out!" Becka cried. "Julie, look— "

But Julie didn't have a chance. By the time she saw the car, it was on top of her.

Everything seemed to go in slow motion.

Julie tried to dodge the car, but the right headlight caught her in the thigh. The impact flipped her into the air until she was sailing over the hood, headfirst. She turned her face, and for the briefest second her eyes connected with Becka's. They were filled with pain and confusion.

When Julie came down, she missed the hood.

She did not miss the windshield.

Her neck and left shoulder smashed into the passenger's side with a dull, cracking sound. She tumbled across the roof, rolling once, twice, before being thrown to the pavement with a loud "Oof!" as the air was forced from her lungs. Then she lay there. Unconscious. Unmoving.

"Julie!" Becka screamed. "*Julie!*"

The car never slowed.

By the time the paramedics arrived, Julie had lost too much blood.

Becka had been the first to reach her friend's side. She was the one who insisted nobody move Julie in case her neck was broken. She was the one who ordered somebody to find a house and call 9-1-1. And she was the one who used her first-aid training to apply pressure to Julie's open wound and try to stop the blood. But the gash was too deep.

"Stay with me," she whispered into her friend's ear. "Don't go! Stay with me, Jules, stay with me ..."

Becka was so involved that she didn't hear the EMS vehicle pull alongside them.

"Please ... there's so much I've got to tell you ..." She didn't hear her friends describing the accident to the paramedics.

"Stay with me! Come on now, fight! You wanted me to tell you about God, and I will, but you have to stay with me. Oh, God ... do you hear me? Stay with me!"

She barely heard the paramedics speaking to her. "Okay, sweetheart, we've got her now. We'll take over."

Becka didn't move. "Please, Jules, don't go, don't go ..."

"Let us in there ...," the voice insisted, but it wasn't until she felt Ryan's firm hands around her shoulders and heard his voice that Rebecca finally allowed herself to be pulled away.

"It's okay, Beck. You've done all you can. It's okay."

Even then, she wouldn't leave. Her hands were covered with her friend's blood, her jeans were stained, and her cheeks smudged—but Becka remained, not caring how she looked, hovering over the scene. She watched as the paramedics took Julie's fading pulse and read her falling blood pressure. She prayed as they shoved IVs into the collapsing veins, lifted the limp body onto a gurney, carefully slid it into the vehicle, and shut the doors.

The one thing Becka didn't do was cry. Not a drop. Until the ambulance started to pull away. Then the sobs came. Hard and gut-wrenching. She could feel Ryan take her into his arms. She could hear him fumble for the words. But nothing helped.

"Why didn't I warn her?" she choked.

"Beck—"

"She should never have come with us."

"Becka, you tried—"

"You, me, Scotty—we're Christians! We can fight this stuff, but—"

"What are you saying? You don't believe what happened out here ... you're not saying it's connected with what happened in the mansion." It was as much a statement as a question. Ryan was new to all of this, and there was a lot he didn't understand.

Becka didn't have an answer. "I don't know." She buried her face into his chest. "I don't know, I don't know, I don't know ..."

It was only a dream. A hallucination.

But it was the most vivid dream Julie had ever experienced.

She was riding in an ambulance looking down at a cute paramedic. He was hunched over some poor soul, working for all he was worth, but the patient wasn't cooperating.

She'd never been inside an ambulance before so she knew she was having to make up a lot of the stuff she saw. For the most part, she was impressed with her imagination. Everything seemed so real, so lifelike.

"No breathing! No pulse!" the paramedic shouted up to the driver. "I'm starting CPR!"

Her dream-self watched as the paramedic ripped open a blue-and-green shirt. His head and shoulders blocked the victim's face, but Julie noted with interest that the person's shirt looked exactly like one she had picked up at an after-Christmas sale.

The paramedic placed his hands on the center of the patient's chest and began to pump vigorously. A growing curiosity tugged at Julie. She leaned past his shoulders to get a better look at the patient's face. It was pale. Lifeless . . .

And it was hers.

Oddly enough, Julie felt no panic. She experienced no fear. If anything, she felt a growing sense of peace. She remembered the speeding car — remembered sailing over the hood and smashing into the windshield — but none of that mattered. She was even losing interest in the paramedic's attempts at pounding life back into her chest.

Instead, Julie's attention was drawn to a gentle stirring. A breeze. It was barely noticeable at first, but it grew stronger by the second. It seemed concentrated around her upper arms and shoulders.

And then she saw it.

It wasn't wind, but a light. It was a light that gently touched and brushed against her shoulders. She turned to watch. Slowly, the light began to take shape until it had formed a person. Or something that looked like a person. Julie could make out a head and long flowing hair. Then a face, then a nose, and a mouth. The mouth wasn't smiling. But it wasn't angry, either.

And, finally, she saw the eyes.

It had been a long time since Julie had seen such tenderness and compassion. But they weren't weak eyes. They had a strength, a depth, and a love — the deepest love she had ever seen. Julie knew these eyes were true, she knew they could be trusted.

She felt a gentle tugging at her shoulders. The being never said a word, but he was making it clear that it was time for Julie to leave.

She took a final look at her body. Funny, but everything seemed so useless, so pointless. The clothes, the hair, the popularity. Weren't school elections coming up in just a few weeks, and hadn't she been fretting about whether or not to run for office? Julie almost laughed. None of that mattered now. It just seemed silly and vain.

Yes, it was definitely time to leave.

Julie looked into the creature's shining face. He nodded and they began to rise.

"Come on, sweetheart. Don't you quit on me!" the paramedic muttered in concentration. Julie looked back at him. He sounded so worried ... but the being was waiting, so she turned to follow.

2

They were in a tunnel.

The sides of the tunnel raced past, but Julie barely noticed. She was too mesmerized by the light at the end — a light that grew brighter every moment. It was the same light that radiated from the being who was escorting her.

But it was much more intense.

It contained every color in the rainbow and then some. Yet at the same time, it was absolutely ... pure. That was the word that kept coming to her mind. There was no other way to describe the light. It was simply ... pure.

As it struck her face and skin she could feel that purity embracing her, washing over her, seeping inside her. Never in her life had she felt so loved, so cherished. And the closer she drew to the light, the more deeply she felt that love.

Suddenly the walls to the tunnel fell away, and she was surrounded by even more light. Julie had heard stories of people dying, of them going through a tunnel and meeting a light. Like everyone else, she figured the light had to be God. But she didn't see him. Instead, she saw a city.

This was no ordinary city. It spread below them for miles.

And in place of concrete and steel were crystal and gems. Glowing crystals and gems. The buildings, the streets, the bridges ... everything glowed with the same light she was feeling.

It wasn't long before she saw the source of the light.

They were approaching a large, grassy knoll, and just on the other side, behind the rise, the light blazed the brightest. Julie couldn't explain it, but as they drew closer, her eyes began to fill with tears. Not tears of sadness; tears of joy. She knew that the light behind the knoll held the comfort to every sorrow and heartache she'd ever felt. She knew it was the answer to all of her pain and emptiness. She knew that in the presence of that light she would never be lonely again.

She also knew that it wasn't just light, but a person.

The paramedic was working silently, determination on his face. He plunged the needle of a syringe into a bottle and drew in a clear liquid. He reached for the Y connection of the IV tubing that led to Julie's arm and inserted the needle. He injected the drug quickly and steadily.

Pitching the syringe into a bag, he expertly slid his fingers down Julie's jawline to her throat and checked her pulse.

There was none.

Julie knew that whoever was on the other side of that knoll was the source of all the light, all the power. And all the love. She wanted to be with this person; she *had* to be with him. It was the most important thing in the world.

She started for the knoll, but to her surprise, her guide stopped her. She looked at him, puzzled. His face still radiated the same strength and kindness, but it was clear he did not want her to approach the knoll.

Julie tried again.

Again, he prevented her.

Her anxiety rose. They were passing the knoll. They were passing the very thing she wanted, the only thing she ever needed.

She tried again, with the same results. Her companion held her back. Fear took hold. Her stomach knotted. And the farther away they traveled from the knoll, the bigger the knot grew. She felt sick—like she was going to throw up. And still they continued moving.

Now different tears burned her eyes as loss and sadness swept over her. Her throat tightened with an unbearable ache of loneliness, and then, when the pain was the greatest, she saw it.

A park.

Directly below them.

But it really wasn't a park; it was more like a garden. A lush, manicured garden. Incredibly beautiful trees towered on every side, shimmering with such vivid color that they made the trees back home seem like shadows. The same was true of the stream that wandered through the garden. Its water was more *real* somehow than any she had ever seen. She thought it looked like sparkling diamonds as it splashed and swirled.

Julie noticed they were slowing down and dropping gently into the garden. She could see human forms of light standing on the lawn, gazing up at her. They waved, and suddenly she recognized faces: her Aunt Marcy, who had passed away when she was eight; a deceased cousin she had never met but whose picture hung in the hallway of her house; Grandma and Grandpa—looking exactly as they had when they were alive, only a lot stronger and happier.

As her feet touched the lawn she was surrounded by these loved ones and many others. Everybody was excited to see her; everybody wanted to hug her.

"Grandma!" Julie embraced her fiercely. "Is this heaven? Am I in heaven?"

The woman continued smiling, but there was no missing the concern around her eyes. She didn't speak, yet Julie could hear her voice.

"You don't belong here, honey. Not yet."

"But, Grandma ..."

"It's for your own good," Grandpa interrupted. "You're not ready, sweetheart. There's something you must do first. A decision you must make."

"But— "

"In good time," Grandma gave her a warm smile. "In good time."

The paramedic snapped on a small machine that quickly hummed to life. He grabbed two metal paddles, then squirted gel from a squeeze bottle onto their flat surfaces. Though his actions were precise and steady, his heart pounded.

"Here we go, sweetheart," he said grimly. He placed the paddles on Julie's chest, then depressed a small switch on one paddle.

Julie's body arched as the electricity surged through it, then slumped back down onto the stretcher.

Suddenly Julie felt a tug. Hard and forceful. Suddenly she was being pulled away—and her dream began to feel more like a nightmare.

She cried out in alarm. "Grandma?"

"It's all right, dear. You must return. You must make your decision."

She was plucked up into the air, flying backward, away from the group, away from the park.

"Grandma! Grandpa!"

But they quickly shrank in size as she flew away. Soon she couldn't see them at all. She was flying faster than ever before. The city blurred as she streaked past. Desperately, she searched for the knoll, the light, but it was nowhere to be seen. She looked for her guide, but he had disappeared. She tried to scream, but she was traveling too fast. Any sound she made was sucked out of her mouth by the roaring wind.

The tunnel closed back around her.

"No." She squeezed out a gasp. "Please ..."

Its sides raced past her at terrifying speed.

"No ..."

Now she was back over the ambulance, being sucked toward it with tremendous force. She covered her face as she approached the roof, but she felt no impact.

For a split second she saw the paramedic. Then her lifeless body.

Then there was nothing.

"We got her back!" the paramedic yelled to his partner. He took a deep breath and wiped the sweat from face. It had been close ... too close. He had almost lost her. But he had finally succeeded in starting her heart.

Becka also dreamed.

She dreamed of the gray car racing over the top of the hill. She dreamed of crying out a warning. And she dreamed of being too late.

It had been twenty-four hours since the accident. The group had followed the ambulance to the hospital and waited all morning and late into the afternoon. But since Julie remained in intensive care and since only her immediate family could visit, there wasn't much they could do.

The police came and asked a lot of questions. Philip and Ryan were able to identify the car as a gray Escort, but no one got the license number, and oddly enough no one could remember what the driver looked like.

By early evening, Julie's dad had convinced them to go home and get some sleep. He promised he'd call if there was any news. So finally, reluctantly, the group broke up and headed home for some much needed rest. Between the accident and the showdown at the mansion, it had been a long two days.

But rest didn't come easily for Becka. Once in bed, she kept tossing and turning. She kept reliving the accident, over and over, in her dreams. Was it her fault? Was there something supernatural she had overlooked in the mansion? Something that came out and attacked Julie on the street? Why hadn't the car slowed? Why hadn't anyone noticed the driver? The questions rolled and tumbled inside her mind.

Each time she dreamed of the accident, she tried to warn Julie, but each time she was too late. She hated it, but there was no way she could help in the dream, and there was no way she could stop the dreaming. Why did it keep returning? Was it guilt? Or was there something she was supposed to see?

By 3:00 a.m. her covers were twisted into a knot, her T-shirt was soaked with sweat—and still she dreamed.

Again the gray car crested the hill. Again in stop-frame slow motion, Becka cried out. Again Julie flew over the hood. But this time as Julie turned her head to see Becka, something changed. It was no longer Julie.

It was Krissi!

Becka gasped. Now it was the group's sweet, super-friendly airhead who looked at Becka in pain and confusion.

The dream shifted and started again. This time Becka was standing in the middle of the road. This time *she* was struck by the car and sent flying over the hood toward the windshield.

Another shift. Krissi was on the road. Krissi was hit. But before the cycle completed, there was another shift. Instead of Krissi flying, it was Becka again. And instead of ending, the dream continued as Becka sailed toward the windshield. She turned to see Julie and Krissi standing off to the side, watching. She looked back to the windshield. It was directly in front of her. She tried to cover her face, but there was no time. Then, a split second before hitting the glass, Becka saw the driver. Stunned disbelief coursed through her. The face looking back at her was ... her own.

She hit the windshield hard, felt the pain of impact, felt the glass shattering and wrapping itself around her head. And then she bolted awake.

Her heart pounded wildly as she sat trying to catch her breath. She reached for the nightstand light and snapped it on. This was no ordinary dream. She and Scott had both had dreams like this before. Something was going on. Something much deeper and more frightening than what appeared on the surface. And by the looks of things, Julie wasn't the only one in danger ... so was Krissi. So was Becka. She glanced at her radio clock.

3:14.

She would not be going back to sleep.

Krissi hated Monday. First there was the usual problem of concentrating on her studies. On good days, this was tough enough. Now, with one of her friends lying in the hospital, it was impossible. To top it off, it was the day of nominations, when each class nominated candidates for next year's student-body officers. Each class had to cram together into a single room and choose their vote.

Since the seniors weren't going to be around next year (well, most of them anyway), they got to go home early. That meant the juniors had the library; the sophomores, the gymnasium; and the freshmen, the cafeteria. When Krissi arrived at the library, it was hot and stuffy with standing room only. She couldn't do anything about the heat and stuffiness, but she knew how to get a seat. In a matter of seconds, she had managed to smile and flirt some guy into offering up one of the prized chairs. She thanked him graciously and took it.

Krissi really wasn't a user. She just figured it was okay to take advantage of the gifts she had. It wasn't her fault that those gifts happened to be a perfect body, perfect long, dark hair, and a perfect smile ... not to mention killer eyelashes. They were her pride and joy.

Krissi sat down and did her best to pay attention to the endless stream of "I nominate so-and-so" and "I second such-and-such." She hated politics almost as much as she hated school. Soon she was reaching down into her bag and pulling out a novel — the type with the handsome hunk in the torn shirt drooling over some babe with even less clothing. But after ten minutes, she closed the book with a sigh and turned back to her handbag for another distraction.

When she and her friends had been at the Hawthorne mansion, a very strange thing had happened: Krissi's hand had written a message all by itself. Back then, losing control like that had been pretty scary, and she had pleaded for it to stop. But lately, over the past day or so, the idea had started to intrigue her. In fact, she actually had begun experimenting to see if she could duplicate the experience.

So far the only words she'd written were "Check him out" and "What a fox," which she suspected came more from watching some college guys working out on the beach than from any supernatural inspiration.

Still, it was worth another try ...

She took out a pen and a spiral tablet, and began doodling. Nothing fancy. Her artistic skills were even less developed than her mental ones.

She glanced at her watch. Would this period ever end? She leaned her head on her free hand and closed her eyes. Somewhere in the background, she could hear Becka's unsteady voice nominating Julie for something.

Good ol' Rebecca, a friend to the end. Krissi thought it was kind of weird that she and Becka hung out together. But Becka had been Julie's friend, and what was good enough for Julie was good enough for Krissi.

Still, she and Becka couldn't be more opposite if they tried. Where Krissi knew every beauty trick in the book, Becka didn't even seem to know there was a book. Where Krissi enjoyed being the center of attention, Becka did her best to blend into the wallpaper.

Even so, Krissi liked Becka's sincerity. During all the time they'd spent together, Becka had never made a wisecrack about Krissi's intelligence. She liked that. Oh, sure, Krissi pretended to laugh when everyone teased her about her smarts, but deep inside it hurt. She appreciated never feeling that hurt around Becka. Oh, and there was one other thing Krissi liked: Becka's "ghostbusting" skills. All the extra attention Becka had been drawing didn't hurt their group's reputation one bit. It did bug her that sometimes Becka seemed to be a supernatural know-it-all, but that was a small price to pay for the fame they all were enjoying. Fame that had continued to grow as Krissi spread word about Becka's performance at the mansion Friday night.

The politics droned on. Krissi yawned loudly. Maybe they'd get the hint. Then again, they might consider the source and ignore her.

They did.

Soon her mind drifted to last summer ... then to the beach ... then to the mall ... until her head dropped forward and she started awake.

Mr. Lowry, the class sponsor, was reading the final tally and writing the winning names on the board. Krissi looked at them. It was pretty much as she suspected. Still, she was pleased to see that Ryan had won their class's nomination and would be running for president.

She glanced to her watch — 2:27. Three minutes to go. Her eyes drifted to the paper in front of her. It was mostly filled with doodles. But toward the bottom, the doodles had gradually turned to writing. And the writing had turned to names … names Krissi's hand had written, all by itself, while she was half-asleep, daydreaming.

Krissi looked back to the board as Mr. Lowry finished writing the last couple of winning nominees. She looked back down to the paper. A cold chill of excitement swept through her body. Excitement mixed with fear.

Her eyes shot back to the board.

The names on her paper were exactly the same as those Mr. Lowry was writing on the board.

3

Mom scraped the remaining macaroni off a plate and into Muttly's bowl. As usual, the puppy inhaled the leftovers without bothering to chew.

Becka stood at the sink, rinsing the dishes and putting them into the dishwasher. It had not been a good day. First, she still couldn't shake her dreams or her worries about Julie. Then there was Krissi, who, in a single day, had managed to spread word of the mansion showdown throughout the entire school. All day she could feel kids gawking at her, she could hear their whispers or — worse yet — the silence that fell over them as she passed. Becka knew some people would think all this reaction was cool, but she hated being the center of attention. She still remembered that time in eighth grade when she spent the entire evening before an oral book report shouting into her pillow, trying to work up a good case of laryngitis.

At dinner Becka hadn't said much. She didn't have to. Scott could rattle on about anything forever, and he usually did. But she knew her mother sensed something. It was simply a matter of time.

Sure enough, as they did the dishes, the question finally rolled around. "Becka, are you all right?"

Rebecca took a deep breath and quietly let it out. She didn't want to get into it. She wasn't ready to get into it.

But her mom wasn't going to let it go. "Beck, what's wrong?"

Fortunately, Scott exploded into the room. As usual he was a flurry of ego and energy. And, as usual, he expected the earth to come to a complete stop over his slightest problem. "Are there any chips?" he asked, throwing open the cupboard and searching. "Hey, who ate all the chips?"

"Scotty," Mom reminded him, "you had dinner twenty minutes ago."

"Exactly," he replied.

Mom and Becka exchanged looks. You can't beat that kind of logic.

Scott settled for a bag of pretzels, which he promptly crammed into his sweatshirt pocket as he started for the door.

"Where are you going?" Mom asked.

"To see Darryl's cousin, Hubert. He's got this cool computer game."

"You'll be back before ten?"

"Or eleven," he said.

"Ten or you won't be going at all."

"Ten-thirty?"

"Of course, you *could* stay and help your sister with the dishes."

"Okay, okay. Ten o'clock." He threw open the door, let it slam, and—just like that—the human hurricane was gone.

Now it was just the two women and the silence, except for the scraping and banging of dishes.

"So . . . ," Mom finally said, "where were we?"

Becka still didn't feel like answering, but she recognized the tone in her mother's voice, the one that said, "We'll-stand-here-all-night-if-you-want-to-but-you're-still-going-to-tell-me-what's-eating-you."

Becka took another breath. "I think ... I think there's more going on with Julie than just the accident."

"Really? Like what?"

"I don't know."

Her mother came to a stop and waited for more. There was none. She persisted. "Beck? What's up, honey?"

"I don't know," Becka repeated, shoving a plate a little too hard into the dish rack. "It's just ... I'm really tired."

Mom hesitated a second, then resumed gathering the dishes off the table. The silence piled up on Becka until she had to answer. "When Dad died, when we moved up here from Brazil, I expected to have a halfway normal life. I knew it would be hard, but ..." Her voice trailed off.

"But?"

"Scotty and I were barely here a month before we got sucked into a fight with the Society. Then there was that hypnotist jerk, then those satanists, then the mansion, and now ..." She could feel her throat tighten, but she wasn't sure why. "Who made us the experts, Mom? Why do we always have to be in the middle of the fight?"

Mom remained quiet.

Becka did her best to hold back, but the dam on her emotions was beginning to crack. Maybe it was the tension of nearly losing her best friend. Maybe it was the stares and whispers behind her back. Or maybe it was just everything.

"I'm sixteen!" she finally blurted. "What do I know about this junk!" Tears began burning Becka's eyes. She didn't know why, and that made her all the madder. "I didn't ask for all this spiritual stuff! I just want to be normal, I want to be like everyone else. Is that too much to ask?"

Mom started to reach for her, but Becka pulled away. She gave an angry swipe at her eyes and leaned both hands on the counter for support.

"Beck, what's—"

"I don't know!" she practically shouted. "How am I supposed to know? Everybody looks at me like I'm some sort of expert. But I don't know anything!"

Mom hesitated, then reached out to touch her daughter's shoulder. That was all it took. Becka turned and allowed herself to be pulled into her mother's embrace. Hot tears spilled onto her cheeks. "I didn't ask for this! I didn't ask to be the freak! Why can't I be like everybody else?"

Mom continued holding Becka as her tears flowed—tears that had been pent up for the past several days, the past weeks, ever since their first encounter with the Society.

Finally Mom spoke. Her own voice was a little thick with emotion. "Beck ... sweetheart. When you gave your life to the Lord, did you just give him part of it?"

Becka didn't answer.

"When you gave him your life, you gave him all of it, didn't you? You didn't keep a part for yourself."

"But I ... I didn't ..."

"I know. You didn't expect this. There are a lot of things we don't expect. I didn't expect your father to die. But isn't that where faith comes in? Isn't that where we have to trust that God knows best, even when we don't see it?"

Becka took a ragged breath. "But it's so hard."

"I know, I know."

"I just don't think I'm cut out for all of this spiritual warfare stuff."

Mom's voice was soft and gentle, but also firm. "That's not your decision, sweetheart. It's not up to you." She paused briefly, then continued. "And, Beck, if you don't tell people, if you aren't willing to help them ... who will?"

Rebecca chewed on the answer, not sure if she really agreed. And then the phone rang.

For a moment neither moved. Becka stirred. Part of her wanted to continue to be held, but part of her was embarrassed over the outburst. The embarrassment part won. She pulled away from her mother.

The phone continued ringing.

Without bothering to look at her mother's eyes (she knew they'd be wet too), Becka crossed to the telephone on the wall. She wiped her face, took a little sniff of composure, then picked up the receiver. "Hello?"

"Becka?"

The voice was a raspy whisper, but Rebecca recognized it instantly. "Julie? Julie, is that you?"

"Beck, it was so beautiful."

"Julie, are you all right? How are you feeling?"

"You were right, Beck. There *is* a God ... and a heaven. I saw them, Beck. I was there."

"Are you out of ICU?"

"It was so incredible, Beck."

"Hold on ... I'll be right over."

"It was so beautiful."

"Hold on."

"Wow!" Scott exclaimed as they entered Hubert's cluttered living room. He'd visited Darryl's cousin a couple of times before. Once when they'd tried to track down their mysterious computer friend Z, and more recently when they'd pulled a trick on the Ascension Lady by reprogramming her computerized astrological charts.

By now he was used to the electronic parts piled in heaps and scattered over the floor like some Radio Shack after a 9.5 quake.

He was even used to the thousand and one empty pizza boxes that never quite made it to the garbage. What surprised him this time were the half dozen people gathered in a circle in front of computer screens. Some had laptops. Others had desktops with monitors. Whatever the setup, each person stared quietly and intently at his screen.

"What are they doing?" Scott whispered.

"Crypts and Wizards," Darryl whispered back. He gave a loud sniff and wiped his nose with the back of his hand. Scott looked at his friend for a moment. He'd gotten used to Darryl's frequent sniffs, but he still couldn't quite appreciate his friend's version of a handkerchief. "Crypts and Wizards? What's that?"

"It's a role-playing game."

"A what?"

"You pretend to be somebody, like a sorcerer or zombie or witch or something. Then you use your powers to try and find the treasure buried deep inside the crypt."

Scott looked at the players. Their faces were glued to their screens, almost trancelike. "They really get into it, don't they?"

"Oh yeah. Sometimes the games go on for hours, days, even weeks. It's like you really become the person. Come on. I asked Hubert to save a couple of places for us." He gave another sniff and motioned for Scott to follow.

"Where is Hubert?" Scott asked. "I don't see him."

"He's upstairs. He's the Crypt Master. He's the guy who drew up the crypt map with all of its traps and monsters and stuff."

"Yeah?"

Darryl nodded. "He basically runs the game." At last they arrived in front of two empty computer terminals. "Here we go."

Scott checked out the screen in front of him. It wasn't too impressive. Just some graphs, the beginning of a maze, and some bizarre figures of people and creatures. "Doesn't look like much," he said as he took a seat behind the console.

Darryl threw him a grin. "Just wait."

"Are you sure it was your grandmother?" Ryan asked.

"Oh yeah." Julie grinned. Her voice was weak and thin. Her hair was stringy in front and matted in the back, and she wore the lamest hospital gown they had ever seen—but inside, Julie bubbled with excitement. "It wasn't just Grandma. My grandpa, my aunt ... people I know are dead were there. It was so incredible. They were, like, all standing in this park with these cool trees and this superclear stream—and the water, it was like diamonds it was so clear."

Rebecca sat on Julie's bed listening to her friend chatter on. It was great having her back. But even as she listened, a tiny alarm started to sound in her head.

"Oh, Becka," Julie beamed. "It was so cool. There was, like, this glowing city, all made of crystal and jewels and stuff. And the light, everywhere there was light. But it didn't come from the sun or anything like that."

"Where did it come from?"

Without blinking Julie answered her directly. "It was God, Beck. The light came from God."

The alarm grew louder. She couldn't put her finger on it, but something didn't fit.

"You saw God?" Ryan asked.

Julie shook her head. "Not exactly. But I was so close I could have, I know it." Becka searched Julie's eyes to see if she was teasing. There was nothing but sincerity in them. "Beck ... he's so cool. I mean, everywhere I went I felt this incredible love, this total ... acceptance. He loves us so much, Becka. You can't even imagine it."

Becka tried to hold Julie's gaze, but couldn't. Her eyes faltered, then looked away.

"Beck, what's wrong?"

Rebecca shook her head. "I don't know ... It's just—I mean,

are you sure it wasn't just a dream? Dreams can seem pretty real."

Julie smiled. "No, Beck, this was no dream."

Becka had her doubts. But this was her best friend. She'd almost been killed. This was not the time to argue. She looked away and spotted a chunk of crystalline rock on the nightstand. It was about the size of her fist, and it was so clear it almost looked like ice. Grateful to change the subject, she turned back to Julie and asked, "What's that?"

"Oh, the Ascension Lady came by earlier and dropped it off." Julie reached over and scooped it into her hand. "It's pretty neat."

"Why'd she bring it over?" Ryan asked.

Julie chuckled. "You know Priscilla. I talked to her on the phone earlier. I told her all about my angel guide and everything, and she got—"

"Your ... angel?" Becka interrupted.

"Oh yeah, I had this angel with me the whole time. Anyway, Priscilla says my spirit has been 'awakened,' or something like that. She says that if I practice with this thing—" she hefted the crystal in her hand and grinned mischievously—"I'll be able to call up my guardian angel anytime I want. I'll be able to evolve to a 'higher level of consciousness.'"

"Good ol' Priscilla," Ryan chuckled. He threw a grin at Becka. "Some things never change."

Becka didn't smile back. The alarm in her head was much louder. She was sure Julie was wrong. That what she had seen couldn't be real. But why? What was wrong?

"Hey, Jules, nice hair."

Everyone turned to see Krissi and Philip enter. Philip was holding an arrangement of red and white carnations they'd picked up from the gift shop downstairs.

"Oh, guys!" Julie exclaimed as she reached out to take the flowers. "They're beautiful." Her voice was getting weaker. She did her best to sound bright and cheery, but there was no missing the exhaustion setting in.

Being his usual sensitive self, Ryan was the first to notice. "Look, Julie, maybe Beck and I should be going. Let you spend a little time with—"

"No, please stay," Julie insisted. She turned to Krissi and Philip. "Ryan and Beck can fill you in on my adventures ... but somebody has to tell me what I've been missing at school. What's the latest?"

As All-School Gossip, Krissi knew it was her duty to give the report. "Kind of a slow day," she said with a shrug. "As far as I know, nobody broke up with anybody. No fights. No arrests. Nobody new is pregnant—"

"But you missed a great chemistry quiz." Ryan grinned.

Philip motioned toward Ryan. "And our boy wonder there, he's about to become the next school president."

"Oh, that's right, nominations were today," Julie said, disappointed. "I really wanted to run for something."

"Becka tried to nominate you," Krissi said, "but she got voted down."

"They didn't know when you'd be coming back," Philip explained.

Julie turned to Becka. She didn't have to say thanks, it was in her eyes.

"Anyway," Krissi continued, "elections are in two weeks, and Ryan Riordan is going to win by a landslide."

Ryan chuckled. "Let's not count our ballots before they're hatched."

"You'll win the election," Krissi insisted. "I know you will."

Ryan smiled. "We'll see."

"No, I'm telling you, you're going to win."

"You been borrowing Priscilla's crystal ball?" Julie teased.

"Better than that." There was no hiding the twinkle in Krissi's eyes. "This afternoon, I knew he was going to win the nomination before they finished counting the ballots." She dug into her handbag. "Here, I'll show you."

The group exchanged glances as Krissi continued to dig. Becka cleared her throat. She tried to keep the question light and casual. "How'd you know that, Krissi?"

"Remember, in the mansion, how my hand was writing that stuff without me controlling it?"

Becka nodded.

"Well, the neatest thing is starting to happen." She kept digging. "I've been doing a little experimenting, and I think I've found a way to get my hand to keep doing it."

"Krissi," Julie warned.

"I know, I know," Krissi answered, "it was scary then, but now I know how to control it."

"Are you sure that's, you know … smart?" Becka ventured.

The word "smart" was a wrong choice, and Krissi immediately shot back, "As smart as any of *your* hocus-pocus stuff." The words stung, but Becka let them pass.

"Ah, here we go." Krissi pulled out the pad and flipped it to the page with all the doodles. "See … down here," she pointed to the bottom of the page. The group moved in closer to look. "Those are the names of everyone nominated from our class. And my hand wrote them *before* Mr. Lowry put them on the board."

The alarm in Becka's head sounded louder. She glanced at Ryan. He was still looking at his name on the sheet. Krissi continued, "Then when I got home, I did it again." She flipped through more pages, found what she was looking for, and ripped it out of the spiral notebook. "It's a message. It's for you, Becka."

Rebecca felt a chill.

Krissi held it out to her. "Take a look. I don't know who's doing the writing or anything, but it's not like what we ran into at the mansion. This guy, or whatever it is, sounds pretty friendly."

Becka took the paper.

"Krissi," Philip said, "after all we went through at the mansion, are you sure you want to play around with something like that?"

"Why not?" Krissi chirped. "I'm the one controlling it. It doesn't happen unless I let it." She turned back to Becka. "Go ahead, read it. Whoever is writing it wanted you to have it."

Becka tried her best to appear calm as she looked to the paper. Unfortunately her hands were shaking. Then there was the familiar chill wrapping itself around her shoulders. There were only three sentences. She read them out loud:

" 'You have awakened their powers. Now you must release them. You must allow them to evolve into a higher level of consciousness.' "

The alarm that had been sounding in Becka's head started screaming. She barely heard Julie exclaim, " 'Higher level of consciousness'? Are you serious? That's the exact phrase the Ascension Lady used!"

4

Ryan eased the Mustang through the wet, foggy streets. Becka's house was only ten or fifteen minutes from the hospital, and they were practically there.

" 'Awakening their powers'? " Ryan repeated. "What's that supposed to mean? 'Evolve to a higher level of consciousness'? Sounds like something from *Star Wars.*"

Becka wasn't smiling. "I knew something was up. When we entered the room ... didn't you feel it? Didn't you feel something was wrong?"

"You mean with Julie?"

Becka nodded. "And with her going to heaven. It couldn't have been real. It has to have been some sort of dream or hallucination or ..."

Ryan looked at her. It was obvious he had doubts. "Beck, lots of people see angels and light. When people die and come back, lots of them have said they were in heaven and saw that stuff."

"That's just it ... What was Julie doing in heaven if she wasn't a Christian?"

Ryan threw her another look.

She shrugged. "I know how that sounds. I love Julie too,

she's my best friend. I don't want to be judgmental or anything, but ..." She struggled to put the thought into words.

Ryan finished it for her, "If she's not a Christian, she's supposed to go to hell."

Becka winced. "That sounds so harsh."

"You bet it does."

Becka looked at him. The scowl across his face told her he disapproved. "But ...," she ventured, "that's the whole reason Jesus died on the cross, so we wouldn't have to go to hell."

Ryan said nothing. The scowl deepened.

She continued, still testing the waters, "I mean, isn't that why you became a Christian?"

"I became a Christian because it was the right thing to do. I read that New Testament you gave me, and it made more sense than anything I'd ever read. But as far as hell and all of that ..." There was a trace of irritation in his voice. "I don't know, Beck. I don't think I can buy that this super-loving God of ours can send innocent kids to hell."

Becka nodded. "It's hard, I know. But the Bible says—"

"The Bible also says there's a heaven ... a heaven that sounds a lot like the place Julie saw." He turned to her. "You know the part I'm talking about?"

"Well, sort of ..."

He motioned toward the backseat. "Go ahead and check it out."

Becka turned to the back. Somewhere underneath all those clothes, books, CDs, and magazines was the Bible she had given him. The one he'd been reading almost every day. She started rummaging.

Ryan was an incredibly gifted guy. Unfortunately, neatness wasn't one of those gifts. She continued the search until Ryan pulled to a stop in front of her house. Then, without even looking, he reached back and produced the book. "You just have to know the system." He grinned.

Becka grinned back. It was good to see him smile again. They'd only had a few small disagreements—not even real arguments—and none of them had gotten out of hand. She was glad this one wouldn't, either. Not that they didn't have discussions and debates. When it came to the Bible, they had lots of them. Ryan always had opinions, but he was also open enough to ask questions or admit when he was wrong. Becka was always honest enough to admit if she didn't have an answer. But this talk on hell ... wasn't hell, like, a major part of the Christian faith? Still, somewhere, deep inside, Becka had to admit she wondered, too, how such a loving God could send people to such a terrible place.

She watched Ryan flip through the worn pages. There was no denying it. She loved being around this guy. Somehow, without even trying, he made her feel warm and secure and a little trembly all at the same time.

She was clueless what he saw in her. It certainly wasn't her thin, mousy brown hair, or her five-foot-six, nearly nonexistent figure. And let's not forget her personality. As best she could figure, she didn't have one. Turn her loose at a party, and you could always depend on her to stand off to the side, doing her best imitation of a potted plant.

But not Ryan. He loved being around people. And they loved being around him. And for some unexplained reason, he especially seemed to enjoy being around her.

As he pored over the pages, his thick black hair fell into his eyes. Becka wanted to brush it back, to tenderly push it aside, but she knew better. Not now.

"Ah, here we go." He tossed his hair back. "It's in the last book of the Bible, Revelation." He began reading: " 'He showed me the Holy City, Jerusalem, coming down out of heaven from God. It shone with the glory of God, and its brilliance was like that of a very precious jewel, like a jasper, clear as crystal.' "

Ryan looked up.

Becka nodded. "It's true, that's exactly what she said she saw."

He continued. "There's more: 'The angel showed me the river of the water of life, as clear as crystal, flowing from the throne of God and of the Lamb, down the middle of the great street of the city. On each side of the river stood the tree of life, bearing twelve crops of fruit, yielding its fruit every month.' "

Again, he stopped and looked up.

Becka took a slow, deep breath. "Then what Julie saw really exists."

Ryan nodded. "So I was right. Non-Christians *do* make it into heaven."

Becka frowned. "I don't understand. I mean, the Bible ... it talks about heaven. We know it's real. But was Julie really there?" She shook her head in confusion. "The Bible talks about hell, too. But ... I mean, it ... " She dropped off, trying to piece it all together. Suddenly she had an idea. She looked at Ryan. "What time do you have?"

Ryan looked at his watch. "A little before nine. Why?"

Becka opened her car door. "I know someone who might be able to help."

"What? Who?"

She stepped out of the car and slammed the door. "Z."

Instantly Ryan was at her side. "That computer guy on the Internet?" He tried unsuccessfully to cover his excitement. "Beck, are you going to finally let me talk to this guy?"

"Come on," she said, "we don't want to miss him."

Julie couldn't explain it, but somehow, some way, she was entering the crystal.

Everyone had left her hospital room. She was all by herself, and she was tired. Dead tired. But not tired enough to ignore the beautiful, clear stone she held in her hand. It was like a diamond, the way it sparkled and refracted the light. Julie's forehead creased in concentration. What had the Ascension Lady said? Her powers had been awakened, and she could use the crystal to summon her angel?

Normally, Julie wouldn't pay that much attention to the woman, but she kept thinking about her grandfather's words: *"You're not ready … There's something you must do first. A decision you must make."* Maybe this whole thing was a part of that decision?

Then there was the fact that Priscilla had used concepts and phrases identical to the note Krissi had written for Becka.

Strange. Very strange …

With that in mind, Julie had begun staring into the rock, looking deeper and deeper into its colors and its light. *"Feel its power,"* Priscilla had said. *"Push aside your own thoughts and merge with its energy."*

At first nothing happened. Julie felt no power, no energy. But as she let her eyes blur, as she relaxed and let her mind empty, a strange sensation started to overtake her. She began forgetting about the hospital — the beige walls, the forest green drapes, the steady roar of the air conditioner, even the bed with its too-firm mattress and too-coarse sheets — everything began to just melt away as though they were no longer there. As though *she* were no longer there.

And for good reason. She wasn't. She had entered the crystal.

She marveled at the incredible colors — their delicate patterns and diversity amazed her. And with the colors came the light. Brighter and brighter it grew, washing out the other colors, overcoming them with its brilliance until there was nothing but the light.

Julie felt excitement surge through her, but as it did so, the light suddenly dimmed and faded. Forcing herself to stay calm, she shoved her excitement aside and again allowed her thoughts to drift. As she emptied her mind, the light returned.

Apparently, it would remain only if she kept her mind free and open.

The light began to condense, slowly taking on a human shape. Immediately Julie knew it was an angel, but it wasn't the one she'd seen before. This one was different somehow ... Julie wasn't quite sure how, she just knew it was.

Then one difference became clear. Very clear.

This angel spoke. It was as though a thought was forming in her mind, but it definitely was not *her* thought.

I am an emissary sent from the Most High.

Julie's heart pounded. She was right! There was no doubting who the Most High was, so this must have been what her grandmother was talking about! But as the excitement came, the light faded. Quickly she pushed her emotions aside, trying to stay calm, trying to stay empty.

More thoughts came.

I have been sent as your new guardian. You are most favored. You have been chosen.

For what? Julie thought back. *Chosen for what?*

There was a pause, then the reply.

You will undergo a spiritual awakening. You have been chosen to enlighten others, to raise them to a higher level of consciousness.

Julie started to tremble. All her life she had felt called to do something, to be a somebody. Of course, she had never told anybody that, but the feelings had always been there, pushed deep down inside.

Again, the light began to waver and fade.

Where are you going? Julie asked, startled.

You are too full of self. The being continued to fade. **You must evolve past your own identity, past the physical.**

Please, don't go. Please ...

The light continued fading. The thoughts grew fainter. **There is too much of you ...**

No, please tell me what to do, I'll do it, just tell me.

The light was almost gone. Only a final thought remained behind: **You must empty yourself. If you are to serve, you must be drained of self and filled with light.**

But—

Suddenly Julie was back in bed. There was no more light, no more voice, just the hard mattress and coarse sheets—and Julie's heartsick emotions. She had failed. She had been called. Called to something great.

But she had failed.

Julie reached over and set the crystal on the nightstand. She was too tired to try again, but she hoped for another chance. In a few hours she would be rested enough to reenter the crystal. She would work for as long as it took to go deeper into the mysteries of her guardian, to understand the great designs he had for her. Even if it took all night. Or the next day. It didn't matter *how* much time it took.

She was not going to disappoint him again.

Becka slid into her brother's desk chair and fired up the computer. The blue glow of the screen lit both her face and Ryan's.

"BEAM ME UP, SCOTTY, BEAM ME UP." Cornelius, Scott's pet parrot, paced back and forth on his nearby perch. He had been with the family for as long as Rebecca and Scott could remember.

"MAKE MY DAY. MAKE MY DAY. *SQUAWK!* MAKE MY DAY."

Becka winced. When she and Scott had first taught the bird those phrases, they were cool and everybody quoted them. Unfortunately, when the sayings went out of style, they neglected to go out of Cornelius's vocabulary.

"BEAM ME UP! BEAM ME UP!"

Becka turned back to the screen as the connection was made

with the chat room. Z was Scott's mysterious friend, the one who had taken an interest in Becka and her brother from the start. No one knew who he was or where he came from, but he was a definite expert on the supernatural.

Becka pulled down the appropriate menu and clicked the mouse.

"You say he usually comes online around nine?" Ryan asked.

"Yeah, or we can just leave each other messages."

Ryan nodded.

"Here we go," Becka said as she entered her brother's password: "Dirty Socks."

Now they were online. She typed:

Z? Are you there? It's me, Rebecca.

They waited. Even though Becka and Scott had talked to Z half a dozen times, it always frightened her a little. Not because Z knew so much about the occult, but because he knew so much about them ... personal things, things that nobody should know ... things nobody outside of the family *could* know.

Finally, the words formed on the screen:

Good evening, Rebecca.

How was your visit with Julie?

Ryan gasped in surprise. "How'd he know we were there?"

Becka shrugged, trying to shake off the uneasiness. "He just knows that stuff."

She turned back to the screen and typed:

Z, Julie said she died and an angel took her to heaven. Is that possible?

After a pause the words appeared:

Opinion regarding near-death experiences is divided.

In what way?

Some experts believe the experience is a hallucination—the effects of chemicals being released into the brain as it begins shutting down.

Becka nodded. Well, at least there was an explanation.

"Ask him about the others," Ryan urged. "He said *some* experts. Ask him what the others say."

Becka typed:

What do other experts believe?

Many believe the soul actually leaves the body. That sometimes it is accompanied by an angel or angels through a tunnel to another dimension where God awaits.

You mean heaven?

They waited. There was no response. Finally Becka typed:

If everybody who dies goes to heaven, then what's the point of being a Christian?

Another pause. This time it was followed by an answer:

Christians believe when they stand before God's throne to be judged, they will be found innocent because Christ paid for their sins. Correct?

Correct.

Where do you suppose that throne is?

Becka looked over to Ryan, then typed:

I imagine in heaven.

Precisely.

"Of course," Ryan slapped his forehead. "We should have known that."

Ryan leaned back in his chair. "Ask him about hell," he said.

Becka nodded.

Z, I know the Bible talks about hell. But how can a loving God send people there?

They waited, but no words appeared.

"Why doesn't he answer?" Ryan asked.

"Sometimes he just doesn't. At least not right away." As she spoke, more words appeared on the screen, but they were not the answer to Ryan's question:

Regarding Julie's experience, please remember that angels, heaven, hell, the supernatural—all are legitimate experiences if they come from God.

How do you know the difference?

We cross the line into the occult when we attempt to create a supernatural experience on our own.

Please explain.

God is the worker of the supernatural. When we take a shortcut and try to create a supernatural experience on our own—through meditation, channeling, Ouija boards, drugs, crystals—we open ourselves up to satanic counterfeit.

The tiny alarm went off in Becka's head again. The same one she had heard earlier in the hospital room. She turned to Ryan.

"What's wrong?" he asked.

"Remember that crystal? Remember Julie said the Ascension Lady had given it to her to call up her angel."

Ryan frowned. "Becka, I really don't think that's—"

Before he could finish, she spun back to the computer and typed:

Z . . . are you telling us that not every angel is a good angel?

There was no answer. Becka felt her hands getting damp, her stomach tightening. Once again that old, familiar chill crawled up her spine.

Z . . . are you there? Z, answer me.

And then, ever so slowly, the final letters formed:

Good night, Rebecca. Tell your friend good night too.

The couple stared at the words in stunned silence.

5

Krissi's folks were at it again. It was the usual rantings and ravings over who was spending too much money on what. Same old screamings. Same old door slammings. As usual, Krissi was hiding out in the safest place to be when the fur flew. Her bedroom.

But tonight she barely noticed the shouting. She was too busy practicing her special writing. She'd already learned the basics. First, she had to stay relaxed. That meant closing the door, drowning out the fighting parents with a CD, and getting nice and comfortable at her desk.

Next came the pen and tablet. She set them on the desk, poised the pen over the paper, and did something she felt particularly qualified to do: She thought of nothing. Of course, all of this still made Krissi nervous—memories of her hand writing on its own at the mansion still gave her the willies—but something even stronger than the fear kept her going.

That something was the thrill. It was exhilarating to play with danger, to toy with and even control the unknown. But there was something even better than that...

There was the prestige.

All her life she'd put up with the airhead comments. All her life she'd endured the "beautiful but dumb" snickerings behind her back. For the most part, it looked like people were right: Thinking didn't seem to be her strong suit. But that didn't mean she wasn't important, that she wasn't a somebody. She was. And if anybody had doubts, let them read that last message. It was beautiful, brilliant, profound … well, at least what she could understand of it.

Krissi closed her eyes and started doodling on the tablet. The arcs were big and wide as she waited for something to happen. After several seconds she looked down.

Nothing but big and wide arcs.

Her parents' voices grew louder. She reached over and cranked up the boom box until the room throbbed with music. It was some alternative group that a guy had given her while trying to put the moves on her. She hated it. Unfortunately, all of her cool CDs were in Philip's car, so …

She resumed doodling. Once again she allowed her mind to drift. Then, gradually, it began. She felt her hand moving on its own. It was an odd sensation, but it only lasted a few seconds before it stopped.

She opened her eyes and looked at the paper. The scribbles had turned to a different and very distinct handwriting. But it was only four words:

Turn that noise down!

Krissi raised her eyebrows. Apparently, her hand had better taste in music than she thought. "All right, all right," she chuckled, "you don't have to get cranky about it." She reached over and turned down the player. Then she repositioned herself, took a few more deep breaths, and closed her eyes.

Instantly, her hand started moving.

She was pleased that the writing came so quickly. She was definitely getting the hang of it. She wanted to peek, but every time she looked at her hand or became conscious of it, everything came to a halt. So she kept her eyes closed and her mind empty.

She wasn't sure how long it was before her hand stopped. But when she opened her eyes, she was surprised to see that she had filled an entire page with the strange handwriting.

Krissi smiled. *Wait'll the others see this.* She pulled the tablet closer and started to read.

Greetings in the name of the Intergalactic Alliance.

She felt a rush of excitement. This was new.

You and your group have been chosen. You will join with other Light Workers on your planet to prepare for our coming. With the guidance of the Ascended Masters, you will teach others to evolve past their three-dimensional levels and achieve a higher state of consciousness.

Krissi stopped reading and stared at the words. She wasn't sure what they meant, but they seemed important. One thing she definitely understood, though: the part that said she had been chosen.

She continued reading.

However, you must be warned of a female in your group. Although she has introduced you to us, her jealousy and insistence upon clinging to outdated religious beliefs will prevent you from achieving your rightful position of power. She is extremely dangerous to you and your group. As a Chosen One, you must avoid her. For your own health and safety, be warned.
Sincerely, Xandrak.

Krissi's heart pounded harder. There was an actual name. An actual person was writing through her! Then she frowned as she reread the last paragraph. A member of their group would be holding her back. A female who had introduced them to the supernatural was standing in Krissi's way.

Not only standing in her way, but this person's — she read the words again — "jealousy" and "outdated religious beliefs" would actually be dangerous to her.

Krissi sat back thoughtfully. Only one person fit that bill. Already Krissi could feel the slightest trace of anger starting to burn. How dare she be held back! How dare someone like Becka stand in her way, especially over something as important as changing the world!

Krissi reached for the phone and hesitated. Should she call and confront Becka? Or should she tell Philip and the others first?

From inside, a quiet, almost imperceptible voice whispered, *Philip.*

She nodded and dialed Philip's number.

At that exact time another phone call was being made. It was late, and Ryan had already gone home. Now Becka was on the phone, pleading with the night nurse at the hospital to ring through to Julie's room. It took some doing, but the woman finally gave in.

When Julie answered, her voice was brimming with excitement.

"Hello?"

"Julie, it's Becka. Are you okay?"

"Becka, it's *so* cool, you wouldn't believe it."

Rebecca swallowed back her uneasiness. "What is?"

"My angel. I've talked to him two or three times tonight. And he's got so much to teach me, so much to teach all of us."

Becka's mouth went dry. She tried to keep her voice steady. "Julie ... listen, are you playing around with that crystal? Are you calling up your ... angel?"

"It's just like the Ascension Lady said." Julie was practically giggling. "He's always there, waiting for me, ready to teach me. There's so much to learn, Beck, and so much love. You wouldn't believe the love."

"Jules ..." Becka tried to swallow again. "Jules, I think you're in danger."

She heard a soft chuckle on the other end.

"Julie, you've got to stop calling that thing up. It's not real, it's a counterfeit."

"No way! He's too loving, too powerful. And he's promised me that same power. He's promised it to all of us."

"Julie—"

"Look, I'd better be going."

"But—"

"I get to go home tomorrow morning. Call me there."

"But, Julie, it's—"

"It's okay, Beck, I promise. You won't know till you experience it. But don't worry. I'll teach you how."

"But—"

"Good night, Becka." There was a click on the other end, followed by the dial tone.

Rebecca stared at the receiver. Her face drained of color. She looked at her hands. They were beginning to shake.

6

No offense, Beck, but it almost sounds like you're jealous."

"Jealous?" Becka said in disbelief. "Me?"

"It's only natural," Philip continued. "Hand me up another piece of tape, will you?"

Becka tore off a strip of masking tape and lifted it up to Philip. He was balanced precariously on a ladder, trying to hang a poster over an archway in the school. Ryan stood nearby, unrolling another poster. It was 7:30 a.m. Thirty minutes before classes started. A few kids were wandering in, but for the most part the place was still empty.

The three of them were hard at work putting up the campaign posters that members of Ryan's campaign committee had made the night before. This one was particularly impressive. Not only for its classy lettering—"Ryan for President" was scripted in gold metallic paint and highlighted by deep burgundy shadows—but also for its location. Philip was hanging it directly over the steps leading to the cafeteria.

Of course, Krissi should have been there too. But, as usual, she was late. Probably something about her hair, makeup, nails, or whatever.

After calling Julie, Becka had been up all night. She tried calling Z back, but it was too late. She tried talking to Scott, but he was too exhausted. Lately, when her brother wasn't in school, he was spending every waking hour over at Darryl's cousin's place, playing some stupid computer game. She barely saw him anymore. Of course, she had tried to call Julie at home the next morning. But for whatever reason, Julie wasn't accepting calls. And now, to top it all off, Philip was mistaking her concern as jealousy.

"I'm not jealous, Philip. I'm just worried about her, that's all. She shouldn't try to make supernatural stuff happen on her own. It's too dangerous."

"But it's okay for you?" Philip asked.

"I—I didn't say that," Becka said, a little flustered.

"Look," Philip continued, "in the beginning it was just you and your brother, and that was cool. You guys were the ones experiencing all the mystical junk. But now Julie is starting to get in on the action. And so is Krissi. I guess it's only natural that you'd be a little—"

"Philip, I am *not* jealous. I'm worried. I mean, if we learned anything at the mansion, it was that not everything supernatural is good."

"But," Ryan corrected, "not everything supernatural is necessarily bad, either."

Becka glanced at him. It was obvious Ryan was still thinking about last night's disagreement over heaven and hell. Philip nodded. "My point, exactly. What's so bad about an angel? Everybody's talking about them. I mean, just look at the TV, movies, magazines, books."

Becka wanted to respond, but at the moment, she was feeling a little outnumbered.

"Remember what Krissi's note said?" Philip asked.

Ryan chuckled. "Yeah. Awakening our powers? Evolving to a higher level of consciousness?"

"Don't laugh. Isn't that the exact thing Julie is experiencing, going into another dimension with her angel buddy? And isn't that exactly what the Ascension Lady predicted?"

Ryan grew more serious. "You think there's a connection? Between Julie and Krissi?"

Philip chose his words carefully. "I think something's been happening ever since the mansion. It's like something's been, I don't know, turned loose in Julie and Krissi. And," Philip tried to soften the next phrase, but there was no missing its sting, "I think Becka has to stay open. She has to be careful not to hold us back."

The words burned in Becka's ears. Hold them back! She was the one who had *saved* them in the first place. She was the one trying to protect them!

Philip leaned farther over the steps and the ladder started to tilt forward.

"Becka!" Ryan reproved. "Hold it steady."

She looked at him, surprised. It was the first time he had ever raised his voice at her.

A little embarrassed, he returned to his work on the other poster and resumed the conversation. "What do you mean, hold us back? How could Rebecca hold us back?"

Philip continued reaching across the stairs. "I got a call from Krissi last night. She received another message."

Ryan and Becka exchanged looks. "Phil," Ryan ventured, "do you think that stuff's okay?"

"You mean is it for real?"

"Well, yeah, for starters."

"The handwriting's not Krissi's, I can tell you that. In fact, it has a left-handed slant to it. Krissi is right-handed. Besides, like I said, it fits with what's happening to Julie and what the Ascension Lady said."

"So that makes all that stuff good?" Becka asked incredulously. She immediately bit her lip, wishing she hadn't sounded so defensive.

Philip looked down at her. His voice was calm, which made her feel even more stupid. "I didn't say they were good or bad, Becka. I'm just suggesting you stay open and not stand in our way."

Becka looked to Ryan, hoping for some defense, but he busied himself with the other poster. She felt a slight tightening in her throat. Ryan didn't have to agree with everything she said, but right now his silence felt more like a betrayal than staying neutral. Once again her mind churned over last night's disagreement about hell and the supernatural. Why hadn't Z answered that question?

Losing herself in thought, she barely heard the chirpy "Hey, guys, it looks great." Philip and Ryan turned to see Krissi round the corner.

It was the turn that did it: The shift of Philip's weight to see Krissi pulled the ladder too far forward, and Becka, still lost in thought, didn't notice.

"Becka!"

She looked up, startled. The ladder tipped; Philip lost his balance.

"Watch it!" Ryan leapt for the ladder, but he was too late. Philip slipped and fell fifteen feet to the hard concrete steps.

"Philip!" Krissi screamed.

The ladder crashed down on top of him as Krissi raced down the steps to his side. Ryan quickly joined them.

Becka looked on, frozen. Krissi and Ryan were both there to help, but Becka could only stand and stare.

"Philip," Krissi cradled his head in her arms. "Philip ... Philip ..."

He stirred slightly and opened his eyes.

"Philip, are you okay?"

"Yeah," he said, trying to move, but wincing in pain. "I'm all right."

A few kids started to gather. At last Becka was able to move. "Philip, I'm so sorry. I don't know—"

Krissi spun around at her. "Stay away!" she ordered. "Get back."

The command shocked Becka, and she came to a stop.

"Krissi," Ryan tried to reason, "it was an accident. Becka didn't— "

"Yes, she did." No one moved. Krissi's voice grew louder and more shrill. "She knew exactly what she was doing!" To prove her point, she dug into her handbag and pulled out a folded piece of paper. The very paper she had written the night before. "See for yourself."

Becka looked on as Ryan took the paper, unfolded it, and read. More kids gathered as Krissi continued her accusation. "It told me you were dangerous!" she shouted. "It told me your jealousy would try to stop us!"

Becka started toward her again. "Kriss— "

"Stay away!"

By now a sizable group of kids had gathered. Becka could feel her face and ears growing hot under their questioning stares.

It was 2:15 in the afternoon. Once again, Julie entered the crystal. But it wasn't really the crystal. Now she understood that the crystal was merely a tool, a way of clearing her mind. She knew she was actually back home. Her folks had picked her up from the hospital earlier that morning, and now she was back in her own bedroom, in her own bed. At least that's where her body was.

Her mind was someplace else.

At the moment it was striving for another level. Summoning her angel was much easier now. She'd been practicing off and on throughout the night, all morning, and into the afternoon. One thing you could say about Julie Mitchell, she was determined.

Her angel, her guardian, was as good a teacher as she was a pupil. Already he had helped her understand the "futility of the physical." Of course, her parents had protested when she refused to brush her hair or eat either breakfast or lunch. But how could they be expected to understand? After all, they were limited to earthly thinking. They had no idea of the great spiritual level to which Julie was evolving. They had no idea that food, clothes, and appearances were merely vain endeavors, earthly weights designed to hamper her evolution to the higher dimension.

Each time Julie approached that dimension, her guardian embraced her with the same warm, accepting light. And each time he gently but firmly encouraged her to give more and more of herself over to that light. Soon she would be able to merge with it. Soon she would become one with the guardian, one with creation, one with God himself.

As she entered the guardian's presence, she felt his light wash over her. Only this time she felt something else. She couldn't put her finger on it, but it almost felt like ... sadness.

Have I done something wrong? she thought.

The guardian glowed and shimmered before her. **Perhaps we are moving too quickly.**

No ... this is what I want. She moved closer. *You promised me. You said I'd soon be joining your level.*

And so you should, except ...

Tell me. What's wrong?

You have been called to a great purpose, this is true. We had hoped for your transcendence to be this very day.

Transcendence?

Your entrance into our level.

Julie's heart leaped. This is what she had been waiting for, this is what she had been working for.

But we are moving too fast ...

Why? What's the problem? Is it my taking a shower? I know you said to forget the physical, but I mean, it's only a shower, and the soap, I know it was perfumed, but—

No!

The thought cut her off with an intensity she hadn't felt before. Apparently, even angels could get frustrated. She waited, almost breathlessly, as the frustration rippled through the light around her and slowly faded.

Finally the creature spoke again. **It is your friend. The one with the dark emotions.**

Who?

The follower of religion.

You mean Becka? Are you talking about Rebecca Williams?

She felt another wave of frustration, more intense than the last, and she frowned. This was more than frustration. It was ... anger. Intense, searing anger. And it frightened her.

Her ways will contaminate you.

Julie frowned. *But she's a Christian. She's the one who—*

I know who she is, the thought interrupted. **But her ways are not ours. She clings to obsolete thinking. Her narrow-mindedness hinders your progress. Her presence will prevent you from reaching and maintaining the god consciousness.**

God consciousness?

Oneness with god.

Julie's mind raced. *Well, then ... let me talk to her. We're good friends. Let me explain that—*

NO!

The anger was there again. Only stronger.

Julie pulled back.

The guardian's next words were more gentle. **The time has come. You must make the decision. If you wish to enter our level, your time has arrived.**

Excitement surged through Julie. *Now? You mean we can do it now?*

Yes, the creature continued patiently. **But you must promise to cut yourself off from the enemy's influence.**

Ever so faintly, Julie heard the phone in her bedroom begin to ring. Instinctively, she sensed who it was. *That's Becka calling, isn't it?*

The light began to fade. The guardian wavered, then began to disappear.

No! Come back, come back!

The phone continued ringing.

Don't go! Come back! Her pleas were urgent, frantic … and, apparently, effective. The light rippled, growing brighter than ever before as the guardian returned.

You are ready, then?

The phone continued ringing.

Yes. Yes, I'm ready. Julie's mind was speaking louder now, practically shouting, trying to drown out the phone. *Tell me, what am I supposed to do?*

It must entirely be your choice.

Yes, yes … Julie was breathing harder now. Both in fear and excitement. The time had come.

Then let yourself go.

But how—?

Let yourself go. Give your will over to me.

The phone continued ringing. Julie hesitated.

Completely.

But—

NOW!

Startled, afraid of losing something she had to have, Julie obeyed. She blocked out the sound of the phone and gave herself over.

Instantly, something flowed into her, filling her body, her thoughts, her mind … her entire being. Her chest stiffened, lifting into the air in an instinctive effort to fight off the intruder. Then she went limp.

As she lay there, stunned, struggling to understand what had happened, one thing became glaringly clear: Something was inside her. Something more powerful than herself.

She was no longer in control.

7

Becka hung up the pay phone outside the school's office.

"Nobody home?" Ryan asked.

Rebecca frowned and shook her head. "She should be there. She said she'd be there."

As they turned and joined the swarm of students heading down the hall and out the door, Becka sighed. It had been a rough day.

Fortunately, Philip had only a few bruises and a sprained hand to show for her stupidity, but that didn't stop the rumors from spreading. And it didn't stop Becka's own self-doubts from growing.

Why had the ladder fallen? Was it really an accident? Or was Krissi right? Maybe she had done something unconsciously, something stemming from her jealousy. But was she really jealous?

The thoughts tortured and chewed at Becka throughout the day. And they were only made worse by her worries over Julie.

Becka followed Ryan out of the school and down the steps toward the parking lot. "Something's up, Ryan. Something's wrong with Julie. I know it."

Ryan took a deep breath but said nothing. He didn't have to.

"You don't believe me, do you?"

"I just think ... well, that you're overreacting a little, that's all."

"Hey, Ry," a jock in a letterman's coat called out, "I'm rooting for you, man."

"Thanks." Ryan flashed a grin. "Just make sure you vote ... and your friends too."

"Count on it."

Before he could turn, two freshman girls approached. It was obvious they were trying to flirt with Ryan. It was equally obvious they were way out of their league.

"Hi, Ryan."

"Ladies."

Unable to think of anything else to say, they quickly scurried off in whispers.

"Don't forget to vote," he called after them.

They giggled and disappeared.

Becka watched Ryan smile. All day he had played the crowd, going for the votes. It didn't really bother Becka, but she did notice a certain insincerity in him that she had never seen before. He was using his smile to win votes and his killer charm to impress everyone. Was there anything wrong with that? She wasn't sure. At the moment there were too many other things to think about.

"How can you say I'm overreacting?" she asked. As her intensity increased so did her volume. "You've seen what demons can do. You've read about them in the Bible."

Ryan cringed and glanced at the passing kids. "Easy, Beck, the whole world doesn't have to hear."

She stared at him. "You're more concerned about what people think than about Julie?"

He kept his voice quiet and low. "I think Julie will be just fine."

"How can you say that?"

Ryan was getting angry. She could tell by the way he fought to keep his voice even. "I can say that because I can see the situation clearly. Because my thinking's not clouded with some competition thing."

"Competition!"

"Yeah, you know ... jealousy."

It was Becka's turn to get angry. The two had never had an official fight before, but there was a first time for everything.

"Ryan, she's in danger! She could get hurt."

"Not any worse than Philip."

"What's *that* supposed to mean?"

They arrived at the Mustang, and he crossed over to unlock and open her door. "Nothing, I ... I'm just glad he's okay, that's all."

Becka stared at him, her mouth slightly open. "You think I did that on purpose?"

"No, of course you didn't— " He ran his hands through his hair in frustration.

"Ryan?"

"I don't— " He started toward his side, then stopped and turned. "All I know is that there's a heaven and that Julie was there, but you wouldn't believe her. You thought she should go to hell."

Becka started to protest, but he continued. "What's more, she had an angel guiding her. And now there's another angel guiding her, but *he's* demonic ... and it's all because you say so." He shook his head and continued toward his door.

Hot tears sprang to Becka's eyes. She hated crying and gave her eyes a swipe. "Ryan— " her voice grew thicker by the second— "you were in the mansion. You saw the demons."

"Julie's not seeing demons!" He unlocked his side and opened the door. "It's an angel, Becka. She's seeing a real, honest-to-goodness angel. Why can't you admit it?"

"Because it's not true."

He turned and leveled a look at her. "We only have your word on that."

"It's evil."

He held her gaze, refusing to back down. "So *you* say."

Becka bit her lip. She was trembling, and she hated that more than the tears. She gave her eyes another swipe.

"Come on," he said. Was it to lighten things up, or because people were staring? Becka couldn't tell. "Let's go."

She stood there, looking at him. How could he think that? After being together all this time, how could he think she was just being paranoid? Or worse yet, that she was hurting people out of jealousy?

Another guy called from a passing car, "Hey, Ryan, good luck Friday."

Ryan cranked up that instant grin of his. "Thanks, man. Don't forget to vote."

"Deal."

Becka could stand no more. She shut the door and turned.

"Beck?"

She began walking away.

"Beck, come on. Becka, come back."

She wasn't sure where she was going, but she had to get away.

"Becka, come on now."

Her pace quickened. She didn't know if he was coming after her or not. She didn't care. The tears spilled onto her cheeks and streamed down her face.

"Becka ... Rebecca!"

She began running.

Julie was glad to have Philip and Krissi stop over. There was so much she wanted to tell them. So much she'd learned. Unfortunately, with her guardian in control, she wasn't allowed to talk.

Not a word. At least for now. Each time she tried to speak, she felt herself being pushed down to someplace deep inside herself. The guardian insisted on running the show. He wanted to do all the talking.

Of course, he never told Philip and Krissi who he was.

Why don't you tell them? she had questioned.

In good time. But right now they are not prepared for such information.

He did his best imitation of Julie. He spoke with her voice and mannerisms as he explained the great calling on Philip and Krissi, and how they would help change the world. Part of Julie was frustrated at having to remain silent, pushed underneath. After all, it was *her* body. But part of her knew the guardian would be able to teach them far better than she.

So Julie let him have his way.

At the moment, they were talking about Krissi's favorite subject.

"I really am special, then?" Krissi squeaked. "I mean, this handwriting, these messages, they really are coming from somebody else?"

"Were they signed?" Julie heard her voice ask.

Once again Krissi dug into her handbag. "You bet they were. But the name is, like, really weird." She pulled out the tablet and flipped through the pages until she found her latest message. "Here it is. His name is ... Xandrak."

Philip smirked. "Sounds like some alien from outer space."

Julie could feel the guardian turning her lips into a smile.

"You're not too far wrong," her voice said.

"It's a real person then?" Krissi exclaimed. "You know who it is?"

"Julie," Philip repeated, "do you really know who this guy is?"

Julie could feel a surge of pride running through her body—a pride that came from having others wait for information only she possessed—but it wasn't *her* pride, it was the guardian's. She felt her throat being cleared and then heard her voice. It wasn't exactly arrogant or haughty. But pretty close.

"Who it is, my friends, isn't nearly as important as what it says."

"You know what it says?" Krissi asked in amazement. "You know about its warning for us to stay away from Rebecca?"

Julie's body took a deep breath and slowly let it out.

"I'm afraid so," her voice said. "The truth of the matter is, we all owe Rebecca Williams a great deal. She is the one who introduced us to the supernatural. But from now on, her selfish ambition and childish jealousy will only stand in our way."

"I knew it," Philip said. "That's exactly what I was telling her."

Julie barely heard. She was too startled at the guardian's lie. She *knew* Becka. She knew there wasn't a selfish bone in the girl's body. Why would he say there was? She tried to surface, to interrupt and correct him, but suddenly she felt herself being thrown down, hurled back underneath.

STAY THERE! The guardian's thought roared in her head.

Julie was shocked. She knew this creature had a temper, but she couldn't imagine it directed toward her. Quickly, she answered him. *That's not true, what you're saying about Becka. She's done nothing that—*

I am warning you, STAY DOWN!

The command outraged Julie. Who was he to tell her what to do? After all, this was *her* body. Outside, in her bedroom, she heard another voice join the group. Ryan had entered. He was asking if anyone had seen Becka. He was saying he thought she might show up here. But Julie barely noticed. Maybe she had made a mistake with the guardian. Maybe she shouldn't have let him take charge. That would be simple enough to correct. She had given up control to let him in, she would regain control and force him to leave. Of course, it would mean giving up all his knowledge and power, but still ...

He was preoccupied, talking more trash about Becka to the group. It was easy for Julie to slip up to the surface without him noticing. When she arrived, she started parting her lips, then she was thrown back down into the blackness. This time harder and fiercer than before. It took a moment to shake off the blow. Now Julie was mad. Real mad. And if there was one thing you didn't want to do, it was make Julie Mitchell mad. Too angry to be afraid, she rose and fought back toward the surface. It made no difference what he said or did, that was *her* mouth, and she would regain control of it.

I AM WARNING YOU! the guardian shouted.

Julie didn't stop. The fight of wills continued. *Let me up!* her thoughts screamed. *Let me back!*

But it made no difference how hard she fought. She could only rise so far before being thrown back down. Whatever control she had given up, she could not regain it. The thought terrified her.

She'd been cut off from her own body.

Let me up!

No.

I want you out! You leave! Now!

You are mine!

Who do you think you are—

I have warned you.

This is my body, and I demand that—

Sleep!

A heaviness fell over Julie. Immediately she lost consciousness. Now the guardian had complete control.

Becka entered her house through the garage's back door.

"Mom?"

There was no answer.

"Scotty?"

Repeat performance.

She sighed and dumped her books onto the kitchen table. *Typical,* she thought, *when I need them, they're nowhere around.*

It was an unfair thought, and she knew it. She knew Mom was still out looking for work. And Scott—well, who knew where Scott was. Ever since he got involved with that stupid computer game at Darryl's cousin's, he'd been practically non-existent. But there was always Muttly. The puppy whined from outside and scratched at the sliding glass door. Becka opened it, and he bounded in with the typical barks and yelps of excitement. She knelt down, and he attacked her with a flurry of licking tongue and wet nose. As he whined and nuzzled, he forced himself onto her lap. Before she knew it, Becka was holding him, hugging him.

Muttly had been Ryan's gift to her when she had returned from the hospital. Her friends had thrown her a welcome-home party. Back when she was everyone's pal.

But now …

Becka hated self-pity, but the emotions were too much. Her eyes began to burn again. Muttly nuzzled and nudged until she tumbled backward onto the floor. And there, lying on the kitchen floor, holding her puppy, Rebecca Williams quietly sobbed.

She was so tired. So lonely. Cut off. And no one cared. Not even Ryan. Why had he turned on her? Why had they all? She could have kept her mouth shut, played along and been like everyone else. And if she'd had her way, that's exactly what she would have done. But oh, no, she had to try and help. She had to be the know-it-all who tried to warn them.

Well, no more. She was through. If they wanted to mess around with that stuff, let them. If they liked playing with fire, fine. Who was she to stop them? She wouldn't. She wouldn't say another word.

Becka shoved Muttly away and, with a loud sniff, rose to her feet. She hadn't asked for the job, and she didn't have to take it.

Let God find somebody else. Let him find another person to be the All-School Oddball. She was through.

Becka headed for the stairs when a sudden wave of compassion struck her.

What about your friends? What about Ryan?

"No!" she shouted at no one in particular. "They're not my worry!"

They don't understand …

"Stop it!" The tears were coming faster now. She headed up the steps.

They need you.

"They don't need me!" she blurted. "They hate me!" She reached the top of the stairs as another set of sobs hit. She wrapped her arms around herself and leaned against the wall. It wasn't fair. None of it!

But that's okay. She'd take no more. She was finished. She pushed away from the wall and started down the hall toward her room.

"*Beck*—" now it was the memory of her mother's voice, of their conversation—"*if you don't tell people, who will?*"

"It's God's worry, not mine!"

"*When you gave him your life, you gave it all.*"

Becka closed her eyes to shut out the words, but they came anyway: "*If you don't tell people, who will? If you don't tell*—"

"Leave me alone!!"

She passed her brother's door and threw a look inside. There was a fresh mound of dirty clothes, evidence that Scott had dropped by. To her surprise the computer screen was still on. Scott was a major slob, but not when it came to his computer. Why was the monitor still glowing?

She hesitated, swiped at her tears, then crossed into his room.

"*SQUAWK!* BEAM ME UP, SCOTTY, BEAM ME UP."

"Shut up, Cornelius."

As though sensing her mood, the bird immediately waddled to the far end of his perch.

She moved to the computer. On-screen there was a message from Z. It was addressed to her. Scott must have thought it was important and left it on for her to see. It contained only four lines. The first two were an address and time.

233 Ramona Street
Basement. 5:00 p.m.

And below that was a single Bible verse:

"Satan himself masquerades as an angel of light."
2 Corinthians 11:14

Becka fought off a shudder. No way. She would not get involved. She stared back at the screen: "Satan himself masquerades as an angel of light."

She turned away. No. It was their choice. Let them live it.

But what about that address? She turned back to the glowing screen. Z never left messages unless they were urgent.

She glanced at her watch—4:37. If she hurried ...

She turned toward the door. All right. Fine. She would go see what Z wanted, but that was it. She would not get involved. Her friends could do what they wanted, but she would not interfere.

From now on, they were on their own.

8

Julie had no idea how long she'd been unconscious, but when she awoke, the guardian was speaking to Philip, Krissi, and Ryan. It was the same con job he'd used on her, telling them how they were chosen, how they had been especially selected to bring the world to greater enlightenment. Only, while she had been asleep, he had apparently revealed his presence to them. Now he was speaking directly to them. He was still using her mouth and lips, but it was his voice, not hers.

"You must give yourself over to the Universal Consciousness," he was telling them. "You must become one with your angels and allow them to guide you into all love and power."

Julie wanted to scream, to cry out a warning. It was the same bait he'd used to trap her. The promise of power, of goodness and love ... all they had to do was give up their wills.

They'd have the power all right; it would only cost them their souls!

"So if you're Julie's angel," Philip was asking, "then where's Julie?"

"Julie is here," she heard her mouth answer reassuringly, "she is just resting. Sudden exposure to such power and knowledge can sometimes be exhausting."

Liar! Julie shouted from deep within the darkness. *You're a liar!* But the thought never reached her lips.

Shut up! came the immediate response. **If you try to speak, I will put you to sleep forever!**

Julie didn't know if that was possible, but she didn't want to take the chance. She had to survive if she was going to find a way to warn her friends.

"So," Krissi was asking, "how exactly do we do it? I mean, become 'one with god' and experience all this cool love and power?"

"You have already started down that path, Krissi Petersen. Your guide has already begun his instruction."

"My writing?" Krissi asked excitedly. "Are you talking about my automatic handwriting?"

Julie felt her lips smile and heard the guardian answer, "With his help and mine, you will all be ushered into the new age."

"When?" Krissi asked.

"This very evening."

No! Julie shouted from inside. *Don't hurt them! You've got me, what more do you—*

SHUT UP! The guardian screamed back down into her. **This is your final warning!**

Julie was desperate. How could she warn them, how could she stop them? Now there was another voice. Ryan's.

"Excuse me."

Julie felt her guardian stiffen with fear. Why? Why would the guardian be afraid of Ryan and not the others? She felt the creature force himself to relax, striving to sound calm and in control. "Yes?"

"No offense," Ryan continued, "but how do we know you're really an angel? I mean, the Bible says a third of you guys were thrown out of heaven with Satan. How do we know you're one of the good guys?"

"Ryan," Krissi admonished.

"It's just a question."

Julie felt more panic seize the guardian. For whatever reason, he was afraid to speak to Ryan. She felt him forcing himself to answer calmly. "The Bible is a great book, but surely you don't believe everything you read in it?"

"Shouldn't I?"

"What about hell?"

Ryan had no answer.

Julie felt a wave of satisfaction wash over the guardian. Apparently, this was something Ryan had been struggling with. That the guardian had this type of information must have sent the guy reeling.

Now that Ryan was off balance, the thing pressed in. "And what of those in your student body? Do you really think they would vote for one with such superstitious beliefs?"

Again Ryan had no answer. With his silence came the guardian's gloating thoughts: He is so stupid. The fool has so much power, yet he doesn't even know how to use it.

Power? Julie thought. He didn't acknowledge her. He seemed too focused on Ryan.

"Your association with Rebecca Williams has darkened your thinking. Others have sensed it. You sense it yourself. Come join with us. Give yourself over. Your power will be the greatest of all."

Julie could only guess that Ryan's silence meant he was still struggling.

She could feel the guardian turning her head to the group as he continued speaking. "See what paralyzing influence she can have over you? This is the danger of which we warned. Rebecca Williams was needed to introduce you to our ways, but now she will only cripple your progress. She will only hamper and destroy your growth."

"But how ... how can we stop her?" Krissi asked.

"She will be ... disposed of. Tonight."

"Disposed of?" Philip's voice was full of alarm.

"But, she's our friend," Krissi protested. "At least, she was."

"She will feel no pain ... in fact, she'll find the experience quite enjoyable. But she will be stopped." Once again Julie could feel her head turning. She knew it was toward Ryan. To scare him, to frighten him. The voice continued, "She and others like her will be silenced."

Suddenly Julie heard a loud crash and the sound of something shattering. Desperately she tried to reach the surface and look out her eyes, but she was held in the darkness.

What was that? she demanded.

One of your porcelain dolls, the guardian answered. **It missed the boy's head by inches.**

You threw one of my dolls!

Not I, fool—one of my associates.

There are others of you in my room?

Before the guardian could answer, Julie heard her door open and someone race out of the room and down the stairs.

Was that Ryan? she asked.

Of course, came the smug, amused answer. **Don't worry, my associates will take care of him. But for now I must take care of your friends ...**

Becka was grateful she'd worn her navy blue hooded sweatshirt. It was getting cold and it had started to rain. The clouds blotted out all light from the moon and stars, and there was a slight wind blowing against her face.

She headed down Second Street, turned onto Ramona, and was surprised at the office building that suddenly loomed before her. It was an old, three-story brick affair. She double-checked the address. 233 Ramona. It matched. But other than a light in the front lobby, the building was completely dark inside. Pitch black.

Becka stood a moment, feeling the chill run across her shoulders. She shook it off, then started for the entrance. She wondered why there was no sign on the building or any lettering on the door's glass window. If this was a business, shouldn't there be a sign or something? Reluctantly she climbed up the concrete steps, then reached for the weathered brass handle.

She hoped it would be locked. She prayed it would be locked.

It wasn't.

The door was left ajar with a small piece of cardboard between the bolt and the hole, preventing the bolt from locking into place. Becka pulled the door open and watched the cardboard flutter to the ground then blow off down the street.

She called, "Hello?"

No answer. There was a deserted counter with an equally deserted receptionist's desk behind it. The lamp above the desk burned brightly, but Becka found little comfort in its solitary light. It just made the place seem more deserted ... more spooky.

"Is anybody here?"

Still no answer. Reluctantly, Becka stepped into the lobby, letting the door close behind her. Suddenly remembering the lock, she spun around to catch the door, but she was too late. It shut and the bolt clicked into place behind her.

She gave the door a push, trying to open it. Then another push, much harder. It did no good. She was locked inside.

"Great," she murmured, "just great." She turned back to the lobby. Now what? She took a tentative step inside, then another. "Hello?" She searched the room. It was absolutely silent and still. There was a frosted-glass door behind the desk, but it was closed. To her right was an old-fashioned drinking fountain, an oak door labeled Restroom, and a set of stairs. What had Z done? He didn't make mistakes like this. If he said meet somebody at five o'clock, there would be somebody at five to meet. That's how he operated. So why wasn't there—

And then she remembered. The message on the computer. It had said to go to the basement.

Becka slowly turned toward the unlit stairway. No way was she going down those. Not in the dark. She turned away.

Still … the message had said, "Basement."

She glanced at her watch—5:06. She stuffed her hands into her pockets. She looked around, then back at the locked door. She sighed. She rechecked her watch. Then, slowly, she turned back toward the steps.

They really weren't *that* dark. The first half, down to the landing, anyway, was lit by the desk lamp. It was a little dim, but she could definitely see where she was going. With another sigh she turned and started for the stairs. Slowly, carefully, one step at a time, she moved downward.

"Hello?" Part of her wanted to make lots of noise so she wouldn't sneak up on someone; the other part wanted to be absolutely silent so no one would know she was there.

She reached the landing. That was the easy part. The lit part. Now the stairs did a sharp about-face in the opposite direction and descended into black shadows.

Still, she had come this far.

"Hello? Is anybody down here?"

There was no response.

Clinging to the rail, she inched her way into the darkness.

"Hello …?"

Step followed step. Gradually her eyes grew accustomed to the darkness, and by the time she reached the bottom, she could see wire-meshed, double glass doors straight ahead. They were newer than the rest of the building. They almost looked like hospital doors. She strained to see through the glass to the other side, but there was only darkness. She moved toward them. Three, four, five steps. She reached out and touched the doors; they were cold. She pushed against the right one, hoping it wouldn't move. It did. She pushed harder. It opened.

"Hello ..." Her voice was much thinner. She stepped inside. It was cold in there. Very cold. Directly in front of her, within touching distance, were more desks. No, not desks ... they looked like tables. She turned toward the wall, feeling. There had to be a light switch somewhere. Ah, there it was. She flipped the switch up. The entire room fluttered as the overhead fluorescents sputtered on. She looked around the room. She'd been right, there were tables in front of her. Three of them.

And on the one closest to her, the one she could reach out and touch, was a body. Human. Dead. The bottom half covered by a sheet. The top half naked.

Becka screamed. She stumbled backward, turned, and ran straight into another body. But this one was alive.

At least, it was standing.

Ryan's Mustang had barely slid to a stop before he threw open the door, leaped out, and headed for Becka's front porch. He was freaked. He'd been okay when the angel told him it knew about his doubts on hell. He'd even managed to hold it together when the thing talked about his desire to be student-body president. It was the threats against Becka's life that did him in.

That and the flying porcelain doll.

Ryan had raced out of Julie's room, not because the doll had barely missed his head, but because he now knew what he was dealing with.

An angel? No way. He'd seen demons try to play that game before. In the mansion. And if the thing—or things—were out to get Becka, and she didn't know ... well, somebody had better warn her. And fast.

Ryan knocked on the front door. Nobody answered. There had to be somebody home. The lights were on. He could see one in the kitchen and one in the upstairs hallway.

He knocked again. "Becka! Scott!"

Impatiently he grabbed the handle and gave it a push. It stuck briefly, then opened. "Becka? Mrs. Williams?" Still no answer. Except for Muttly. The little guy bounded toward him at full speed.

"Hey, fellow," Ryan bent down for the onslaught of slurping tongue and wiggling body. "Where is everybody? Huh, fellow? Is anybody home?"

The dog whined and continued the licking attack.

Ryan rose and moved toward the stairs. Somebody had to be there. They wouldn't have left with lights on and the dog in the house. "Becka? Scott?" He started up the steps. "It's me, Ryan. Is anybody home?"

Muttly did his best to follow, but he still hadn't mastered the fine art of stair climbing. Not that he didn't try. But each attempt was met with slips, spills, and some very impressive backward somersaults.

"Beck ..." Ryan reached the top of the steps and looked down the hall. What had happened? Had Julie's guardian already struck? Steeling himself for the worst, he started down the hall.

He'd barely reached the first door before he heard: "BEAM ME UP!"

Ryan leaped out of his skin.

"BEAM ME UP! *SQUAWK*. BEAM ME UP!"

He turned to Scott's room and saw Cornelius strutting back and forth on his perch. "MAKE MY DAY. MAKE MY DAY. MAKE MY DAY."

Ryan took a deep breath to steady his nerves, then spotted the computer screen. It was still on. "Scotty?" he called.

Still no answer.

Cautiously, he entered the room, stepped over the mound of dirty clothes, and moved to the screen. It read:

TO: Rebecca
FROM: Z
233 Ramona Street
Basement. 5:00 p.m.

And below that, a Bible verse:

"Satan himself masquerades as an angel of light."
2 Corinthians 11:14

Ryan stood there, puzzled. Not about the verse. It only confirmed what he already knew. It was the address. It seemed familiar. He couldn't put his finger on it, but somehow he'd heard it before. He glanced at his watch—5:12. That must be where Rebecca was. Maybe that was why everything was left on and Muttly was still in the house—she'd dashed out to try and make the meeting in time.

If he was right, he was probably just a few minutes behind her. He turned and headed out of the room, darted down the hall, and took the steps two and three at a time.

233 Ramona Street, 233 Ramona Street . . .

The address kept ringing in his head. Why did it sound so familiar?

It wasn't until he was out the door and running for his car that it clicked.

233 Ramona Street. That was a place they used to tease each other about as kids. That was the place they used to dare each other to visit at Halloween.

233 Ramona Street was the city morgue.

9

Sorry, didn't mean to startle you."

Becka looked up. She opened her mouth, but no words would come.

"I was upstairs in the men's room."

She still couldn't find her voice.

"You must be Rebecca Williams."

She finally managed a nod.

"I'm Dr. Gary Woods." He stuck out his hand for a shake.

Becka numbly took it. He seemed a nice enough man. Balding, late fifties, a little on the overfed side. Not at all what you'd expect for a serial killer. Then again, what exactly did serial killers look like?

"Are you ..." She cleared her throat. "Z said I was to meet someone."

The man chuckled. "Z? Is that what he's calling himself now?"

"You're not him, are you?"

The man shook his head and continued to smile.

"But you know him?"

"Oh yes, I know him." His smile slowly faded. "I owe him a

great deal. In fact, you might say I owe him my life. Please," he motioned to a couple of stools across the room, "let's sit down."

Becka looked nervously at the body lying, half-naked, on the table beside her.

"Oh, don't worry about John." Woods grinned. "He's in no hurry."

"John?"

"John Doe. That's what we call the bodies we can't identify."

"Identify? Are you, like, a ..." Becka searched for the word.

"I'm the county's assistant coroner. I investigate deaths, perform autopsies, that sort of thing. Please." Again he motioned to the stools across the room.

Becka turned. But as she walked past the body on the table, she couldn't help staring. It was amazing how white and lifeless the thing appeared. The thing? She gave a shudder. This was no thing, it was a person. Well, at least it used to be a person. Somebody who ate and laughed and cried and loved, just like herself. Still, just to be safe, she gave the table a wide berth. Sensing her uneasiness, Dr. Woods pulled the sheet over the body. It helped some, but not much.

Becka glanced about the room. It wasn't big. The three steel tables filled most of it. Over each table hung a large light. Two of the walls were lined with laboratory-type counters that had various pieces of medical equipment resting on them. The farthest wall was made of the same stainless steel as the tables. It looked like a giant freezer. But instead of one door, there were a dozen, three feet wide and two feet high. They were stacked side by side and on top of one another. Almost like a giant filing cabinet. A giant freezer/filing cabinet with drawers just wide enough to hold a ...

Becka gave another shudder.

"May I get you some tea or anything?" Dr. Woods asked.

"Uh, no, thanks." Becka took a seat on one of the stools as

Woods approached the nearby counter. He filled a coffee mug with water from a faucet and set it in a microwave.

"So you, uh ..." Becka cleared her throat. She had lots of questions, but she wanted to be delicate, just in case he was a part-time serial killer. "You work here at night ... all alone ... by yourself?"

The doctor laughed. "It's actually quite peaceful when you get used to it. The folks here—" he motioned toward the stainless steel freezer—"they don't give me much trouble. Most cooperative patients I've ever had." He punched the time on the microwave and pressed start. "Besides, they give me a much clearer perspective on life: what's important, what's not, that kind of thing."

Becka forced a nervous smile.

"But ... that's not why Z wanted us to talk. He said you had some questions about hell?"

Rebecca looked at him and blinked. She'd completely forgotten about that question. With all that was going on, it no longer seemed important. But Z must have thought it was. Well, since she was here and since she really had no other place to go ... or friends to go there with ...

"Well, yeah." She shrugged. "I had a few questions."

"Such as, does it exist?"

"For starters, yeah. And if it does, why would a loving God send people there?"

Woods leaned against the counter and folded his arms. "First of all, let me be very clear about something, Rebecca. Hell does exist. It is very real, and it is very terrifying."

"But how can you be so sure? I know the Bible talks about it, but how can—"

"Because I was there."

Becka stopped cold. She could only stare. Before she could respond, she heard a muffled pounding and banging. She threw a nervous look to the freezer drawers. "Wh-what's that?"

"Did you leave the front door ajar?" Woods asked.

"No, it locked before I could catch it."

"Well," he turned and headed for the double glass doors at the other end. "It sounds like we have another visitor. I'll be right back." Before Becka could protest, he threw open the doors and bounded up the stairs.

Becka fought off another shiver. No way was she thrilled about being left alone in this room. She stole a glance at the body covered with the sheet, then turned back to the giant icebox behind her. Come to think about it, maybe she wasn't all that alone after all. The thought gave her little comfort.

A minute later, Dr. Woods came back down the stairway. Beside him was a very anxious and agitated Ryan.

Once Becka told Ryan that Dr. Woods knew Z and that he could be trusted, Ryan quickly explained what was happening at Julie's.

"You were right, we're not dealing with angels," he said. "We're dealing with one of the bad guys. He's already got control of Julie. And Krissi and Philip, well, who knows what's going to happen to them."

Rebecca felt an unbearable heaviness in her chest. Those were her friends he was talking about. People she loved. She bit her lip and looked at the floor.

They were also people who would no longer listen.

"If we go now," Ryan continued, "maybe we can stop them before anything else happens."

She did not answer.

"Becka?"

Slowly, sadly, she looked up.

"What's wrong?"

She didn't answer.

"Beck, we've got to do something."

When she spoke, her voice was thick and husky. "I've been trying, Ryan. All week I've been trying."

"I know that, but together, maybe—"

She shook her head. "It won't work."

"So what are you saying? That we just sit here and do nothing?"

"Ryan ..." She tried to swallow, but there was a large lump in her throat. "Don't you get it? They don't want my help. They don't want anything to do with me."

Ryan stared at her.

Unable to hold his gaze, she looked back to the floor. "I'm sorry." She shook her head. "I'm ..." She trailed off, still shaking her head.

A long silence followed. Finally Dr. Woods coughed slightly and spoke. "I don't mean to intrude here, but perhaps I can be of some help."

They looked at him.

"Perhaps our meeting is more timely than either you or Z imagined. Rebecca, you said there was nothing to be done, and you may be right. Your friends may not listen to you. But to stop talking to them, to stop telling them the truth, well, maybe that's not your decision to make. Maybe they deserve as many chances as God decides to give them. As many chances as he gave me."

"What do you mean?" she asked.

Woods drew in a deep breath and slowly let it out. "Two years ago, my wife and daughters were killed in an automobile accident."

"That's terrible!"

He nodded. "I—I was driving." A moment of silence hung over them. Becka could tell the memories were hard on him, but he forced himself to continue. "Lisa ... she was a religious woman. You know, church, Bible studies, Sunday school, the whole nine yards. But I never had the time or, quite honestly, the inclination. I was too busy being a successful surgeon."

"You used to be a surgeon?" Ryan asked.

The man seemed to barely hear. "It was late and I was bone tired, but I insisted on getting home. There was some big conference or something I was to speak at in the morning. I remember trying to keep my eyes open, and then ... suddenly there was the horn and the bright lights of the semi. I tried to swerve out of the way, but ..."

He grew silent.

Ryan and Becka exchanged looks.

Finally, he continued, "The next thing I knew, I was being sucked out of my body—as though I was fluid in a syringe. I remember looking for Lisa, for the girls, but they were nowhere to be found. I was falling. It was a deep pit, a hole that went on and on forever. I was terrified. I tried to scream, but I was too frightened. When I looked at the sides of the hole, the walls weren't made of dirt as I'd expected. They were made of people. Living carcasses. Human corpses. Thousands of them. They were all on fire. Their clothes, their bodies, their faces ..."

"So you were in hell?" Ryan asked softly.

The man seemed too lost in memories to answer. He went on, "I remember trying to breathe, but the stench was suffocating. The smell of rotten eggs. I believe it was sulfur. Brimstone, they used to call it.

"After falling for what seemed like hours, I hit a lake, but it wasn't a lake of water. It was made of fire. It's hard to explain, but it wasn't wet. Only hot." He closed his eyes for a moment. "The heat was intense, searing. I was engulfed in it. Every inch of me was covered by flame. Every nerve of my body screamed out in agony, but there was no relief. I wanted to pass out, I wanted to die, but I couldn't.

"And then I saw them ... hideous ... thousands of them. Like giant, leathery gremlins with razor-sharp fangs and knifelike claws."

Again Ryan and Becka looked at each other. They'd seen such creatures. During their encounter in the mansion.

"They flew back and forth through the flames, urgently, as though they were coming and going on important missions. Most of them paid little attention to me. Though a few would claw or take bites out of my burning flesh, as if for fun.

"It was then I noticed that the flames weren't just fire. They were also scenes. They were events from my life. Somehow, all of my past actions, even my thoughts, had been turned into flames and tongues of fire that burned and tortured me. Needless to say, they weren't pleasant memories. They were my failures. My sins. Every bad thing I'd ever done or thought was transformed into these relentless, burning flames. Times I had lied, cheated, hated; acts of unkindness and immorality. Everything was there. And each memory became a scorching flame that seared and charred my remaining flesh.

"I screamed for help. I begged someone, anyone, to take away the pain. And then I heard a voice. It was the kindest, most loving voice I had ever heard. And its kindness made my agony all the more unbearable. 'I have taken your pain,' it said. 'I have endured all of this suffering for you, in your place.'

" 'Who are you?' I cried. And the response washed over me. 'I am the Lamb who was slain for your sins.' " He looked into Becka's eyes. "I knew who that was. Immediately. The voice went on to explain how he had offered to take my punishment—and I wouldn't let him. I cried out in pain and frustration. I asked him why he'd sent me to that place. And his answer ... it was so full of love. And so sad."

"What did he say?" Ryan asked.

"He told me, 'No, dear friend, I have not sent you. You have made this choice yourself. This is your decision. How desperately I wanted to save you from it. My desire for you to avoid this place was so great that I came to earth and suffered in your place. But you would not accept my offer.' "

Becka saw tears in the man's eyes, and she felt her own eyes growing moist. Dr. Woods drew a deep breath and continued.

"I told him I didn't know, that no one had told me about him. But he said he'd spoken to me many times, through my friends, through Lisa, even through my daughters. As I listened, I knew he was right. And then he said, 'But so far, you have refused my offer.' "

"So far?" Ryan echoed, and Dr. Woods smiled grimly.

"I grabbed on to that too. Believe me. When he said that, I cried out, 'Do I still have a chance? Are you giving me another chance?' His answer was the most wonderful thing I've ever heard. 'Yes,' he said, 'your time has not yet come.'

"When I asked about my children … about Lisa, he assured me they were safe." His voice choked with emotion. "He said they were at his side, enjoying his love and goodness. And then he said, 'When it is your time, you may join them. But it must be your choice, your decision. Not mine. I love you. I want you to join us. But it is up to you.' "

Dr. Woods grew quiet. The three sat in absolute silence.

Finally Ryan cleared his throat and spoke. "And then?"

"And then I regained consciousness, in ICU, where I remained for nearly a month."

"The voice," Becka ventured, "was it …?"

He nodded. "Yes, it was Jesus Christ."

"So there *is* a hell," Ryan half whispered.

Dr. Woods nodded. "But it is not a place God sends us to. It's a place we choose when we refuse him. Don't you see? *That's* why Christ died, to pay for our wrongs so we don't have to go there. To save us from ourselves, from the penalty we've earned through our sin."

"But when you died," Becka asked, "why did you go to hell? Aren't you supposed to be judged first?"

"Who said I died?" Woods shook his head. "My heart never stopped, they never had to revive me. The best I can figure is that I had a vision. But whatever it was, it was a gift from God, a warning about what was in store for me if I didn't turn to him."

He looked at Becka, his expression and voice earnest. "It was another chance, Rebecca. God gave me chance after chance, and when everything looked hopeless, he gave me yet another chance. He never stopped reaching out to me. Never. And if he never stops reaching out, how can we do any less? With our friends, our loved ones ... how can we do any less?"

Tears filled Becka's eyes. "But— " her voice was barely above a whisper—"I'm not God."

Woods' voice was equally soft and filled with compassion. "No, you're not. But you are his hands on earth, and you are his feet. As believers, we make up his body. Each one of us is a part of his body. Someone has to tell those who don't know him, Rebecca. It may mean more pain. It may mean more rejection. But if you love your friends, what other choice do you have?"

Becka stared at the floor. He was right.

"If you don't tell them," he continued gently, "who will?"

The words rang in Becka's ears. They were the same words her mother had used. She looked up, tears streaming down her face. "What more can I say? What more can I do?"

Dr. Woods shook his head. "I don't know, but it's late. And if Ryan's right, every minute counts."

Becka nodded and turned to Ryan.

There was moisture in his own eyes. "Come on." He reached for her hand. "We'd better go."

Becka nodded. Dr. Woods was right, there wasn't a minute to waste.

10

Becka looked at the clock on the dash of Ryan's Mustang—6:00. As Ryan sent his car speeding toward Julie's house, Becka knew they'd used up valuable time at the morgue, but it had been necessary. It had helped her find her second wind.

She was ready to try again. To reach out, regardless of the cost.

"Remember," Ryan asked, "before our showdown at the mansion, remember that section in Ephesians we read?"

Becka grabbed his Bible and flipped through it. "You mean the different pieces of armor we're supposed to wear when fighting the devil?"

"Yeah, let's go down the list."

She found it. "Ephesians 6:14. Here we go: 'Stand firm then, with the belt of truth buckled around your waist, with the breastplate of righteousness in place.' "

"Got it." Ryan nodded. "We're holding on to God's truth, and we're doing what God wants, right?"

"Right," she said. "We've got his approval." She continued reading: " 'And with your feet fitted with the readiness that comes from the gospel of peace.' "

"We're definitely preaching the gospel," Ryan said.

Becka continued: " 'Take up the shield of faith, with which you can extinguish all the flaming arrows of the evil one.' Satan. "

"Faith. We've got that."

" 'Take the helmet of salvation.' "

Ryan nodded. "Our heads need to keep remembering we're saved. Got it."

" 'And the sword of the Spirit, which is the word of God.' " Becka looked up.

Ryan was already chuckling. "Remember how crazy quoting the Bible made those little critters in the mansion?"

Becka nodded. "That's all Jesus used when he fought Satan."

Ryan agreed. "No guns, no missiles, just the Bible. That was his sword, his only weapon."

"And ours," Becka added.

Ryan nodded as he turned the last corner and headed up Julie's street.

Becka looked back to the book: "The last piece of armor: 'Pray in the Spirit on all occasions.' "

Ryan threw her a chagrined look. "Guess we've kinda left that out lately, haven't we?"

Becka nodded. It was true. In all of the emotion flying around, they'd completely forgotten about prayer.

Ryan eased the car to a stop in front of the house, and before Becka could move, he reached out and took her hand. Then, to her astonishment, he closed his eyes and began to pray.

"Lord ..."

Becka looked on, stunned. It was all she could do to say grace in front of people. But here was Ryan, praying out loud as if it was the most natural thing in the world. What an incredible person this guy was! She closed her eyes as he continued.

"I'm not real good at this kinda stuff ... but you know what we need here. There's some kids in that house who don't know what they're dealing with. Show them, God. Let them see what's really happening. And, uh ..." He hesitated, unsure where to go. Becka couldn't help but give his hand a squeeze of encouragement. That's all it took. "And help us too. Show us the right thing to do, keep us safe, and don't let us mess up too bad. In Jesus' name we pray. Amen."

"Amen," Becka repeated softly.

They opened their eyes and looked at one another. The lump had returned to Becka's throat, but this time it had nothing to do with sadness or even fear. It had everything to do with her feelings for Ryan.

They stepped out of the car and headed for the house. It was fancy, three stories, and worth a lot of bucks. They reached the door, knocked, and endured the hellos and pleasantries from Julie's mom. Becka knew she should try and explain what was going on, but she also knew the woman wouldn't believe them. Fortunately, she saved Becka the trouble by explaining that she and her husband were just heading out to catch a movie.

Becka's eyebrows raised. How convenient.

Or was it?

"Go on upstairs," Julie's mom said while slipping into her coat. "And if you and the rest of the gang want any munchies, feel free to help yourself in the kitchen."

The last thing Becka or Ryan wanted to do was eat, but they thanked her and started up the stairway. Rebecca could feel her heart pounding. She'd had lots of encounters with the enemy lately, but she was still frightened. Maybe that was good. Maybe the fear was a reminder that this stuff wasn't something to play with.

She reached out and took Ryan's hand. It was as cold and damp as hers.

They arrived at the top of the staircase, turned, and headed for Julie's room. Fourth door on the left. Once there, they stopped and looked at each other. There was no missing the anxiety each was feeling. Becka took a deep breath and nodded.

Ryan reached for the knob, turned it, and pushed. Neither was prepared for what they saw.

The room looked normal enough. It was large and painted in robin's egg blue. On one side was a dresser and a white vanity with a huge mirror surrounded by a dozen softly glowing bulbs. The next wall contained a closed window with white chiffon curtains that stirred in a strange sort of breeze. Beside the window was a towering bookshelf that ran from the ceiling to the floor, also in white. Next to the bookshelf was a desk with a top-of-the-line computer on it. The final wall was nothing but a giant walk-in closet. None of this was surprising. Becka knew Julie had money. She also knew Julie never showed it off, which was why they were such good friends.

What *had* surprised Becka was seeing Philip and Krissi standing at the foot of Julie's bed, staring in awe. The reason was pretty clear. Julie was no longer in bed. In fact she was no longer *on* the bed. Instead, with her eyes closed in blissful peace, Julie Mitchell was floating above her bed. Not too far above it, only four or five inches. But it was enough.

Julie's eyes fluttered and opened, and Becka went cold. Whoever was behind those eyes was not her friend.

When Julie saw Becka, her face twisted and contorted. Immediately, she fell back down onto the bed. "Youuuu," Julie hissed. But it wasn't Julie's voice. It was as twisted and contorted as the face. And as full of hate. "You are not welcome."

Rebecca could feel the waves of hostility press against her. She took another breath, trying to calm herself.

"Becka," Philip spoke up. He tried his best to sound casual but was doing a lousy imitation of it. "What brings you here?"

Ryan stepped forward. "Listen, what you have here, it's not what it looks like."

"Silence!" the voice inside Julie ordered.

Ryan turned toward his friend. "This ... thing ... it's not an angel."

"Of course he is!" Krissi squeaked. "He's teaching us all sorts of cool things so we can band together and help save the—"

Ryan cut her off. "Do you remember all the stuff that happened in the mansion? Remember all those little creatures?"

"You mean the demons?" Philip asked.

"Exactly. That's what we've got here. This is no angel. This thing is nothing more than—"

"Liar!" Julie hissed.

"It's just another demon, but this one is disguised to make you think it's an angel."

Suddenly the bookshelf behind Ryan began to vibrate. Everyone turned and watched as the shaking grew more violent.

"Maybe it's an earthquake," Krissi said hopefully. But she knew it wasn't. Nothing else in the room moved.

As the books vibrated forward, Becka stole a glance at Julie. The concentration on the girl's face made it clear that she was the one responsible, that the shaking was an extension of her anger.

The wind had picked up considerably. Then, one by one, the books began falling to the floor.

Philip motioned for Ryan to look at Julie's face. "Don't you see—look how you're upsetting her."

"That's right," Krissi whined. "You're wrecking it! You're going to make her mad and ruin everything." The books continued tumbling out, faster and with more force. The wind increased, causing the curtains to flap and whip noisily. Becka prepared herself. She was about to speak, she was about to step forward and put an end to all of these special effects. Unfortunately, Ryan had other plans.

He turned and addressed Julie. "Is that all you can do?" His voice was a little high, the way it got when he was nervous, but he did his best to cover it. "Kinda bush league, aren't you?"

"Ryan," Becka warned. "Don't mess arou— "

Julie's voice cut her off. "Bush league, am I?" Her lips curled into a sneer.

Ryan crossed his arms and shrugged. "I've seen better."

"Ryan ...," Becka whispered.

He spoke to Becka, but was loud enough for all to hear. "We don't have to be afraid of this garbage. We're Christians. We've got the authority."

"Oh, you are a Christian now, are you?" Julie's voice smirked.

The tone gave both Ryan and Becka the creeps. But Ryan rose to the challenge. "Yeah ... I am."

Julie began to laugh.

"What's so funny?"

"Do you honestly think you qualify? In your wildest dreams, do you really believe you are good enough to be a follower of the Christ?"

Ryan threw a look at Becka and shifted his weight. "Well, yeah ... sure."

"Perhaps you should tell that to the Johnson children."

"Who?"

"You remember the Johnsons. It was their dog you ran over on New Year's Eve."

Ryan glanced to Becka. "It ... it was an accident."

"Is that why you never told anyone? Is that why you didn't even try to find the owner?"

"He was—he was already dead, I-I didn't know who he belonged to. I— "

"Just like you didn't know you were shoplifting that car stereo last spring?"

Ryan looked like he'd been punched in the gut. "It-it was a dare. Just a— "

"Or just like you could have passed geometry last year without those cheat sheets?"

"Ryan?" Krissi asked in surprise. "You cheated your way through geometry?"

His eyes darted to his friends; he was breathing faster, trying to catch his breath. "Not all the time, I, uh ..."

"Yes, Ryan Riordan, you are a fine example of a Christian. Just ask Nancy Haldermen."

The color drained from Ryan's face. "Wh-what ...?"

"Sweet Nancy, in the backseat of your car. You remember."

Philip looked to Ryan in disdain. "You and Nancy Haldermen?"

Ryan took a half-step back and turned to Becka. His eyes were wide, like the eyes of an animal trapped in a car's headlight. His voice trembled.

"Beck, it was a long time ago ... I ... I ..." He stumbled back into the desk and half-fell, half-sat beside the computer.

Becka looked on, stunned. Part of her wanted to help Ryan, but part of her was repelled at what she was hearing. Was this the real Ryan Riordan?

The voice persisted, bearing down with glee, going in for the kill. "Yes, everything is 'I' in your life, isn't it? 'I' this, 'I' that. The truth is, you are arrogant and self-centered to the core. Ryan Riordan, Mr. Popularity. Ryan Riordan, everybody's friend ... but it's all a lie, isn't it? Just a sham. Just a way to use people to get what you want."

"Please ..." His voice was weaker.

"Just like your parents' divorce!"

Ryan gasped. "That wasn't my—"

"Of course it wasn't. At least that's what they tell you. But we know better, don't we? We know it was your constant demands. I, I, I! It was your fault, not theirs. You are the one. It is you who pushed them over the edge! You are the one who drove them apart, you are the one who destroyed your family!"

"No! It's ..." Ryan's voice was small, helpless. "It's not ..."

"Of course it is! You're no Christian! You'll never be a Christian. You're not good enough!"

The thing began to laugh. It was loud and hysterical, filling the room, so shrill that the computer monitor beside Ryan resonated until it suddenly exploded, sending glass flying in all directions. Krissi screamed. The wind howled through the room. The giant bookcase creaked forward.

"Look out!" Philip cried. He pushed Krissi aside just as it crashed to the floor, missing her by inches, scattering books everywhere.

She began screaming hysterically.

"Let's get out of here!" Philip shouted. He grabbed Krissi and raced for the door. "Come on, let's go! Let's get out of here!"

"You are no Christian!" the thing shrieked. "You're not good enough. You destroy everything you touch, even those you claim to love!"

"Stop it!" Becka shouted over the wind, pulling her eyes from Ryan's tormented face. "Stop it this instant!"

The thing ignored her. It tilted Julie's head back and laughed louder than ever, sounding less and less human, more and more like an animal.

"Ryan," Becka spun back to him, but he sat, his head in his hands, defeated. "Ryan!" Becka was in his face, shouting over the voice that still laughed and raged at Ryan. "We've got to get out of here!"

Suddenly the bulbs around the vanity mirror began to explode, each one showering the room with hot, broken glass.

"Ryan!"

The laughter increased.

Becka grabbed his arm. "Ryan! We've got to go!" He nodded almost numbly and allowed her to help him to his feet. Suddenly the mirror exploded, firing thousands of razor-sharp splinters at them. Becka covered her face as they stumbled across the books, the broken glass, the splintered wood.

They reached the door, but the wind's force held it shut.

The laughter increased as they struggled and pulled. Now the window exploded. Inward. Glass flew everywhere. Becka ducked, and she and Ryan continued fighting the door until finally they managed to pry it open an inch, then a foot.

They squeezed through, Becka first, then Ryan. Once they were on the other side, the door slammed shut with a powerful force.

Becka looked down the hall. "Philip? Krissi?" she called, then she turned to Ryan. "Where'd they go?"

He just stared at her. "Beck ... I'm sorry." The words caught in his throat as he fought back the tears. "Some of that stuff—it happened so long ago."

"It's okay. Look, we've got to go back in and—"

"No, it's *not* okay!" He sniffed and wiped at his eyes. "I can't go back in there. I'm too ... Beck, I'm too dirty. That thing was right. I'm no Christian."

"Ryan, that's all the past."

He shook his head. "No. Who do I think I am, anyway? I'm not good enough. Don't you see? Didn't you hear what she was saying? I'm a hypocrite. A fraud."

"No, that's the whole point. We're all failures—one way or another. Don't you remember what Dr. Woods said? Jesus died to take our punishment for messing up. That's the whole point. It doesn't matter what you've done. None of us is good enough."

"I can't do this."

"Listen to me."

"I—"

"Listen to me!" Her intensity surprised them both. "It doesn't matter what you've done! If you're sorry and you've asked Jesus to forgive you, it's over! Forgotten."

"But—" There was a loud crash behind the door, followed by hellish laughter.

"Ryan, Julie needs us! We're God's hands, remember? We're his feet. If we don't help Julie, who will?"

"But you heard what she said."

"It's just like at the mansion, when the demon came after me, making me feel guilty. The only power it had was the power *I* gave it because I forgot my 'helmet of salvation.' Just like you forgot yours in there."

Ryan looked at her, not understanding.

"You forgot you're saved. That thing inside Julie was playing a mind game with you." Becka could see the lights slowly coming on. "None of that stuff matters anymore. You're forgiven. Jesus said the past is gone, and it is!"

He looked at her, slowly catching on. "I can't believe I didn't see what it was up to. All I could think about was that I wasn't good enough."

"And you're not. None of us is. That's why we had to get saved."

He nodded. Another crash came from the room, followed by more maniacal laughter. Ryan met Becka's gaze, then said, "We have to go back in there, don't we?"

Becka nodded. "But we can't argue with it. We can't even listen to it. We need to let God do the fighting."

Ryan nodded.

Becka took another long, deep breath, then reached for the door.

11

Back at home, Becka's mom was about to step into the shower. It had been a grueling day of job hunting. She was looking forward to letting the warm water work out some of the tension in her neck. But as she opened the shower door, she was suddenly hit with a feeling of uneasiness. She stopped midstep.

Something was wrong. With Becka.

"Is any one of you in trouble? He should pray." The verse hit her as hard as the uneasiness.

These kinds of feelings didn't happen often, but over the years, Mom had learned to trust them. She reached in, shut off the water, slipped on her robe, and headed for the bedroom. She found her Bible, held it close to her chest, and began to pace the hallway.

"Dear Jesus ... dear Lord. Protect my baby. Protect Rebecca ..."

She continued pacing, her prayers growing more and more urgent. "Give her the faith, Lord. Whatever she's going through, give her the faith to get through it."

She pushed open Becka's bedroom door and looked inside. Waves of memories flooded her ... memories of God's faithfulness, of his protection in the past. "Help her, God, don't let her go through this alone. Be there for her, in Jesus' name."

She flipped open her Bible to Psalm 91, one of her favorites, and read it out loud: " 'He who dwells in the shelter of the Most High will rest in the shadow of the Almighty. I will say of the LORD, "He is my refuge and my fortress, my God, in whom I trust." Surely he will save you from the fowler's snare and from the deadly pestilence. He will cover you with his feathers, and under his wings you will find refuge; his faithfulness will be your shield and rampart. You will not fear the terror of night ...' "

Mom leaned against the door frame and gently eased herself down to the floor outside Becka's room. She continued reading. And praying.

The wind suddenly let up, and Julie's door opened easily. Almost too easily. Inside, everything was dark except for a streetlamp shining through the broken window. What was left of the tattered curtains danced and flapped in the breeze, throwing eerie shadows across the room.

Ryan and Becka quietly slipped in, trying their best to avoid the pieces of broken glass and mirror covering the floor. They peered through the darkness and saw Julie sitting on the bed. Her eyes were closed ... until a shard of glass crunched under Ryan's foot. Immediately her eyes popped open, wide and expectant.

Becka tried to swallow, but her mouth was bone dry. She cleared her throat, then spoke. "Julie?"

No response.

She tried again. "Julie?"

The mouth moved mechanically. "Julie is not here."

"You're a liar!" Ryan said, stepping forward.

Becka reached out and touched him. It was a reminder to stay cool. Turning back to the bed, she repeated, "We want to speak to Julie."

The eyes locked onto Becka. "Pity about Philip falling off that ladder."

"What?"

The sneer returned to the mouth. "A smarter person would have asked themselves why it happened just as Krissi entered the hallway."

Becka's surprise turned to anger. "That was you?"

Now it was Ryan's turn to reach out and touch her. "Watch it," he whispered, "it's baiting you."

Becka looked at him, then nodded. He was right. She'd almost fallen for it again. *Help us, Lord,* she prayed, then turned back to Julie. "We demand to speak to Julie."

"I told you, Julie is not— "

"By the power and authority of Jesus Christ— " Becka's voice grew stronger— "we demand to speak to Julie."

Immediately Julie's eyes rolled up into her head, her eyelids twitching and fluttering. A moment later, her eyes rolled back down—and Becka and Ryan could tell it was Julie. She looked lost and confused, like she'd been wakened from a dream. She searched the room until she spotted Rebecca.

"Beck ..." Her voice was husky and frail. "Becka help me, you've got to— " Suddenly her body jerked and her stare went blank.

"Julie," Becka cried. "Julie!"

The sneer returned.

Now it was Ryan's turn. "In the name of Jesus Christ, we order you to leave Julie's body. Now."

Nothing happened.

Ryan and Becka exchanged glances. What was wrong? In the past, they'd had total authority through Christ. The things had to obey.

Once again the voice started to chuckle.

Ryan repeated himself. "Leave! Now!"

The chuckle turned to laughter ... mocking, cackling. "You have no authority."

Ryan knew better. "Oh yes, we do, and in the name of Jesus, I demand you—"

"Julie wants me here," the voice interrupted. "Julie invited me here."

"You're a liar," Ryan shot back. "You leave her, and you leave her now."

No reaction.

Again Becka and Ryan traded looks. What was going on? Finally Becka leaned to Ryan and whispered, "What if it's right? What if Julie wants it to stay?"

Ryan frowned. "Are you saying there's nothing we could do to help then?"

"It's her choice. She's the one who has to decide. It's just like Dr. Woods going to hell. If he wanted to go there, God wouldn't stop him. If Julie wants this thing, then—"

"That's right," the voice hissed, "Julie wants me here, she wants my knowledge." The voice grew more confident. "She wants my power, she wants my—"

Becka interrupted, "I want to speak to Julie."

There was a moment's hesitation.

"Now!" Becka demanded.

Instantly the eyes rolled up and then down. Once again Julie was back on the surface.

Becka approached the bed. "Julie ... Julie, you've got to listen to me. We can't make this thing leave on our own. You invited it in, you have to want it to go."

"He won't let me. He keeps pushing me under, threatening to put me to sleep. Besides, I had to do it. Grandma—"

"No," Ryan interrupted. "This isn't what your grandmother was talking about, Julie! This thing has nothing to do with heaven! Becka and I, we can make it leave, but you've got to want it to go!"

Julie's eyes started to flutter.

"No," Becka shouted. "Fight it, Julie ... fight it!"

The girl's body tensed. Her face twisted and scowled as her head tossed back and forth. Somewhere, deep inside, a fierce battle was raging. Julie began to sweat profusely. Her body convulsed. She began coughing, gagging, until, finally, she vomited—all over her pajamas, all over the bedding. She took a deep breath then convulsed again, spewing even more vomit. "Help me!" she gasped. "Please."

The wind in the room was growing stronger again.

"Julie," Becka cried intently, "you've got to deny this thing. You've got to refuse it. All of it! The power, the knowledge, everything. You've got to give it all up."

"But—"

"Everything!"

"Stop it!" the other voice growled. "She wants me! She wants—"

"You're a liar!" Becka cried. "Satan 'is the father of lies.'"

The Scripture verse hit its mark. An agonizing scream escaped Julie's lips. Her body writhed as if acid had been thrown on it.

Becka pressed in, shouting over the rising wind. "Julie, refuse this thing! Deny it! We can't make it leave unless you want it to!"

Julie came back to the top, only for a second, but long enough to gasp, "Yes ... yes!"

That was all they needed. With full confidence Becka shouted, "By the power and authority of Jesus Christ, I command you to leave Julie."

Nothing happened.

"No more games. Now!"

Julie's body doubled over.

"Now!"

Julie threw her head back. Her voice screamed. It was unearthly—full of agony, torment, betrayal.

"Stop it!" Becka shouted. "Leave her *now!*"

Instantly, the scream faded, and Julie collapsed onto the bed. She was totally limp. It was over. Just like that, the battle had been won. Rebecca closed her eyes. The demon was gone. She knew it.

"Thank you, Jesus … thank you …," she whispered gratefully. Once again, the enemy had done everything possible to make them doubt the authority they had in Christ, to test their faith, to throw them off. But, once again, God had stood by his promises and given Becka and Ryan the strength to win.

Becka glanced at Ryan. He nodded, knowingly. "I'll get some stuff to wash her up."

Becka nodded, then watched as he headed into the hall. She closed her eyes again and took a very deep breath. She was tired. Very tired. It had been a long, exhausting day—a long, exhausting week.

Julie stirred, and Becka stepped up to the bed. The girl moaned and opened her eyes.

"Oh, Beck …" Her voice was weak and feeble.

"It's okay, Jules. It's over now."

A worn and beaten Julie looked up at Becka, her eyes full of helplessness and shame. Becka knelt on the bed and wrapped her arms around her friend. Julie began to weep. "It was so awful," she sobbed, "so awful. I tried to come up, I tried to warn them, but …"

"Shh, it's okay now, it's all over." She felt the girl's back grow rigid, then the grip around her own body tighten. Becka tried to pull away, but Julie's grasp increased. Suddenly Becka felt herself being lifted off the floor and pulled onto the bed.

"Julie, what are you— " Becka's words were cut off as the air was forced from her lungs. She tried to free herself, but the grip was too strong—and growing tighter by the second. She tried to breathe, but it was becoming more and more difficult. She squirmed and twisted.

"Julie ... I can't breathe!"

The grip tightened even more, and what air she had was forced out. Fear swept over Becka. She fought—twisting, turning, rolling—but the hold could not be broken.

"Julie ...," she gasped.

But Julie didn't hear; Julie was no longer in charge. Becka's lungs burned for air. She had to get some oxygen. She kicked and thrashed for all she was worth. The edges of her vision began turning white, growing fuzzy. She needed air. She was passing out.

There was another hellish laugh, but it was slightly different from before. Becka could feel Julie's mouth draw near to her ear. And then, ever so quietly, the voice whispered: "Did you really think there was only one of us?"

Adrenaline surged through Becka's body. She twisted, rolled, jerked, kicked. By arching her back, she managed to roll them off the bed and onto the floor. They hit hard and began thrashing back and forth over the broken pieces of glass and mirror. The fall had momentarily broken Julie's grip. Becka breathed just enough air, she found just enough faith to gasp, "Stop ... in Christ's name, I ... command you to stop!"

Instantly, the struggle ceased. Julie's grip relaxed. For a long moment the two girls lay on the floor, panting, trying to catch their breath. The wind continued to blow. Becka started dragging herself toward the door. She had to get out of there. She didn't think she could withstand another attack.

Then, slowly, with seemingly superhuman strength, Julie sat up. Her head swiveled toward Becka, and once again the mouth distorted into a hideous grin.

Becka froze. "How many— " she fought to catch her breath— "how many of you are there?"

Julie's face slowly changed. But not like before. This time the change was complete ... and inhuman. Images superimposed themselves over the girl's face. Hideous images. First a grotesque gargoyle, then a wolf's head, then a half-snake, half-monkey, then a giant rat.

Becka's heart pounded wildly as the faces continued, one after another after another. She had her answer. It was true, the guardian had obeyed the command she and Ryan gave it. It had left. But it had opened the door for others. He was gone, but there were a dozen more remaining.

Becka rose unsteadily to her feet. The wind stung her eyes and made them water. She tried to call to Ryan, but she was too weak and too afraid. Unable to take her eyes off the changing face, she started backing toward the door. She was exhausted and afraid.

Suddenly, the wind ripped the curtains off their rods. They flew from the window directly at her. She screamed and tried to duck, but they hit her, instantly wrapping around her face, her body, her arms. She clawed at them, staggering blindly, trying to pull them away, trying to scream. But the terror was too great.

She lost her balance. She stumbled once, twice, then crashed to the floor.

More hellish laughter: deafening, chilling, paralyzing. It was drawing closer. The thing had raised Julie to her feet and was approaching. Unable to see, crazed with panic, Becka tore at the curtains, but it did no good.

God! God! her mind screamed in panic as the laughter roared above her as the creature prepared to strike.

Mom continued reading and praying.

"'A thousand fall at your side, ten thousand at your right hand, but it will not come near you. You will only observe with your eyes and see the punishment of the wicked. If you make the Most High your dwelling—even the LORD, who is my refuge—then no harm will befall you, no disaster will come near your tent. For he will command his angels concerning you to guard you in all your ways, they will lift you up in their hands, so that you will not strike your foot against a stone. You will tread upon the lion and the cobra; you will trample the great lion and the serpent.' "

Somewhere in the back of Becka's terrified mind, a small spark of reason ignited ... a microscopic ember that the panic had not completely put out ... a tiny point of light that could not be extinguished. She drew deep, rapid breaths of air through her constricted throat. She would try again.

The words were faint, barely audible, more thought than spoken. "In the name of Jesus Christ, I command you to stop ..."

The wind ceased. The curtains went limp.

Becka fought with the material, tearing it off her face, away from her body ... only to see Julie standing above her, snarling, preparing for a final lunge. Suddenly Becka heard another voice.

" 'The Lord rebuke you!' " Ryan shouted as he entered the room.

Julie's voice shrieked. Her body reeled backward until it crashed into the far wall.

Ryan wasted no time. "By the power and authority of Jesus Christ, we command you to leave—all of you! Leave Julie this instant. We cast you into the abyss, we cast each of you into the lake of fire, never to return!"

Julie's head flew back, and a screeching howl erupted from her throat ... and then, slowly, limply, she slid to the floor. There was only silence. The howl had stopped, the wind had faded. Now there was nothing except quiet weeping. Becka rose to her feet. Slowly, cautiously, she crossed to Julie, who was huddled against the wall in a broken heap.

"I'm sorry ...," Julie cried softly.

Becka knelt to her side. "Julie?"

Julie looked up, her face smudged with sweat and blood and tears. "Becka ... I'm so sorry ..."

This time Rebecca knew it was over. Completely. This time she knew she was talking to the real Julie. And this time, as the two fell into an embrace, Becka also began to cry.

"'Because he loves me,' says the LORD, 'I will rescue him; I will protect him, for he acknowledges my name. He will call upon me, and I will answer him; I will be with him in trouble, I will deliver him and honor him. With long life will I satisfy him and show him my salvation.'"

Mom closed her eyes. "Amen," she prayed, breathing a sigh of relief. "Amen, dear Jesus, amen, amen ..."

12

The last period of the day was over. News that Ryan had lost the election had just been announced over the school intercom. Now everyone was shuffling out into the halls and heading for home. If the defeat had been announced two weeks earlier, it would have surprised everyone. After all, Ryan Riordan had been everybody's pal, the All-American Good Guy. But it hadn't taken Krissi long to spread the dirt she'd learned about him in Julie's bedroom. And it hadn't taken long for that dirt to destroy Ryan's chances of winning any type of election.

As Ryan and Becka moved down the hall, a couple of guys offered him a "Tough break, Riordan." But that was about it for sympathy. Everyone else just passed without speaking. They were either unsure of what to say or figured Ryan wasn't worth the effort of saying anything.

"I can't blame them," Ryan sighed as they rounded the corner and headed for their lockers. "I did kinda let everyone down."

Becka reached out to take his hand. "Not me," she said quietly.

He looked down at her and smiled. It was the killer smile. The one she'd missed seeing for so long. The one that put that warm glow in the center of her chest.

She knew the last few days had been rough on him. Losing the election was tough, but going to Mr. Patton, the geometry teacher, and offering to do makeup assignments wasn't so easy, either. Nor was visiting the stereo shop and working out a payment plan for the stereo he'd stolen. Yet he never told a soul. The reason was simple. Ryan wasn't doing it to earn back his reputation. He did it because he thought it was the right thing to do. Becka held his hand tighter.

"Ryan ... hey, Ryan!"

They both recognized the voice and turned to see Krissi making her way through the crowd. "Hi, guys," she chirped. Becka watched in wonder. After all but single-handedly causing Ryan to lose the election, after managing to trash both of their reputations, here she was acting as if nothing had happened! Good ol' Krissi. Good ol' empty-headed, who-can-help-but-love-her Krissi.

"How you guys doing?" she asked, pulling up alongside them.

Ryan shrugged. "Could be better."

A frown almost creased her perfect brow. "Oh, that ... Sorry, but Xandrak says we should always live in truth."

"Xandrak?" Ryan asked.

"Yeah, you know, the alien who's writing messages through me."

"Alien?" Ryan repeated. "Listen, Krissi, I don't think Xandrak is such a—"

Krissi raised up her hand. "I know what you're going to say. Xandrak has already told me. That's why he said I should stay away from you two. He says your way of thinking is old-fashioned. That it's holding us back from entering the new paradigm shift."

"The new ... what?" Becka asked.

"You wouldn't understand." Krissi turned to her bag and began digging. "Your minds have been too polluted. Listen, are you going to see Julie?"

"Yeah," Ryan answered. "We've been having a Bible study with her."

Krissi continued to rummage. "So she's become a Christian?"

"Yeah," Becka responded. "After all that happened she couldn't wait."

"She sure felt embarrassed, though," Ryan added. "I mean, being sucked into all that counterfeit stuff."

Becka nodded. "I told her we've all been sucked in at times." She cast a glance at Ryan. It was true. They'd all been fooled by the lies at one time or another. Becka went on, "I'm just relieved she knows it was lies now. From that supposed trip to heaven—"

Ryan interrupted, "Which she now realizes was either a total dream or another major deception."

"—all the way to that demon creep," Becka finished.

Krissi raised her eyebrows. "Hmmmm," was her only comment.

"But she's still got a lot of questions," Ryan said.

"I'll bet she does," said Krissi as she pulled a note from her bag and shoved it into Becka's hand. "Here."

"What's this?"

"It's from Xandrak. It's about your little brother. I shouldn't be letting you read it, but I figured, what the heck, I won't be staying on this planet much longer anyway, so what does it matter."

"I'm sorry, what?"

Krissi turned. "I'll be in the mother ship."

"Krissi, what are you—what do you mean?"

Krissi had already turned and started off.

"Krissi?" But she disappeared into the crowd.

Ryan looked to Becka. "Mother ship? Aliens? She won't be on this planet much longer? Any idea what she's talking about?"

Becka could only shake her head. Then, remembering the note, she unfolded it and took a look.

Greetings in the name of the Intergalactic Alliance: One enemy is no longer a threat. His mind has been ensnared by his own imaginings. Unlike his older sister, he has been neutralized. He is ours. Soon she and her kind will follow. Peace and prosperity. Xandrak.

Becka's knees began to weaken.

"What's wrong?" Ryan asked.

Her hand trembled as she passed the note to him. She closed her eyes. She had no idea what it all meant.

But she had a sickening feeling she would be finding out.

The Encounter

The coming of the lawless one will be in accordance with the work of Satan displayed in all kinds of counterfeit miracles, signs and wonders, and in every sort of evil that deceives those who are perishing. They perish because they refused to love the truth and so be saved.

2 THESSALONIANS 2:9–10

1

How are you coming?" Philip asked as he peered over the stack of library books at Krissi.

The girl sighed and lifted her perfectly manicured nails to brush her perfect dark hair out of her perfect green eyes. "If you keep interrupting my concentration," she complained, "nothing will happen."

"Sorry," he said.

"Xandrak only writes through me if I relax and keep my mind clear."

Philip chuckled and returned to his books. If there was ever a person who would be able to keep her mind clear, it was Krissi. As far as he knew she hadn't had a deep thought in years. But getting her to relax was another thing. Let's face it—opening yourself up to the influence of aliens and allowing them to write messages through you would tend to make anyone a little nervous.

But that's what Krissi was doing, and she was getting good at it. Very good. The process was called automatic handwriting, and during the past week its effects had grown stronger than ever. Often the writing would repeat the same phrases over and over again. Phrases that always emphasized Krissi was a specially chosen Light Worker, that she would help usher in the New Age of spiritual enlightenment, and that if she listened carefully to the Ascended Masters, she could help cleanse the planet and rescue it from its self-destruction.

Of course, neither Philip nor Krissi was sure what all of this stuff meant, but what they did understand sounded pretty cool.

Krissi also had been warned, over and over, to stay away from people with "dark emotions"—especially narrow-minded Christians like Rebecca Williams, Becka's boyfriend, Ryan, and now Julie Mitchell. It made no difference that they all used to be friends. Their old-fashioned way of thinking, their "clinging to outdated religion," could pose a real threat.

At least, that's what the messages kept saying.

They said one other thing too—and this was the phrase that had Krissi the most excited. They told her she would be "making contact with an intergalactic race." Soon.

That's why Krissi was so busy trying to connect with Xandrak, her alien guide. And that's why Philip was poring through every book on UFOs that he could find in the public library. If there was even the slightest chance of actually meeting inhabitants from another world, he wanted to be prepared.

At first Philip didn't buy into all of this UFO nonsense. As an intellectual type, he believed everything had to be proven. Sure, he knew Krissi's automatic writing was legitimate—they'd tested it a dozen times. Not only was the handwriting entirely different from her own, but whatever or whoever was moving her hand knew things Krissi couldn't possibly know.

Still, to believe it was actually somebody from another planet, to believe that an extraterrestrial was actually writing through his girlfriend, well, that was a bit much for Philip. But as the information in her writing continued to line up with his research, Philip was finding it harder and harder to deny what Krissi was telling him.

"Check it out," he said, referring to the book in front of him. "It says here that one out of ten adults in the United States has seen a UFO."

"No kidding?" she asked.

He nodded. "And not just crackpots. It says here that the pharaohs of Egypt saw them, as well as Christopher Columbus, Andrew Jackson, and NASA astronauts."

Krissi nodded and repositioned the pencil on her writing pad so it would flow more smoothly. Still, nothing happened.

Philip continued. "Ninety-five percent of the sightings can be explained, but there's still five percent that no one has an answer for. Oh, and listen to this: 'Currently there are over one thousand documented cases of personal contact with alien creatures.'"

"You mean where people actually meet them?"

"Uh-huh. It also says there are UFO channelers and automatic handwriters around the world."

Krissi's excitement drooped. "So there are more people than just me doing this type of writing?"

"Yeah, tons. In fact, it says—"

"Philip," she interrupted. "Look at my hand. It's starting!"

They both looked down at the paper as her hand began to write letters. It was the same handwriting they'd seen before.

"This is so cool," she chirped. "I'm not having to zone out or daydream or anything. Now it's just happening as I sit here talking."

Philip cocked his head to watch the letters form. "I guess that means it's getting stronger."

"He," Krissi corrected. "*He's* getting stronger."

Philip shrugged. He still wasn't entirely convinced.

They continued watching, but instead of the New Age ramblings that Krissi's hand usually wrote, this message was short and to the point:

Greetings in the name of the Intergalactic Alliance. The time for our rendezvous has arrived. Prepare for encounter at old logging road off Highway 72, north of Seth Creek. 8:00 p.m. Peace.
Xandrak

The pencil came to a stop. Philip's and Krissi's hearts pounded as they stared at the message. Neither fully believed what they saw. Finally, Philip looked at his watch. "It's 7:07 …"

Krissi nodded, swallowing back a wave of both fear and excitement. "If we're going to meet him we better hurry."

👁 👁

"Sweetheart, I'm just a little concerned, that's all."

"Everything's fine, Mom."

"But you're spending all your evenings there. And Becka and I, we hardly ever see you anymore."

Scott could feel his mother closing in. If he didn't hurry and ease her fears, she could stop him from going over to Hubert's at all. He reached across the dinner table for the casserole dish and piled up an extra portion of Hamburger Whatever onto his plate. Eating was a good way to stall while he thought of the best approach. Come to think of it, eating was good for just about anything these days. At fifteen, Scott Williams was growing faster than a weed, and food was one thing he could never get enough of.

Food and playing Crypts and Wizards.

The game had been going on for about two weeks now. Darryl, his best friend, had invited him over to his cousin Hubert's house. As a part-time computer whiz and full-time weirded-out genius, Hubert had modified an incredible fantasy role-playing game. Each night, he would lock himself away in an upstairs bedroom and run the master computer while Scott and a half dozen other players plugged in their own computers downstairs and tried to track down the treasure Hubert had hidden in a special crypt—a crypt that only he had the map for.

The game was incredible. Not only did it give Scott a chance to really use his mind, but he could put that incredible imagination of his to work as well. Each of the players played a character with special strengths, personalities, and magical powers. Some were elves, others werewolves, warriors, warlocks, wizards, zombies, and the list went on. You could be anything you wanted. And nothing matched the excitement of battling as a supernatural character who had special weapons, spells, and magical powers.

Of course, Scott knew some of this stuff could be pretty dark at times, and it did make him just a little bit nervous. But, hey, it was only a game. Just make-believe. All in his imagination.

The character he had created for himself—a mystical holy man by the name of Ttocs (Scott spelled backward)—had many of the same personality traits he did: a strong sense of justice, a belief in the supernatural, and a love for people. As the game continued over the hours, the days, and on into the weeks, Scott had grown more and more attached to the little guy. Together the two fought off the ghouls and monsters that Hubert—and other players' characters—threw at them. All this while carefully planning their route to get to the treasure.

"Scotty, are you sure it's really that healthy?" Becka asked from across the table.

"What's that supposed to mean?" Scott didn't exactly snap at his older sister, but he wasn't smiling, either. What business was it of hers? Sure, the two of them were extra close. There was something about growing up in the Brazilian rain forest and only having each other as playmates that created a bit of a bond. Then there was losing Dad in the airplane crash less than a year ago. And, of course, all that occult stuff they'd gone through since they moved to the States. Still, that didn't give her the right to meddle.

Becka shrugged. "It just seems like spending all your time doing something like that isn't so smart."

Scott tried to hide his irritation. "Relax. I'm just honing my computer skills. Besides, I'm getting a chance to exercise my imagination and—" he threw her a pointed look—"make a few friends along the way."

Becka glanced down.

He'd hit his mark. It was a little mean, but he'd had to find some way of telling her to back off. He knew Becka had a hard time making friends; on the self-image scale of 1 to 10 she was about a –3. He also knew that Philip and Krissi, two of the few friends she did have, had just cut her off.

Becka grew silent. He knew she'd caught his drift. Now there was only Mom to worry about.

"Well—" his mother wiped her mouth and rose from her chair to get dessert—"I'm not saying no. Yet."

Scott relaxed.

"But," she continued, "I want you to give the matter some serious thought."

Scott nodded, grateful the inquisition had come to an end. He snuck a peek at his watch. 7:45. He had to hurry. The game would be resuming in fifteen minutes, and he couldn't miss a second of it.

The Jeep Wrangler raced down Highway 72 with the CD blasting an old Doors tune. It wasn't Philip's favorite music, but since his car was in the shop and the Wrangler was borrowed from Dad, he had to listen to whatever tunes Dad had. The moon was full and shrouded with only a thin layer of fog coming in from the coast. There was plenty of light to see the logging road ... if they only knew where it was.

He glanced at the dashboard clock. 8:10. They were already late—thanks to Krissi's insistence that they stop by her house so she could change. Let's face it, the last thing in the world you want to do when meeting aliens from another planet is to be seen wearing a shirt that's three months out of fashion. Not when you have a new vest and capris to wear. Philip sighed and pressed down on the accelerator.

He loved Krissi. Everybody knew it. They didn't understand it, but they knew it. It seemed so odd that Philip, with his superintellect, would show the slightest interest in Krissi, with her superairheadedness. Maybe it had something to do with her impulsive way of life. Philip had to think everything through five times before he even considered doing it; Krissi just up and did. When this approach didn't make him crazy, Philip loved the excitement and freedom it brought.

But his feelings went far deeper than that.

Maybe it had to do with growing up next door to her and being best friends all their lives. Or maybe it had to do with Philip's mom taking his two sisters and deserting him and his dad without a word. Krissi had been the only one there for him. Feeling for him. Aching with him. Holding him for hours one afternoon when he couldn't stop crying.

Whatever the reason for their love, if the phrase "opposites attract" had ever applied to a couple, it applied to them. Krissi was Philip's breath of freedom and fresh air; he was her rock and reality check.

"We must have passed it," Krissi shouted over the music. "Turn around."

Philip threw her a look. "Did you see anything?"

She shook her head. "No, but we passed it. I know we did."

"Krissi …"

"Don't ask me how I know, I just—I just know it. I feel it, okay?"

Philip gave her another look.

"We haven't got much time," she insisted. "Please, trust me on this."

He glanced at the clock. 8:11. They were going to be late anyway, and if Krissi was so sure …

He slowed the Wrangler, pulled to the side, and threw the vehicle into a sharp U-turn. The gravel sprayed as he gunned the engine and slid back onto the road going the opposite direction. Once again he looked at Krissi. She was concentrating, staring out her window.

There were no other cars in sight. Philip clicked on the high beams and picked up speed. Ever since their little supernatural encounter at the Hawthorne mansion, Krissi's automatic handwriting wasn't the only thing that had grown stronger. Her intuition, her ability to sense things she didn't know, had increased. She could perceive things others didn't.

Philip smiled. Of course, some of this was just her natural spontaneity, like the time she'd felt "impressed" to take the day off and go to the beach instead of taking a geometry midterm. Or the time she felt "directed" to order silver-plated hunting knives on the shopping channel. He shook his head slightly. She'd never hunted in her life and didn't know anyone who did. But that was all some time ago. Lately ... Philip glanced at her. Lately Krissi's insights tended to be right on the money.

"There!" she shouted. "Right there!"

Philip looked just in time to see a secluded opening whisk by. He hit the brakes, threw the Jeep into reverse, and quickly backed up. Sure enough, there it was. With all the underbrush, it had been practically invisible. But now you could clearly see it was the remains of an old logging road.

"It looks pretty overgrown in there," Krissi said.

Philip grinned at her and reached down. "That's why we've got four-wheel drive, kiddo." He pulled a smaller gearshift forward, turned the Jeep toward the opening, and they began bouncing and jostling up the remains of the old dirt road.

Bushes scraped the sides of the vehicle and an occasional tree branch slapped at the windshield. Philip took it slow in case there were also rocks or ruts hiding, waiting to rip out his oil pan.

"What do you think we'll see?" he asked. "Flying saucers? Little green men?"

Krissi craned her neck to look up into the sky. "I'm not sure." The fog had grown thicker, allowing only the most determined stars to burn through. She turned and looked out her window at the passing brush and trees. "Xandrak wouldn't tell us to show up here if it wasn't something ... hold it! What was that?"

"What?"

"Stop the car!"

Philip hit the brakes. He reached over to turn off the CD. Now there was just the quiet idling of the motor.

Krissi looked over her shoulder through the window of the backseat. "It looked like ..." She hesitated.

"Like what?"

"A cow."

Philip chuckled. "Krissi, there aren't any cows around here. The nearest ranch is twenty miles away."

"It was a cow, I'm sure of it. It had four legs, horns, everything." She reached for the door and opened it.

"Krissi, don't— " But he was too late. The door was already open and she was stepping out. Philip sighed and followed suit, uncoiling his six-foot frame from behind the wheel.

Once outside, he talked to her over the roof as she walked away. "Even if it is a cow, that's not exactly what we're looking for."

"I know." Krissi delicately pushed aside a branch that threatened to mess her hair or, worse yet, soil her vest. "But doesn't it, like, surprise you that a cow would be way out here in the middle of the woods?"

He gave no answer.

"Philip?"

Still no response.

"Philip, answer me." She turned back to the car and saw there was a good reason for his silence.

Philip was staring at a diamond-shaped object that hovered a hundred feet above them in the sky.

Krissi moved for a better look. It wasn't just one diamond-shaped object, but three. Three craft hovering in a perfect triangular formation. They were absolutely silent, but they pulsed various colors—first red, then green, then yellow, then back to red.

She watched as Philip continued to stare for another half minute. Even then he never took his eyes off the objects. "Okay," he said hoarsely. "Now what?"

2

As if answering his question, the formation of lights started moving forward.

"They're going!" Philip cried. "They didn't see us. Hey!" he shouted. "Hey, we're down here!" He waved his arms. "We're down here. Hey! We're— "

"They know," Krissi said quietly. Her voice was so calm he turned to look at her. She stood on the other side of the Jeep. "They want us to follow."

"They what?"

"They want us to follow them. They're staying above the road so we can follow."

Philip stared at her, then looked back to the moving objects. Sure enough, they were moving forward, but very slowly and directly over the road that stretched before them.

He climbed back into the Jeep. Krissi slid into the passenger seat. He started to put the vehicle into gear, then turned and asked, "You sure we want to do this?"

Krissi smiled. "What do you think?"

Philip had no choice. He wished he had, but the time to chicken out would have been back at the library or at Krissi's house or on the highway. Not here, not now. He nodded, dropped the Jeep into gear, and they started forward.

Krissi's eyes stayed glued to the windshield, focused on the pulsing lights that led them. They never grew brighter, they never grew dimmer. They just continued the same pulse from red to green to yellow and back to red.

As Philip drove he felt a chill start somewhere in his gut and slowly work its way up his back and into his shoulders. It was uncanny, the way the lights stayed in perfect formation, the way they kept the same distance from them, slowing when he had to slow, speeding up when he sped up.

The only sound was the jarring and bouncing of the Jeep as it dipped in and out of the holes and ruts. Neither Philip nor Krissi spoke. They remained as silent as the lights.

The road finally opened onto a large grassy area half the size of a football field. The lights slowly veered from the road and crossed to the far left side of the field, near a stand of pine trees. There they came to a stop and waited.

Philip hesitated. He was not about to get out of the vehicle and follow the hovering craft. Nor was he crazy about turning off the road and traveling through some unknown field at night. Who knew what ditches, stumps, or drop-offs lay ahead. Still, what other choice did he have? Reluctantly, he eased the Jeep off the road and crept through the field. It took several minutes, but at last he pulled to a stop twenty or so feet from the lights.

"Krissi?"

"Shh ..." She was still staring up through the windshield.

Philip looked at her. Was she sensing something? Was she hearing something? He glanced back up to the silent lights.

Suddenly the Jeep's engine began to sputter. Then cough. Then it quit altogether. Philip glanced at the gas gauge. There was still a quarter tank left. Then he realized it wasn't just the motor that had stopped. The headlights were gone too.

He reached over to the key, switched it off, then back on. The engine turned but would not start. He turned the ignition off, then tried again. Same result.

"Don't worry about it," Krissi said.

"What?"

"It's okay."

He looked at her, not understanding. He gave the ignition a third try, this time grinding the starter over and over again.

Suddenly, there was a blast of light — so bright and intense that he thought the craft above him had blown up. But it wasn't an explosion; it was a light beam, five feet in diameter and as bright as the sun. It slowly extended from the center of the three crafts toward the stand of pine trees.

Philip and Krissi shielded their eyes as the light continued to stretch toward the trees, but when it hit the top branches, it did not illuminate them. It ignited them. Instantly. They exploded into a giant fireball.

Krissi screamed as they covered their faces from the light and heat that blasted through the windshield.

Philip fumbled for the ignition. He had to get them out of there! He turned the key. Nothing.

He looked back at the beam of light and froze. It was moving — so slowly that at first he thought it was the hot wavy air from the fire playing tricks, like a mirage. But this was no trick. The beam was moving off the blazing trees and inching its way toward them, igniting everything in its path.

"Philip, get us out of here!"

Philip pumped the accelerator. Still nothing.

The light continued toward them.

"Philip!"

"I'm trying!" he shouted. *"I'm trying!"*

Now the beam was fifteen feet away …

"PHILIP!!"

His hand was shaking. It was so sweaty that the key slipped as he tried to turn it.

Twelve feet, ten . . .

Now they could hear the moisture from the grass and shrubs hissing and sizzling under the approaching heat. Pieces of wood cracked and popped as if in a fireplace.

Eight feet . . .

"Philip!"

Five . . .

He reached for his door. "Let's get out of here!"

"What?"

"Run! Get out of the car! *Run!*"

Then, as instantly as it had started, the beam stopped. There was no light. Only the blazing trees ahead of them and the burning undergrowth beside them. Philip stared. The fire would not spread. He knew that. Everything was too damp and wet. He leaned against the wheel, trying to catch his breath, trying to steady himself.

Krissi sat beside him, shaking like a leaf.

They sat in the car, unable to move, as the pines continued burning. Both followed the line of charred vegetation, cut with razorlike accuracy from the trees to within five feet of their Jeep.

Philip turned to Krissi. The light from the fire danced and played across her frightened face. With one hand he wiped away the sweat that had fallen into his eyes. With the other he reached out to her. "You okay?"

She nodded.

He craned his neck to look back up through the windshield.

When Krissi finally spoke, her voice was weak and thin. "Are . . . are they still there?"

The light from the fire was so bright it was impossible to see anything in the sky.

"It's too bright," he said. "I can't tell." He heard the handle to the passenger door move. His eyes shot to Krissi, who was opening the door and getting out. "Where are you going?!"

"I can't stay in here. I've got to go."

"Krissi, we're safe in here. At least safer than—"

But Krissi would not listen. "I can't stay in here!" She stepped down into the knee-high grass. She tilted her head up toward the sky. Whatever expression she had on her face suddenly froze. "Philip ..." Her voice was high and faraway.

"What? What is it?"

"Philip ... they're coming ..."

"Krissi, get back insi—"

The car pitched violently to the right.

"Philip!"

With the jolt came another light. Glaring. Powerful. Overcoming every shadow, every inch of darkness. But this light was different from the first. It was blue and carried no heat. Only power. The vehicle heaved under another impact and began to rock.

"Philip!!"

When he spotted her, she was still outside but clinging to the door with all of her might. Her feet were parallel to the ground and rising. Something was sucking her upward!

"Philip!" she screamed, terrified.

He lunged for her, but the shaking of the car tossed him like a pinball. One minute he'd grabbed her arm through the open window, the next he was thrown to the floorboard.

Krissi's grip on the door had been broken. She was now clinging to the side mirror, screaming hysterically. Philip struggled back up into the seat. He reached out the window and grabbed her wrists—both of them. They were so slick with sweat that he could barely hang on. He could no longer see her legs. They were above her head as she clung to the door, screaming.

"Don't let me go! Don't let me go!"

The car continued to lunge back and forth. For a brief second their eyes connected. There was no mistaking Krissi's helpless horror. Adrenaline surged through Philip. He would save her.

He would not let go of her, not at any cost. Still clinging to her wrists, he pulled himself to her window. But his grip was slipping.

"Hang on!" he shouted. "Hang on!"

"I can't! Philip, help m—"

The car lurched violently. Krissi screamed as her hands slipped away from the mirror. The pull was too great. Philip could no longer hold her. She slid from his grip and disappeared into the night.

"Krissi! *Krissi!!*"

Becka bolted awake in her room. She'd gone to bed early and had barely dropped off when she had a dream. But this wasn't just your run-of-the-mill dream. It was another one of those dreams. She couldn't remember any specifics. Just terror.

And Krissi. Somehow she knew the terror involved Krissi.

For days Becka had tried to warn her onetime friend about playing with automatic handwriting. Becka knew the experience was legitimate. She knew somebody or something was moving Krissi's hand.

She also knew that the somebody or something was evil.

Becka, Ryan, even her other friend Julie, had all tried to warn Krissi. But the autowriting messages had said the three of them were not to be trusted. So Krissi cut them off. It had been painful for Becka, but it was far from the first time she had been snubbed because of her faith.

Actually, it went further than just her faith. Over the past several months Becka had been developing a certain skill, a "calling" if you will. It wasn't something she wanted. On the contrary, what she really wanted was to blend into the crowd and be like everyone else. But that didn't seem to be her lot. Instead, with all the supernatural battles she'd been involved in, she had developed a reputation as someone who was all too familiar with the occult. Someone who knew what to look out for, and if necessary, someone who could battle it.

Kids at school had started calling her the All-School Ghostbuster.

Now, as she lay in the darkness of her room, she could feel her gift at work again. The old, familiar dread surrounded her—but it wasn't dread for herself. It was dread for Krissi.

Prayer wasn't something Becka was great at. Truth was, she knew she should be doing a lot more of it than she did. But with schoolwork, friends, TV, and the fast-paced life of high school, it was usually pretty hard to find time. Still, she tried.

Especially tonight. She had to. When she felt this kind of dread, she knew she had no option. It was the only way she could battle ... whatever was going on. And, at least for tonight, it was the only thing she could do for Krissi, the only way she could help.

So Becka started to pray.

Scott stared intently at the computer screen. Ttocs, the mystical holy man he had created, was locked in mortal combat with a blood-drinking banshee. According to Hubert, the Crypt Master, the ghoul had been lying in wait for just such an attack. Now the monster leaped onto Ttocs's neck, dug her fangs into his arteries, and sucked with all her might. Not only was she drawing Ttocs's blood, but his brains were also being sucked through the hollow, needlelike fangs.

Scott hit the Alt, Shift, and R keys on his keyboard and watched numbers flash across his screen. This was the computer's version of throwing dice.

The numbers appeared: 11, 4, and 3. Scott groaned. The 11 meant he got away, but not without losing most of his mental abilities. The two low numbers meant he had lost his armor and long sword. In short, Ttocs had survived. Barely.

Scott thumped his desk in frustration.

Darryl, who was sitting in the station beside him, gave a loud sniff. "So, it's just a game, huh?" He grinned.

Scott ignored him. "What good is it being a holy man when there are goons like that who can destroy you in one round?"

"You shouldn't have used your sword."

"What do you mean?"

"You're a mystic, right? A holy man?"

"So ..."

"So, use your telekinesis powers—your magic. Instead of fighting them with swords, use your spells."

Suddenly Scott's screen began to flash. One of the other players was challenging him to combat. He'd obviously smelled blood and was close enough to go in for the kill.

Again Scott rolled the dice. Again the numbers were too low. And thanks to the attack of a common, everyday flesh eater, the great Ttocs suddenly died. His internal organs had been devoured and the rest of his brain sucked out. Scott slapped the desk again. He was out of the game.

"And another thing," Darryl sniffed while pushing up his glasses, "you were only playing halfway."

"What do you mean?"

"To really win at this thing, you have to play body, mind, and soul."

"I was."

"No way. Your character was too nice. Next time make up somebody ruthless and bloodthirsty. Save the nice-guy act for reality."

Scott gave him a look, then turned back to his screen and watched as his name and location were bleeped from the map. His face flushed with anger. He knew it was only a game, but still ... part of him had been up on that screen. Part of him had just been destroyed.

He folded his arms and leaned back. *So Darryl thinks I'm*

holding back, does he? That I was too nice? Okay, fine. Next time I'll create a better character. Next time I'll play with everything I have. They want bloodthirsty and ruthless, they'll get bloodthirsty and ruthless. He smiled grimly. *The new and improved Ttocs will be unstoppable.*

As he waited for Darryl and the others to finish for the evening, Scott grabbed a paper and pencil, rose to his feet, and crossed to the Game Book on the center table. This was a book that listed various types of characters, explaining their abilities, weapons, powers, personalities, and so forth. He flipped the book open. He would need all the help and hints he could get. He would still keep the name Ttocs. But this new version would be the best player they had ever seen.

3

"Krissi!"

Philip threw open the car door and staggered into the blinding blue light. She was his life, his reason for living. If she had to meet some awful fate, he would meet it with her. If he had to give up his life to save hers, he would.

But once he stepped outside, the light was no longer blue. It was orangish white, like the sun. And it no longer hovered above him. It was rising over the mountains in the east, right where the sun would rise.

Philip shook his head and blinked. It *was* the sun. He was staring at the rising sun!

He rubbed his eyes and took half a step back. But instead of grass under his feet, he heard the crunch of gravel. His mouth opened in surprise as he saw he was no longer standing in grass, but on asphalt.

What was going on?

He looked around. He wasn't in the field anymore. He was standing next to his dad's Jeep on Highway 72!

"What are you doing out there?"

He spun around to see Krissi sitting up in the passenger's

seat. Her eyes were puffy from sleep, but other than that she looked perfectly fine.

"What ...?" He swallowed. "Are you okay?"

She gave a long stretch. "Yeah."

He looked back into the sky. It was blue and gorgeous and clear. Not a flying saucer in sight.

"Why didn't you wake me?" she asked. "What time is it?" Before he could check his watch, she squinted at the dash clock. "Six twenty-five! My folks are going to kill me. Hurry up, we have to get home."

Philip nodded numbly and crossed to his side of the Jeep. As he climbed inside, Krissi scolded him again. "You should have woke me."

He reached for the ignition. "I, uh, I didn't know you were asleep."

"Yeah, right," she scoffed. She pulled down the vanity mirror to check her hair and makeup. "I must have really zonked out."

Philip fired up the Jeep. It started on the first try. "What, uh, what was the last thing you remember? Last night, I mean."

She scowled, trying to think. "I was getting out to look for that stupid cow."

Philip took a deep breath to steady himself. "You don't remember seeing those lights? You don't remember getting sucked into the air?"

Krissi gave him a look. "What's that supposed to mean?"

He could find no answer.

"I remember getting out of the car and you telling me I couldn't possibly have seen a cow. You said the nearest ranch was twenty miles away and that—hey, wait a minute."

Philip turned to her.

Krissi was looking into the vanity mirror. "Did you brush my hair?"

"Did I what?"

"My hair, when I was asleep, did you, like, try to brush it or something?"

"Why would I—"

"I never part it on the left."

"What?"

"My hair. That's my worst side. I never part it on the left."

Philip stared. She was right. In all the years he had known her, he had never seen her hair parted on the left. He'd seen it up, he'd seen it back, he'd seen it cropped ... but he had never seen it parted on the left.

Krissi turned back to him, puzzled, her voice sounding more and more uneasy. "Philip, what's going on?"

"Just talk to her, that's all I'm asking."

"Philip," Becka sighed, "she doesn't want to talk to me. She doesn't even want to see me."

"I know ... but if I can arrange something, if I can get the two of you together?"

Philip stayed glued to her side as Becka arrived at her locker and opened it. The last thing in the world she wanted was another encounter with Krissi. The screaming bout in the hall last week had been enough. The girl was always so dramatic. Normally that didn't bother Becka, but the fact that Krissi's dramatics had been directed at her and that they'd been loud enough for everyone to hear did bother her. A lot.

"Please, just a word," Philip persisted.

"She thinks I'm the enemy," Becka answered. "You know that. She says I'm holding you guys back from evolving to your next spiritual level, whatever *that* means." Becka dumped her books into her locker and grabbed her lunch.

"I think it means we're in way over our heads."

Becka turned to him. "Something happened?"

Philip nodded and looked away. “Last night.”

Becka waited, remembering her dreams, remembering her prayers.

“We were supposed to have a meeting with that alien thing, that Xandrak guy.”

Becka closed her locker slowly. Philip, the intellectual—Philip, the always confident, always perfect Ken to Krissi’s perfect Barbie—was looking very pale. And scared.

“Are you okay?”

He tried to smile, but with little success.

“What happened?”

He cleared his throat and glanced at the floor. But before he could answer, another voice called out.

“Philip?”

They turned to see Krissi standing there, her hands on her hips.

“Hey, Krissi. I, uh, I was just talking to Becka.”

She took a step closer. The two girls nodded to each other. Becka could already feel the hall temperature drop several degrees.

Philip continued, trying just a little too hard. “I was telling her about what happened last night, at least what I thought happened, and, uh, she wanted to go out and visit the place. You know, see for herself.”

Becka threw him a look, but his eyes did not meet hers.

Krissi turned from one to the other. Finally she shrugged. “I suppose.” Then, zeroing in on Becka, she continued, “I mean if it’s going to help convince you that it’s really happening.”

Becka opened her mouth. She was about to explain that she had no doubts something was happening, but Philip stepped in. “That’s right, I think it would really help convince her that it’s for real.”

“Oh, it’s real,” Krissi repeated. “I called up the Ascension Lady, and she said it was a classic case of alien abduction.”

"Of what?" Becka asked.

"You wouldn't understand. But the Ascension Lady does, and she's going to explain it all to us tomorrow."

The Ascension Lady was the woman who owned the New Age Bookshop in town and who dabbled in the occult. At one point, up at the Hawthorne mansion, Becka had actually helped her, saving her from a ruthless demonic attack. But it hadn't taken long for the woman to return to her old ways. When Becka found out she'd gone back to the occult, she'd felt a type of defeat—with plenty of pain and regret.

She suspected that was why Krissi was bringing up the Ascension Lady's name—to rub a little more salt in the wound.

"Good." Philip jumped in a little too quickly. "Then we'll meet after school, okay?"

"Whatever." Krissi moved away. "Just as long as she doesn't try any of her hocus-pocus junk. Are you coming?"

"Yeah." Philip turned. Continuing to avoid Becka's gaze, he quickly moved to join Krissi as she entered the moving swarm of students heading for the cafeteria. At the last second he turned and called over his shoulder, "Tell Ryan we'll meet him in the parking lot right after school."

Before Becka could respond he turned and continued down the hall. She stood a long moment, silent and thoughtful.

She didn't like what was happening. Not one bit. But if Krissi and Philip needed her special type of help, did she really have any other choice?

The books had cost Scott nearly fifty bucks—a month's worth of lawn mowing and handyman jobs—but they were worth every penny. He'd gone downtown at lunch to pick them up from the local comic-book store. The first was simply a rule book: *An Encyclopedia for Crypts and Wizards.* But the second book, that was what really held his interest. It was a careful, step-by-step description with charts and diagrams explaining how to create the very best characters for the game.

Scott had started reading it on the way back to school, and thanks to the book's size (small enough to fit behind his geometry text), he continued reading and studying it well into fourth period. Carefully, he went through page after page, jotting down notes on armor, weapons, kill abilities, sexual bent, ruthlessness, passion, using curses, casting spells, speaking with the dead, calling up plagues, divining animal entrails ... and the list went on.

Of course, he knew these weren't characteristics you'd necessarily want in real life, but, hey, it was just make-believe. Truth is, it was a rush being someone he could never be, doing things he could never do. In fact, when it came right down to it, fantasizing he was Ttocs had been the high point of the last few weeks.

At the moment he was deeply involved in the "Vengeful Characteristics"—when and how to be vengeful, why it can benefit you during a specific round. It was so fascinating that he hadn't even heard Mr. Patton call on him.

"Mr. Williams?" the stocky, bald man repeated. "Mr. Williams?!"

Scott looked up, startled.

"I trust you're not too bored with our discussion."

Still coming out of the daze, Scott answered, "Yes, sir."

The class chuckled.

"What?"

"I mean, no, sir. I mean, yes, sir, I'm not too bored."

"Good. Then do try to stay with us. Given your performance on last week's quiz, I think you'll find the investment well worth the effort."

"Yes, sir," Scott said, feeling his ears start to redden.

Mr. Patton returned to the theorem on the board, and Scott was grateful everyone redirected their attention to the front.

Everyone but Bonnie Eagleman.

Bonnie sat one row up and to the right. In the past she'd made every effort to let Scott know she was interested in him. And, though flattered, Scott had made every effort to avoid her. She was a good kid, just not his type. Now he felt her eyes on him, and she was probably grinning away with those braces.

It was irritating, and Scott was in no mood to deal with it. He'd just been chewed out by Patton and—after spending twenty minutes immersed in vengefulness—he realized he didn't have to put up with it. Ttocs certainly wouldn't.

"Hey," he whispered, motioning for her to come a little closer.

She obeyed, her heart obviously atwitter.

"I've got a question."

She waited eagerly.

"With all that metal in your mouth, when you sleep, does your head, like, point north?"

Bonnie's smile twitched slightly, then faded. The student in front snickered as Bonnie's cheeks turned crimson red and she looked back to the front.

It was one of Scott's better jabs, but he instantly regretted it. He'd hurt her feelings. Actually, destroyed them was more like it. He hadn't meant to be cruel. He just wasn't thinking. Okay, okay, he *was* thinking, but more like the new Ttocs than Scott. He frowned, trying to fight off the guilt and uneasiness.

What had happened? Being cruel wasn't his style. Not at all.

But it *was* Ttocs's style.

"So you think this stuff's, like, demonic?" Ryan asked.

Becka took in a deep breath and slowly let it out. The two were riding in Ryan's vintage Mustang and following Philip's Jeep up Highway 72.

"I don't know," she finally said. "You can't say everything is from the devil just because you don't understand it. That's stupid. I don't understand electricity, but that doesn't make it demonic."

Ryan nodded. "Even so, after all the stuff we've been through ... at the mansion, that so-called angel in Julie's room, Krissi's automatic writing ... and now whatever Philip claimed he saw ..."

Becka closed her eyes. Why did she always end up here, involved in something she didn't like? Pulled into the world of the supernatural?

She felt Ryan's hand take hers, and she looked at him. Emotions washed over her. She admired him so much — his honesty, his sensitivity ... and, of course, his looks didn't hurt, either. Especially the way that thick black hair constantly fell into those gorgeous blue eyes.

He'd only been a Christian for a few weeks, but he'd been exposed to more spiritual warfare than most would have to face in a lifetime.

The thought didn't exactly thrill her.

"I'm sorry," she said quietly.

"For what?"

"For you always being pulled into this sort of stuff."

Not missing a beat, he flashed her his killer grin. "Seems a small price to pay for the company I get to keep."

Becka couldn't help but smile. Once again that wonderful warmth spread through her body. What was with this guy? Couldn't he see that she was just your basic nobody with your basic nobody figure and looks? And let's not forget that wonderful nobody hair ... thin, mousy brown, and unable to hold a style for more than thirty seconds.

He squeezed her hand. She gratefully returned it. Apparently she was a somebody to him.

Up ahead, the Jeep slowed and pulled off the road.

"Looks like we're here," Ryan said as he pulled in behind it.

The two climbed out of the Mustang and walked up to Philip and Krissi.

"It's pretty overgrown in there," Philip said, motioning to the brush-covered logging road.

"How far is it?" Ryan asked.

"'Bout half a mile. Hop in and we'll four-wheel it."

Ryan and Becka climbed into the backseat. "What happened to your convertible?" Ryan asked.

"It's in the shop," Philip said. "My dad's letting me borrow this."

"Cool."

Philip dropped the Jeep into four-wheel drive, and they started the tooth-rattling, bone-jarring journey up the road.

Before too much silence could fill the car, Ryan asked, "It's still a little unclear to me. What exactly is it you two saw?"

"Philip saw it," Krissi corrected. "Not me."

"But ... you were with him, right?"

Krissi nodded. She looked straight ahead, searching the road. "I just don't remember. The Ascension Lady says with that type of memory lapse, I'm probably repressing something."

"I'm sorry, what?"

Philip explained, "There are about ten hours of time that neither Krissi nor I can account for. One minute it was 8:20 at night, the next minute it was 6:30 in the morning."

"So how do you know you weren't dreaming?"

Philip tried to smile. "What I saw last night—the lights, the field, the burning trees—it was no dream."

Ryan frowned. "How can you be so sure?" He turned to Krissi. "And you don't remember any of it?"

"Not yet," Krissi said. "But I talked to the Ascension Lady, and she's going to hypnotize me and help me remember all the forgotten stuff."

Ryan and Becka exchanged uneasy glances. They remembered

all too well what had happened when Becka had been hypnotized … and the way she'd almost been killed because of it.

Becka leaned forward. She had promised herself not to talk during the trip, and definitely not to preach, but this was important. "Krissi?"

The girl turned, giving her half an ear.

"Hypnotism is kind of tricky. Are you sure that's something you want to go through with?"

Krissi's expression hardened. "Please—"

But before she could continue, Philip hit the brakes and brought the Jeep to a sliding stop. "What in the world?"

"What's wrong?" Ryan asked.

"Up ahead … lying in the road."

Ryan and Becka craned their necks to see what looked like a cow.

"Is it dead?" Krissi asked.

"Looks like." Philip opened his door and stepped out.

Krissi followed. "See, I told you I saw a cow."

Ryan and Becka traded looks and climbed out after them.

"What's a cow doing all the way out here?" Ryan asked.

"That was my question," Philip said as he and Krissi continued in the lead. "In fact, that's exactly what I asked Krissi just before I saw the lights." They arrived at the cow and came to a stop. "Will you look at that." Ryan and Becka approached as Philip kneeled down to examine the carcass. "It's been gutted."

"What?" Ryan asked.

"See for yourself." Philip picked up a nearby stick and pushed a flap of skin aside. "All of its organs, they've been removed."

The four stared in silence.

"And look at those incisions," Ryan said, kneeling down to join him. He motioned to the cut sections in the hide. "Look how clean they are."

Philip nodded. "They've been burned in, like with a laser or something."

Becka tried her best to stay calm, but once again she could feel an icy chill grip her shoulders. She looked up, searching the woods, peering down the road. Something was there. She knew it.

"You think someone, like, butchered it?" Krissi asked. "For the meat?"

"That's a possibility," Philip said.

Ryan shook his head. "I don't think so."

"Why not?"

"There's no blood. Do you see any blood around?"

The question brought Becka's attention back to the carcass. She searched the ground. Ryan was right. There wasn't a drop of blood to be found anywhere.

"Guys ..." It was Krissi. Her voice sounded very thin, very frightened. Becka saw she was trembling and looking down the road. "I, uh, I don't ... I don't think we should go any farther. I don't think we should go in there at all."

The other three looked at Krissi, exchanged glances, then followed her gaze down the road.

4

BEAM ME UP, SCOTTY, BEAM ME UP! *SQUAWK*. BEAM ME UP!"

Scott reached over and stroked Cornelius with the eraser tip of his pencil. The parrot craned his neck this way and that, making sure Scott hit all the right spots.

Ah, ecstasy ...

It was 5:30 p.m. Friday night. Scott didn't have to be at Hubert's for the next campaign of Crypts and Wizards until 7:00. On his desk was a tablet of carefully planned characteristics for the new and improved Ttocs. It had taken him most of the afternoon to create this new character, and for the most part he was happy.

For the most part.

Still ... something was gnawing at him. He couldn't put his finger on it, but he was pretty sure it had something to do with the game. And with the way he had acted toward Bonnie Eagleman in geometry class.

He reached over to flip on the computer. A moment later he was in the chat room. He was hoping to connect with Z, the mysterious figure who had taken him and Becka under his wing.

There seemed to be nothing Z didn't know—even in personal areas where he shouldn't know anything. That's what made him so interesting.

And, at times, so spooky.

Z didn't normally log on until 9:00 p.m., but from time to time he could be contacted earlier. Scott was hoping this would be one of those times. A moment later the screen came up, and he typed in his handle:

This is New Kid. Z, are you there?

He waited. Finally the words formed:

Hello, New Kid. Are you enjoying the game?

Scott sucked in his breath. No matter how many times Z pulled stunts like that, it still gave him the willies. He wanted to ask Z how he got his information, but he knew Z's response would be the same as always: silence.

Reluctantly, Scott plowed ahead with his next question:

What do you know about role-playing games?

The response came quickly:

I know there are several available and that they are quite engaging.

Scott nodded. Z had that right. He typed:

What about problems? Have you ever heard of any?

There was a long pause. Scott typed:

Z, are you still there?

Finally a question appeared:

Do you find yourself relating too closely with your created character?

Scott fought off another shiver and typed:

Maybe. How did you know?

It is quite common among fantasy role-playing games. Psychologists have proven that extended time of living in fantasy can make it difficult to distinguish between fantasy and reality.

Scott felt himself growing defensive. He typed:

That's only for children or the weak minded.

Perhaps, but Gary Gygax, the creator of one such game, Dungeons & Dragons, is quoted as saying: "You can get very emotionally involved. I've got several characters I've nurtured through many tension-filled, terror-fraught D&D games, and I'd be really crushed if I lost one of them. They can become very much a part of you."

Scott stared at the words, then typed:

But that doesn't make it unhealthy.

There was a pause. Finally:

Please stand by for data:

Scott knew Z was checking his resources. Sometimes this would take a few minutes, a day, or even a week. Not this time. This time the information appeared in just a few seconds:

The National Coalition on Television Violence has linked heavy involvement with the violence-oriented fantasy role-playing war games to over 90 deaths. These include 62 murders, 26 suicides, and 2 deaths of undetermined causes.

Scott studied the screen. More information appeared:

Psychiatrist Thomas E. Radecki states:
"While perhaps a hundred young people have been led to murder and suicide, the evidence suggests that thousands have committed more minor anti-social behavior, and hundreds of thousands have become desensitized to violence."

Scott typed:

But I'm smarter than that. I'm not going to go out and kill somebody after playing Crypts and Wizards.

Probably not. However, if your created character is involved in sex, violence, witchcraft, greed, or any other type of immorality, a small part of you actually participates with him in those acts.

Scott snorted.

It's just fantasy; it's just in my head. I'm not really doing it.

What you frequently think, you start to become.

How can you say that?

It's a psychological fact. It's also in your Bible.

Where?

Christ states that if you hate someone, it's as if you've committed murder. If you lust after someone, it's as if you've committed adultery.

Scott paused. It was true, that was basic Sunday school info he'd heard all his life. But still …

Z's final words appeared on the screen:

"For he is the kind of man who is always thinking about the cost. 'Eat and drink,' he says to you, but his heart is not with you" (Proverbs 23:7). Good night, New Kid.

Scott stared at the verse, then glanced at his watch. 5:56. The game would start in an hour. He had to make a decision.

Krissi continued gazing down the overgrown road. Becka could see she was trembling and moved to her side. "Are you all right? Krissi?"

She finally turned, but when her eyes met Becka's they had changed from wide-eyed fear to narrow, suspicious anger. "This is your doing, isn't it?"

Rebecca frowned. "What?"

"You're trying to frighten me. You're trying to stop me from making contact."

The others exchanged discreet glances. Philip cleared his throat and reached out to put his arm around her. "Krissi—"

She shrugged him off and continued glaring at Becka. "You know they're down that road, don't you? You know they're waiting for me, and you're trying to scare me off."

"Krissi," Philip repeated, "nobody's trying to do anything. If you don't want us to go any further, then we don't have t—"

She spun around to Philip, her eyes widening in surprise. "You're in on this too?"

"What?"

She started backing away, looking first at Philip, then Ryan, then Becka. "Why are you doing this? Why are you trying to stop me?"

Philip took a half step toward her. "Krissi, come on! Nobody's—"

"Liar!"

The accusation stopped him cold.

She looked over her shoulder, back down the road. From the look on her face, whatever was there both attracted and horrified her.

"Krissi ..."

She took another step back. A look of determination filled her face.

Philip continued. "Krissi, please, you're acting really weird. You're scaring all of—"

Before he could finish she spun around and sprinted down the road.

"Krissi!" Philip was the first to start after her. "Come back!"

Ryan and Becka followed.

Krissi disappeared around the bend, but they knew she was still running. They could hear the brush rustling and twigs snapping.

"Krissi!" Philip's tone was both frantic and angry.

When they finally reached the bend and rounded it, they slowed to a stop. There, before them, was the field. The field Philip had described. But Krissi was nowhere in sight. Obviously she had left the road. But which direction had she taken?

"Krissi!" Philip shouted. "Krissi, answer me!"

There was no sound, only the group's heavy breathing. Becka reached out to touch Ryan's shoulder, directing his attention across the field, to the left side ... to a stand of burned trees. The charred trunks looked like poles, the bare branches reached out like blackened skeleton arms.

"See?" Philip said, nodding. "It's exactly like I told you. No way was it a dream."

The three continued to stare until Becka motioned for them to be still. "Listen."

They did. There was a scratching, digging sound.

Philip shouted, "Krissi? Krissi, is that you?"

No answer. Only more digging.

Becka pointed. "It's coming from the trees."

They started through the tall grass toward the burned trees. Becka wasn't sure whether her heart was pounding from excitement or fear. She had no time to decide. Immediately they came upon a long strip of burned grass about five feet wide.

Philip slowed to a stop. They took his cue. "This is the path the beam of light cut. It started at those trees and ran all the way to my Jeep."

Ryan stooped to the ground. He picked up a piece of burnt wood and gave a sniff.

The digging sound resumed. It was louder than before and mixed with another sound. Gasping grunts.

"Krissi!" Philip started up the charcoal path toward the trees. Ryan and Becka followed. A moment later they arrived under the trees and discovered Krissi. She was on her knees, holding a large stick, and digging and drawing in the blackened dirt. With each stroke of the stick she grunted and groaned.

"Krissi …" Philip dropped to her side, but she did not notice. She was in another world, too preoccupied to notice anyone or anything. Her clothes were covered in ash, her face smeared with charcoal.

"Krissi …" Philip grabbed hold of her shoulders. She continued drawing. He shook her. "Krissi!" Still no response. "Krissi, listen to me!" The shaking knocked the stick from her grasp, but she did not stop. She dropped onto her hands and began clawing the dirt with her fingers, grunting and groaning like an animal.

"Krissi!" He forced her to look at him. "Can you hear me? Can you hear me?!"

She blinked. Once, twice …

"Krissi!"

Recognition slowly filled her eyes. She looked at the others, her expression lost and confused.

"Are you all right?" Philip asked, his voice husky with concern and fear.

Suddenly, she threw her arms around him, clinging to him

for all she was worth. "Help me," she gasped. "Don't let me go again! Don't let me go!"

"It's okay," he comforted. "We're here. We're here."

She began sobbing. "Don't let me go ... Don't let me go ..."

"Shh, it's okay. You're not going anywhere. Shh ..."

Rebecca looked on. She wanted desperately to help but knew there was nothing she could do. It wasn't until Ryan touched her arm and pointed toward the drawing in the dirt and ash that her concern gave way to another emotion. The markings were several inches deep. Only now it was clear they were not drawings. They were words.

WE AWAIT AT CABIN.

Over at Hubert's, Scott stared at the screen as the Crypt Master took roll, typing each of the players' names.

Arzule?

Present.

Wraith?

Here.

The game was about to begin. Scott was more than a little uneasy about being there, especially after talking with Z. But he'd gone to so much work preparing and perfecting his character, he couldn't just quit now. Not until he saw how well the new and improved Ttocs performed.

The roll call continued.

Ashram?

Here.

Scott had decided he would play one more game, that was all. Just one more. Only this one he'd play as Darryl had suggested: with everything he had, with his heart, his mind, and his soul. If he lost, fine. He'd walk away knowing he'd given it his best shot.

Quantoz?

Yo.

Drucid?

Here.

If he won, so much the better. He could walk away knowing he had beaten the Master. But to stop after his first defeat ... well, let's face it, that just wasn't Scott Williams' style.

Phantasm?

Here.

He trusted Z, of course, but what Z had written was still one man's opinion. And it wasn't like there was some specific verse in the Bible that said, "Thou shall not play Crypts and Wizards."

Shredder?

I'm here.

Ttocs?

Scott stared at the screen. His name appeared again.

Ttocs?

Scott continued to hesitate. If he was going to play this thing, he was going to play all out. He heard a loud sniff to his right and Darryl's squeaky voice.

"Scott, you're up."

He nodded.

Ttocs?

He reached for the keyboard and slowly typed:

Present.

There. It was done. One more time. And this time he was going to play for all he was worth.

5

There he is."

Becka turned to see Philip exiting Krissi's house. He spotted their car and headed down the walk to join them. Rebecca rolled down her window. The night air was chilly but not cold. It looked like rain. Of course. It always rained on weekends.

"Is she okay?" Becka asked.

Philip ducked his head through the window and rested his arms on the door. "Yeah, she'll be okay. Pretty tired though." He glanced away, trying to sound casual. "'Course she wants to see the Ascension Lady tomorrow. You know, get hypnotized, find out what really happened and everything ..."

Becka nodded. She wanted to say something, but her last comment on hypnotism had nearly caused a fight.

"When she wrote *cabin,*" Ryan asked, "any idea what she meant?"

Philip shrugged. "Maybe her folks' cabin."

"At Cougar Creek?"

"Maybe." Silence stole over the conversation.

"You going to be all right?" Becka asked.

Philip forced a smile, but there was no missing his concern. It was obvious he really loved the girl. "Sure."

More silence.

"Listen, uh—" he cleared his throat—"I really appreciate you guys being there for her tonight. I know she hasn't been the nicest person to be around, especially to you two."

Ryan shrugged. "No prob."

Philip continued, "I haven't said much ... but, well, you need to know that I really respect your guys' faith and stuff."

Becka watched him struggle to put his feelings into words.

"I mean, what you've got—your belief in God and all that, it's pretty cool ... and sometimes, I, uh, well, I envy you."

Before she could catch herself, Becka quietly laid her hand on his arm. It was a small gesture, but she saw it was one he appreciated.

"Anyway, maybe, when you pray and stuff, maybe you could say a little prayer for her too."

Becka nodded.

"Philip?" Ryan asked.

He looked over to him.

"You could join us if you wanted. In praying, I mean."

There was that smile again. Sad. Tired. "Thanks," he said, "but I was there once ... remember?"

Ryan looked at him and nodded.

Another moment of silence.

"Well," Philip finally pulled from the window, forcing another grin and trying to bring the conversation to a happy ending. "You guys take care, and we'll let you know what happens tomorrow."

But Ryan wouldn't let go that easily. Philip had just shared his heart with them, and he wasn't going to slip away that easily. "Philip?"

He stooped back down. Ryan's voice was gentle and quiet.

"He's still there for you, man. All you have to do is reach out. He's still there."

Philip's grin faded as he searched Ryan's eyes. His friend was speaking straight from the heart, and he knew it. Finally he nodded. "I know ..."

With that he rose from the window and started toward the Jeep.

Becka watched him cross to the driver's side and open the door. "What did he mean, he'd been there?" she asked. "Been where?"

"Philip used to believe in God ... a long time ago. His whole family."

She turned to Ryan. "Philip?"

Ryan nodded, watching as Philip climbed into the Jeep and started up the engine.

"What happened?"

"His folks divorced. He stopped believing in God." He shrugged. "He stopped believing in anything."

Becka felt like she'd been hit in the stomach. Her heart leaped out to the boy as she turned and watched his Jeep pull into the street, then head down the road. "That's terrible."

Ryan nodded.

They watched the taillights disappear into the night as rain started splattering on their windshield.

Scott stared at the screen.

The dice had been good to him. Very good. He'd scored enough points to purchase plenty of weapons, spells, armor, poisons, and hexes at the Wizard's Shoppe. Not only had Ttocs become one of the biggest and most powerful players, but thanks to Scott's careful planning, he was also one of the most ruthless. Already he had severely crippled one player and completely disemboweled a mischievous warlock. But that was only the beginning.

It was his turn, and once again he chose "Combat." This time against Darryl's character, Drucid.

"Oh, man!" Darryl gave a loud sniff from beside him. "Why pick on me? Look how weak I am. I'm no threat."

That didn't matter to the bloodthirsty Ttocs.

They rolled, and Ttocs began the attack.

First he hit Drucid with a mace, a spiked metal ball on a chain. Drucid was able to hold off the first couple of blows, but his armor was like paper when pitted against the mighty Ttocs. He soon began to crumple.

"Give me a break," Darryl moaned.

Scott barely heard. He wanted to save his armor points for another encounter, so he released his pet vampire, Rabid, to continue the assault.

Drucid tried to run for cover, but the dice worked against him. He'd barely turned before Rabid swooped down out of the sky, slashed into his neck, and began gulping Drucid's steamy black blood.

Scott could see Darryl fidgeting beside him. It was obvious Drucid's life would be over before it had a chance to begin. "Come on!" Darryl whispered. "You gotta let me play a little longer."

Scott glanced at him with a sly grin. No way did he intend to let up. He rolled for another attack. Once again he won. Now Ttocs began a brutal karate assault on Drucid. The creature was able to deflect the kicks and punches, but he didn't see the dagger Ttocs had hidden in his belt ... until he felt its icy blade slip between his ribs. Drucid staggered. Ttocs threw him into a headlock. And there, with his bare hands, Ttocs crushed Drucid's skull like an egg.

Darryl groaned and stared at his laptop. It was over. Just like that. His character was dead.

Darryl was definitely not happy.

Scott, on the other hand, was ecstatic. The rush of excitement was so great that his fingers were actually trembling. What a game! Ttocs had just annihilated another victim. Gloriously. Ruthlessly. But there were plenty more. Scott grinned with glee.

Ttocs was unstoppable. He would not be held back.

It was Rebecca and Ryan's turn with Z. Since it was Friday, Mom had no problem with Becka having late-night company, just as long as the door stayed open and they said good-bye by midnight. Becka had already logged on to the computer, connected with Z, and started asking questions about Krissi and UFOs.

But are they real? UFOs, I mean?

Evidence indicates that all but 5% of reported sightings have a normal, logical explanation.

And the other 5%? Are they really spaceships from outer space?

Yes and no.

Please explain.

Most reputable researchers believe the appearances are real, but not physical.

I don't understand.

If they are physical, they would have to follow physical laws.

Such as?

1. Most sightings have been reported to travel between 1,000 and 18,000 miles an hour. Yet no person has ever reported hearing a loud boom.

Ryan nodded. "He's right. The speed of sound is around seven hundred miles an hour. Anything traveling faster than that would create a sonic boom."

Z continued:

2. The objects are often seen coming to instant stops.

Why is that a problem?

What happens when you are inside a car traveling at 20 or 30 miles an hour and it suddenly stops?

You get thrown forward.

Imagine that same effect if you were traveling several thousand times faster.

Your body would be trashed?

"Hamburger city," Ryan chuckled.

Z wasn't finished.

3. Many UFOs are seen streaking across the sky, then making abrupt right-angle turns.

Becka typed:

Wouldn't the same thing happen? Whoever was inside would be destroyed.

Correct. The force of making a right-angle turn while traveling at only 5,000 miles an hour is strong enough to shear in half a solid steel ball, let alone destroy any living creature inside.

So what are they really?

Most researchers believe UFOs are not extraterrestrial but inner-dimensional.

Meaning?

They don't come from other worlds; they come from other dimensions.

Becka swallowed hard. She didn't like the sound of that. Slowly she typed:

The only other dimension we know is the spiritual world. Are you saying these things are spiritual?

UFO author Michael Lindemann is quoted as saying that Dr. Jacques Valle, the leading UFO researcher in the world, believes that "so-called aliens don't fit any logical pattern of extra-terrestrial visitors." Tracing back through the long history of reported humanoid superbeings in religious and folkloric literature, he suggests that today's aliens might be a modern analogy to ancient gods, demons, and fairies.

Becka tried to swallow again, but this time there was nothing left to swallow. The word *demon* stuck out like a flashing road sign. She typed:

Those are just opinions, right?

Expert opinions. Consider the following points:

1. Most "alien" messages are autowritten or spoken through humans in exactly the same method that occultists use to channel demons.
2. Their messages frequently emphasize the nondeity of Jesus Christ.
3. They generally insist man will never be judged by God.
4. Many of these channelers experience the exact physical and mental symptoms of people who are possessed by demons: nausea, hallucination, antisocial behavior, and hearing voices.

Ryan leaned back in his chair. "He's describing Krissi to a T."

Becka nodded and was already typing:

What about people who claim they've been taken by aliens?

Reports of so-called alien abductions are increasing. However, it is interesting that every abducted person I've studied has had previous involvement with the occult.

Ryan moaned, "Krissi again."

Becka nodded and continued typing:

Every one has dabbled in the occult?

Without exception.

Becka was almost finished, but she had one last question:

What sorts of things happen in an abduction?

Sometimes the person is returned physically injured. Sometimes not. But there are always psychological scars. Worst of all, once an abduction happens, the victims frequently find themselves being taken over and over again.

Becka and Ryan stared at one another. Each knew what the other was thinking. If it had happened to Krissi once, it would probably happen again.

6

Philip sat, nervous and edgy, in the back room of the Ascension Bookshop. The room was full of shadows. A couple of worn sofas were shoved against the maroon walls, which were decorated with astrological signs. This was the meeting room of the Society, a group of kids who dabbled in the occult. Philip had heard about them, but he'd never taken them seriously. Come to think of it, he had never taken the Ascension Lady or this bookshop too seriously, either.

Until now.

Now the woman had Krissi sitting in a chair and in some sort of trance.

Philip didn't like that. Not that he was a control freak—Krissi was free to do whatever she wanted—but he had always been there to protect and defend her. Not this time. This time there was nothing he could do except sit and listen as she recalled the logging road, the cow, the lights, the fire, and stepping out of the Jeep.

Beads of perspiration covered her face as she gasped for breath. "I'm hanging on to the mirror. I'm screaming to Philip, 'Don't let go; don't let me go, please don't let me go!' "

The room seemed to be charged with electricity, but the Ascension Lady kept her voice even and calm. "And then what happened?"

Suddenly Krissi burst into tears.

Philip rose to his feet, but the Ascension Lady motioned for him to stay back. "It's okay," she reassured him in a whisper. "This is what she has been repressing; this is what her subconscious needs to uncover."

"Philip ..." Krissi's voice sounded very far away, like a lost little girl.

"What happened?" the Ascension Lady asked. "Where's Philip?"

Tears streamed down Krissi's cheeks. "He let go. He let go of me ..."

The accusation—the idea she would think he let go on purpose—cut deep into Philip's heart. He wanted to set the record straight, to tell her he'd hung on as long as he could, but the Ascension Lady's look told him to remain quiet.

Suddenly Krissi's face filled with horror. "No! Stay away, stay away from me!"

"Where are you?" the Ascension Lady asked. "Where are you now?"

"I'm inside. The light, it pulled me inside. They're all around me."

"Who is? Who is all around?"

"Stay back!"

"Who are they, Krissi? What do they look like?"

"Their eyes! They're so big ... like insects. Black. Shiny. Stay away!"

Philip started to stand again, but the Ascension Lady threw him another quelling look. "What else?" she continued. "What else can you tell us about them?"

"No hair. Big heads, like upside-down teardrops. Two little

holes for a nose. And their mouths, they don't have any lips, just a thin line."

"How many of them do you see?"

"Six … no, eight. They're short. Four feet. And they're so skinny, just skin stretched over bone. Gray skin and bones."

"Gray? You said gray?"

"Yes."

"Are you certain they are gray?"

"Is that common?" Philip whispered.

The Ascension Lady nodded.

"Yes," Krissi said. "Smooth, powdery gray. Like they've never even seen the sun." Suddenly she cocked her head as if listening. "What? What do you mean?"

"What's happening now?"

"One of them is talking. He's telling me not to worry. They've come to help us, to help me." Again her expression changed. "No … no! Stay away. No, please."

"Krissi, what's happening?"

"They're touching me. Their fingers are long and skinny. They only have three on each hand. No, please … I'm not ready for this. Please, you're scaring me."

"Krissi?"

"No!" Krissi tossed her head first one way, then the other. "No, please …" She gulped in air as if she were fighting.

"Krissi, what's going on?"

No answer.

"Krissi, talk to me."

Her thrashing increased. Back and forth. Sweat streamed down her face.

"Krissi, what—?"

"They're taking off my vest. No! I try to fight, but my arms, they've done something to my arms! I can't move my arms! No! *NO!*" Her whole body writhed and convulsed, but her arms stayed perfectly limp at her side. "No … no!"

That was it. Philip had to do something. He lunged from his seat and rushed to her side.

"Krissi!"

The Ascension Lady reached out to grasp his arm, shaking her head fiercely. "You'll only make it worse!" she hissed. She turned back to Krissi, fighting to keep her voice calm. "Krissi, can you hear me?"

"Machines ... they've got machines. They're all over me. The machines are touching me everywhere. No. No! Make them stop. Please make them stop!" She shuddered, her face contorting in pain. "Nooo ..."

"That's enough!" Philip shouted.

The Ascension Lady shook her head without looking at him. "No, it's important she— "

"I said that's *enough!*"

"She's there," the woman argued. "This is what happened. You can't just— "

"Augh!"

They spun to see Krissi shrieking at the top of her lungs. "*AUGHHHHH!*"

Philip knelt beside her. The Ascension Lady tried to block him, but he pushed her aside. He grasped Krissi's arms and shook her. "Krissi! Krissi, wake up!"

She continued to fight and struggle and cry.

"Krissi, it's Philip." He shook her again, harder. "It's me! Krissi, wake up."

"No ... no ... please ..."

"Krissi— "

Suddenly her body went limp. She was still gasping for breath, but apparently whatever she had seen was gone.

Philip touched her face gently, not even noticing the way his hand trembled. "Krissi ... can you hear me? Krissi?"

Her eyes fluttered, then opened. They darted back and forth as she tried to get her bearings. Once she realized where she was, her face scrunched into a frown. "Why did you stop me?" Her voice was hoarse from the screaming.

"What?"

"You stopped me. Why did you stop me? They were giving me instructions. They were telling me— " She stopped, noticing the Ascension Lady behind him. "Why did you let him stop me?"

The woman only shook her head.

Krissi's eyes shifted back to Philip. "We've got to go."

"What? Where?"

"My folks' cabin. Cougar Creek."

Philip scowled.

"It's too crowded here. Too many interferences. They want me to meet them at Cougar Creek, where it's isolated, where we can be alone."

"Krissi, that's a two-hour drive into the mountains. We can't— "

"They want to give me more information. They said I need further instruct— "

"After all you've been through?" Philip exploded. He'd had enough. "No way. It's over."

She met his eyes. He felt a chill at the icy glare. There was a determination in her eyes that he'd never seen before.

"If you won't go with me," she said, "I'll go by myself." She started to rise from her seat, but she was a little shaky.

"Whoa." the Ascension Lady moved in to steady her.

"I'm fine," Krissi said, pushing her aside. "I'm fine." Then turning to look at Philip squarely, she asked, "So are you coming, or am I going alone?"

Twenty minutes later Becka hung up the phone. She'd just talked to a very nervous and very worried Philip.

"I don't know what's going on," he'd said. "But … we can't

face this thing on our own. We need your help. Can you and Ryan come to Cougar Creek? Can you meet us there? We really need you guys."

Rebecca's first instinct was to say no. The last thing in the world she wanted was to face more spiritual warfare. It had only been a week or so since her last encounter. An encounter that had left Julie, her best friend, still in bed, recovering.

And if that cow, the burned grass in the field, and the destroyed trees were any indication of the power she would have to face ... well, who could blame Becka for thinking overtime to find an excuse not to go.

If only Philip hadn't sounded so ... frightened.

She finally managed to hang up, but not before promising that she'd run it past her mother. With any luck Mom would freak at the idea of her and Ryan taking a two-hour drive into the mountains, and that would be that. With any luck Mom would encourage her to avoid any more spiritual encounters.

Then again, Mom was always full of surprises.

"I think you should go, Beck."

"*What?*"

"I think you and Ryan and Scotty need to go up there and help."

Becka followed her into the kitchen. "But, Mom ..."

"I don't like the idea any better than you, but you said it yourself. They need you."

"But why ..." She struggled for the words.

"Why you?"

Becka nodded.

Mom turned to her. They'd had this conversation more than once. Her answer was gentle but firm. "I think you know the answer."

Becka looked down.

"You've known it for months. Even when Dad was alive,

when we used to pray over you—even then we knew you would be called to something like this."

"But ..." Becka could feel her throat tighten. She looked up at her mother. "I'm really scared."

Mom paused, then nodded. "Me too, sweetheart ... me too. Every time you get involved in something like this, it makes me go cold inside." She turned as though she was looking out the kitchen window—but Becka knew she was trying to control her emotions. After a minute, Mom went on. "Believe me, if I had my way I'd say no. But ... part of loving is letting go." Finally she turned to face Becka. "And part of trusting the Lord is letting go too."

Becka looked into her mother's eyes.

Mom reached over and brushed her hair behind her ears. "He hasn't failed us yet, sweetheart. He won't fail you now."

Before she knew it, Becka had wrapped her arms around her mother. She loved this woman with all of her heart. She knew this was as hard on Mom as it was on her. She also knew she had a lot to learn from the woman—especially when it came to loving and trusting God.

Now she needed to talk to Scott.

"No way."

"Scotty, they need us."

"I'm busy."

Becka stayed on his heels all the way up the stairs and down the hall into his room. "Listen, what's going on at that cabin is a lot more important than some stupid game."

He snorted. "A lot you know."

Her voice raised a notch. "I know you've been like the invisible man ever since you started playing it."

He turned on her. "Is that some sort of crime?"

"It's a crime when there are people who need help and you'd rather sit around and play some stupid game."

"Stop calling it that!" The resentful outburst surprised them both. Scott continued, obviously forcing himself to calm down. "Listen, this is more than just a game, all right?"

Rebecca simply looked at him.

"It's ... Beck, there's nothing like it. When I play, it's like ... I don't know, it's like I've got this power, like I can do all these incredible things I could never do in real life."

"It's just a game, Scotty. Make-believe."

"I know, but sometimes ... sometimes it seems so real. More than real. Like I'm really there. Like I'm really this guy with all this power." He shrugged and turned to stroke the sleeping Cornelius. "I just don't feel like giving it up. Especially for some wild-goose chase up in the mountains."

Becka continued to stare. This was not like her brother. Not at all. He was always the first to jump in and help people. "Scotty, we're talking about real people here. Real flesh-and-blood people who need our help. Mine. *And* yours."

He fidgeted. "You don't need me. You've done it before without me."

She shook her head slowly, her expression thoughtful, almost apprehensive. "This is different. This one is really different." She looked at him. "We need you there."

He glanced up at her. She held his gaze. He looked over to the computer, and Becka could see wheels starting to turn.

"Hold on," he said. "Wait a minute. Who says I can't do both?"

"What?"

"Sure. Darryl's got his laptop and he's out of the game."

"What's that got to—"

"There's a telephone up there, right?"

"Yeah, I suppose."

"I bet I could call in and hook up with the modem. Then I can play from wherever we're at."

"Scotty, I don't think that's exactly what—" She broke off. Scott wasn't listening. He was picking up the phone and dialing Darryl's number. Becka stood, watching. She wasn't too sure this was a good idea.

Still, having part of Scott there was better than having none of him …

She watched the excitement on his face as Darryl agreed to loan him the laptop, and a chill of doubt ran through her.

… or was it?

Shaking off her concern, she looked at her watch. It was 3:05. As soon as Scott was off the phone she'd call Ryan. They could be on the road within an hour.

7

Scott knew something was wrong. Here he was, riding in the backseat of Ryan's Mustang, going up into the mountains for some sort of major showdown with some sort of major evil, and all he could think about was what Ttocs' next move would be in the game. Amazing. Part of him knew Becka was right when she said it was just a game. But part of him knew it went much deeper than that. Much, much deeper ...

For the hundredth time he shuffled through Darryl's laptop computer case to make sure he had everything necessary to call up on the modem. And for the hundredth time he asked Ryan about the phone situation. "You're absolutely sure Krissi's folks don't have a telephone?"

"Will you relax," Ryan chuckled. "The General Store is just ahead. I guarantee you, the owner will let you call from there."

"It can't be a pay phone. It's got to be a line I can plug in to the computer."

"He's cool. I'm sure he'll let you use the store phone just as long as you pay for it and don't take too long."

"It won't be long. Just a few minutes every half hour or so."

"Every half hour?" Becka turned to Scott from the front. "How long do you plan to spend there?"

That was the question Scott had been dreading. Fortunately, Ryan slowed the car and was turning into the General Store's parking lot. A perfect time to change the subject. "Are we here?" he asked.

"This is the place."

It was an old-fashioned store with rough wood planking and a long front porch. The sun was just thinking about setting, and the warm glow of the lights inside looked inviting. Even more so when they stepped out into the cold.

"It's freezing!" Becka shivered as she fumbled with the buttons on her coat.

Ryan grinned. White plumes of smoke escaped from his mouth as he spoke to Scott. "The cabin is just a mile or so up the road. There's this big orange trout for a mailbox, and the driveway winds up a little hill. You can't miss it."

Scott nodded.

"Well, let's get you settled," Ryan said as he started up the store's steps. "How long did you say? A few minutes every half hour?"

Scott nodded, doing his best to avoid Becka's glare. He knew he was cheating. He knew by agreeing to come he'd led her to believe he'd help. Well, he would. Sort of. He hoped. He readjusted the computer strap on his shoulder and headed up the stairs after them.

"What a jerk," Becka said as they pulled out of the store's parking lot and onto the road. "He won't even stop long enough to help. It's like that stupid game's got a hold on him."

Ryan nodded. "I had a friend that really got caught up into that stuff too."

"What happened?"

"He just sort of dropped out."

"Dropped out?"

"I still see him around school and stuff, but it's like he's not really there. Like, he's in a different world."

Becka turned to look back at the store as it disappeared around the bend. Her anger and frustration had already turned to concern.

Becka and Ryan had barely left the store before Scott had situated himself in the back office and connected with Hubert's computer. The other players in the group had agreed to let him accumulate turns while he traveled, so when he finally got online, Scott was ready to give it everything he had. Unfortunately, the dice had other ideas.

On his first move Ttocs was attacked by a living corpse. The hideous creature began shredding his flesh and devouring it. Each time Scott rolled the dice for a counterattack, he lost. Each time he tried to defend himself, he gave up more and more of his power.

Things were not going well. Not well at all.

Finally, through a complicated incantation, Ttocs was able to conjure up a fireball. The light exploded in all directions, raining flames down upon the undead monster and sending it scurrying for cover. But the damage was already done. Ttocs was far weaker than when he'd started.

And still they came at him. This time it was one of the players. Ttocs had barely taken a step before the infamous Quantoz, an offspring of Satan himself, went in for the kill. It was unbelievable the way the dice kept rolling against Scott. Each time Ttocs tried to defend himself, he lost. And each time he lost, Scott grew more and more depressed.

Finally Quantoz's turn was over. Nearly half of Ttocs's armor had been depleted and almost all of his magic had been neutralized. It had been a bloody series of attacks, but at least for now it was over.

Scott leaned back in the office chair and rubbed his neck. His face was wet with perspiration, and he was breathing hard. "Just a game," Becka had said. Hardly. Not when he was fighting for his life. And it was his life. Ttocs was his creation. Ttocs was a part of him ... Ttocs *was* him.

But that was okay. His turn wouldn't be for several more minutes. He would have time to rest, to get his bearings and, now that he was so much weaker, find a way to stay in the game without being destroyed.

Suddenly his thoughts were interrupted by another player signaling to attack him. It was obvious the player thought he might be able to finish Ttocs off. Maybe he could.

Scott took a deep breath and sat up at the keyboard preparing for another assault ...

"Here we go." Ryan turned left onto a dirt road and started winding up the steep, tree-lined driveway. The sun had just set and the temperature was dropping quickly.

"How do you know about this place?" Becka asked.

"Krissi's folks used to invite us up every summer. Me, Julie, Krissi, and Philip."

Becka nodded, once again remembering how she was the new kid. Once again feeling like the outsider, the one who had come in and ruined everything. As if reading her thoughts, Ryan reached out and took her hand. She gratefully accepted it. It was warm, strong, and reassuring.

At last the cabin came into view. It was one story, not too big, and covered with worn brown shingles. Philip's Jeep sat in front.

"That's weird," Ryan said.

"What?"

"The chimney, there's no smoke coming from it. In this

weather you'd think they would have started a fire. It's the only way to heat the cabin."

"And check out the Jeep," Becka said, pointing toward it. Both doors were wide open. Ryan pulled up alongside it, turned off the ignition, and climbed out. "Philip? Krissi?"

Becka followed, feet crunching on frozen gravel, clouds of breath hovering above her head. They looked inside the Jeep, but it held no clues. Just the usual guy clutter and—

"Ryan!" She motioned to the passenger seat. "It's Krissi's bag."

Ryan nodded, barely listening.

"You don't understand. Krissi would never go anywhere without her bag. It's got her makeup, her brush, all the bare essentials for her life."

Ryan stared down at it a moment. Then they both turned to the cabin. It looked completely deserted. No lights. No sign of activity. Once again Ryan reached out to take her hand—and once again Becka was grateful for its warmth and strength.

They started forward. This time it was Becka's turn to call out. "Krissi? Philip?"

No answer.

They arrived at the porch steps. The railing was covered with a thin layer of frost.

"Krissi!"

The air was dead still. No sound, no movement. Just the shuffling of their feet and the creaking wood as they started up the stairs.

"Philip!"

They reached the door. Ryan looked at Becka, took a deep breath, and reached for the handle. Becka wasn't sure if the shiver that raced across her shoulders was from the cold or from what awaited them inside.

She would soon find out.

8

A wave of relief washed over Philip as he heard Ryan and Becka calling his name outside the cabin. He wanted to shout an answer, but he was afraid to send Krissi into another fit. The last one had wiped her out. They had barely arrived when she had suddenly jumped out of the Jeep, run into the cabin, and thrown herself down on the floor, screaming. It was like an epileptic seizure, only worse.

It had taken all of Philip's strength just to stop her from crashing into the furniture and walls and hurting herself. When she had finally reached exhaustion, he did his best to quiet her. Soon her screams had turned to soft, helpless whimpering.

"Philip," she'd moaned, "I need a pencil—they need to write something. Please, get me a pencil."

But he had no pen or pencil on him, and he wasn't about to leave her to find one.

"Please, they want to communicate. We've got to let them communicate."

"Shh," was all he could say as he sat with her on the floor. Holding her. Rocking her. "Shh, it's going to be okay." He fought back the tears. It had been a long, long time since he had cried.

But he was scared. More scared than he could remember—not of UFOs or aliens or whatever, but of losing Krissi. He'd lost his mother and sisters. That had nearly destroyed him. He wasn't about to lose the only other thing he cherished.

They stayed that way, huddled together on the floor, for he didn't know how long. It was freezing, but he didn't dare let go of her to start a fire. At least not yet. Maybe after she fell asleep. She was so exhausted she was nearly there.

Then he heard Ryan and Becka calling. The cabin door creaked open and there they stood.

"Over here," he called softly. "We're over here."

Ryan was the first to step inside. "Are you guys okay?" He fumbled for the switch on the wall and snapped it on. Welcome light flooded the room. Becka entered behind him, but as soon as her foot touched the floor, Philip felt Krissi's body grow rigid.

"Who-who's there?" she asked, squinting from the light.

"It's us, Krissi," Ryan answered. "Me and Beck."

She looked up to Philip accusingly. "You told them where we were? You invited them?"

It was time to face the music. "Krissi, I don't think what's happening ... I'm not convinced it's good."

"They'll scare him off!" She struggled to sit up. "You read what Xandrak wrote. He won't be able to help us if their beliefs hold us back."

"Maybe holding us back ..." Philip searched for the words. "Maybe that's not such a bad idea."

"*What?*"

"After all that's happened to us, maybe there's something about their beliefs we need."

"How can you *say* that?" Her voice rang with hurt and betrayal. "They're going to ruin everything. Don't you see?"

"Krissi," Ryan said, "we're not here to ruin—"

But he was interrupted by his car horn honking in short bursts, over and over again. Everyone turned toward the open door. Outside, bright lights flashed on the trees, off and on, off and on.

"What's that?" Krissi demanded.

"I think it's my car alarm." Ryan stepped outside for a better look. "That's weird."

"Something bump into it?" Becka asked, joining him.

Ryan shook his head. "I never armed it. How could the thing go off if I never set it?" He shrugged, stuffed his hands into his pockets, and headed down the steps to investigate. Becka followed.

Philip wanted to call out, to beg them to stay. But he knew how weak and stupid that would sound, so he remained quiet.

He wished he hadn't.

As soon as Ryan and Becka were out of sight, Krissi rose unsteadily to her feet.

"Where are you going?"

"He's here," she whispered.

Immediately Philip was beside her. "Who is? Who's here?"

"Xandrak."

He fought off a shiver and looked around the room. "I don't see any—"

Suddenly the table radio blasted on at full volume. Philip spun toward it, but no one was there. He looked back at Krissi. She was staring off into space again, her eyes starting to glaze over. He gave her a little shake. "Krissi? Oh, not again! What's going on?"

She didn't respond.

The TV on the bookshelf suddenly came on and began to blare. There was no picture, just lots of snow. And static. Very loud static.

"Krissi?" He shouted over the noise. He gave her a harder shake. "Krissi!"

But Krissi didn't even seem to hear him. She slowly turned toward the door.

"Krissi! Answer me!"

No response.

"Ryan!" he shouted, more alarmed than ever. "Becka!"

Instantly the radio and TV shut off. Along with the light in the room. Once again they were immersed in darkness. And silence. Even Ryan's car alarm had stopped.

"Krissi?" Philip whispered.

Still no answer, but he could feel her body start to tremble.

"Krissi?"

Then, ever so slowly, she raised her hand until it was pointing directly at the door. Philip's eyes followed her gesture; then he sucked in his breath. Someone was there. Standing in the open doorway. It was impossible to make out much detail, but there was a silhouette of a short creature, maybe four feet tall. He was grotesquely skinny with long arms and a strange, triangle-shaped head.

"Xandrak?" Krissi's voice was barely a whisper.

The creature said nothing but raised his arm. At the end of it were three long, wiry fingers.

Krissi started to move. Philip's grip on her shoulder tightened.

"Philip ..."

He held her firmly.

"Philip, let me go. He wants to talk to me."

But he held tight. Nothing would make him let go. Not this time.

Without warning, there was an explosion of light. It blasted through the doorway and windows. Blinding. Overpowering. Exactly the same light that had assaulted them in the Jeep. The energy was so strong it knocked Philip to the ground. He barely hit the floor before he was scrambling to his knees, fighting to get back to his feet and grab Krissi. But by the time he stood, she was gone. He spun to the door. So was the creature.

"Krissi!" he screamed.

The light vanished.

"*No!*" He bolted toward the door and out onto the porch just in time to crash into Ryan.

"What was *that?*" Ryan exclaimed. "It was like lightning!"

"They've got Krissi!"

"Who? What?"

Then Philip spotted it. For a split second a ball of silvery light hovered over the ridge of the driveway—and then it was gone. There was no time to explain. He raced for his car.

Ryan grabbed him. "Philip, wait!"

"They have Krissi. Don't you understand?"

"Yes, but—"

"Let me go."

"You can't fight this stuff on your own."

He tried to pull away, but Ryan held him tight. "You don't understand!" Philip shouted. "I let her down once. I can't do it again!"

"You've got to let us help you!" Ryan shouted back. "You can't fight it on your own." Again Philip tried to break free, but Ryan held on. "You said it yourself. You need our help. You need our faith."

"I tried it."

"This is different."

They continued to struggle. "Let go!"

"Philip, you've got to trust—"

"Let go!"

"Phil—"

Philip clenched his fist, drew his arm back, and hit Ryan with everything he had. Becka screamed as Ryan flew across the porch, hitting the window with the back of his head. The glass shattered, and he slowly slid to the floor.

Philip did not stop to watch.

Ttocs' new attacker, Wraith, was a ghoul, fifteenth class. Normally he wouldn't waste time on someone as weak and defenseless as Ttocs had become, but Scott had been pretty ruthless in the beginning, and what goes around comes around. It was payback time.

The dice fell worse than before. Wraith relentlessly stripped Ttocs of his armor and weapon points, smashing, parrying, and dissolving them with deadly acid from his fangs.

Scott hunched over the keyboard in the back room of the store, typing for all he was worth. Sweat dripped from his face, but he didn't notice. His heart pounded furiously, but he didn't care. It was no longer his sweat or his heart. It was Ttocs'. And he was no longer in the General Store; he was somewhere in the crypt, fighting for his very life.

He rolled the dice to retreat, but Wraith was far too clever. He cast a spell on Ttocs, paralyzing him. Then, assisted by the powers of hell, he levitated Ttocs and turned him around, forcing him to face a giant sword made of dragon teeth. Teeth that would embed themselves into an opponent's throat and eat his flesh.

The sword flew swiftly toward his neck. Ttocs tried to move, to duck, but the spell was too powerful. The sword hit its mark. Scott cried out in pain, grabbing at his own throat. Now the teeth began their deadly job, gnawing and tearing. Ttocs gasped for breath, but it did no good. He staggered and clutched at his neck, coughing and wheezing. Everything around him started to spin, the light grew dim, color faded.

He fell. Hard. Try as he might, Scott could not get him to move. His unbeatable creation lay motionless.

It was over. Ttocs was dead.

Scott stared at the screen, his heart thundering in his head, his breath coming in short gasps. It couldn't be! Ttocs was too great. Scott had spent too much time making him powerful, unstoppable, undefeatable. But there on the screen lay the character, his eyes frozen in what had been a brutal, agonizing death.

Scott closed his own eyes. How could this be? How could Ttocs be gone? He lowered his head into his hands as a lump of emotion rose into his throat. His friend was dead. His creation. His self …

Scott sat there silently a long, long time. And then he began to weep.

Philip bounced out of the driveway and slid onto the main road. He tromped on the gas and the Jeep fishtailed. He fought the wheel and managed to bring it back under control. A hundred yards ahead, the silvery ball of light hovered ten, maybe fifteen, feet above the road. It seemed to be waiting for him to catch up. Philip was happy to oblige.

He pushed harder on the accelerator. But as he picked up speed, so did the light. It was the same cat-and-mouse game they'd played before. The faster he went, the faster it went. Philip barely saw the road. He kept his eyes fixed on the object. It was hard to make out its exact size and shape. Sometimes it seemed as round as a ball, maybe seven feet across. Other times it looked like a flattened saucer, twenty feet in diameter.

But none of that mattered. All Philip knew was that somehow, some way, Krissi was a part of that light—and somehow, some way, he had to help her.

They hit the bend in the road. It curved to the right. He straightened it by cutting into the other lane. The General Store lay ahead. He screamed past it, doing between sixty and seventy miles an hour.

Suddenly, just past the store, the light took a hard left and disappeared into a newly cut driveway that wound deep into the woods.

Philip hit the brakes. Immediately he knew he'd made a mistake. The damp fog had frozen, leaving a thin, icy glaze on the road.

The Jeep started to slide.

Everything turned to slow motion. He could feel the car sliding out of control. Spinning. Instinctively he cranked the wheel. It did little good—he was going too fast.

Carnival rides flashed through his mind—the rides you have no control over, where you can only sit and scream until they're over—but this ride was short-lived. The left front wheel caught the loose dirt of the shoulder. That was all it took. The dirt slowed the wheels, but the Jeep kept flying sideways.

The Jeep began rolling!

Philip clutched the wheel with his right hand and threw his left arm over his face. Tree trunks, the steep bank, and the road were all jumbled as his body slammed into the driver's-side window, then was thrown up into the roof. The steering wheel jabbed into his legs as glass sprayed in all directions. He wondered dazedly how many times the vehicle was rolling when suddenly it came to a bone-jarring stop.

He'd hit a tree.

Thank God! He was upside down, but at least he wasn't rolling anymore.

No sooner had Philip thought this than the Jeep shuddered and slid down a bank a dozen or so more feet before it finally came to a complete stop. A few pieces of glass tinkled; some clods of dirt fell from the spinning tires. But other than that there was silence ... except for a faint crackling and popping.

Philip opened his eyes. He was inside, lying on the roof. A blue light flickered in rhythm with the crackling and popping. It took a moment to register before he realized he hadn't hit a tree—he'd hit a power pole.

He tried to move along the inside of the roof, but the shifting of his weight caused the car to creak forward. He looked out the windshield—and froze. A drop-off loomed directly ahead—seventy-five feet of sheer nothing.

Fear rose within him, but he fought it back. He moved again, more cautiously, and again the Jeep started to tip. He stopped. Now he understood. The car was on its top, balancing on a rock or ledge or something. He was safe, but just barely. One wrong move, and he'd send the whole thing plummeting off the cliff.

9

Scott heard the squealing tires and the sickening sound of crunching metal. He knew there'd been an accident just outside the store, but he didn't care. How could he? His best friend had been brutally murdered. *He* had been brutally murdered. With that type of tragedy, how could he pay attention to bothersome things like reality?

Still, he heard customers shouting to one another and rushing outside, so he figured he'd better join them. Reluctantly he snapped off the laptop, rose, and headed for the front door.

He hadn't felt this bad since his father had died.

Becka and Ryan bounced down the driveway in the Mustang, heading as fast as they could toward the main road. Ryan threw the car into a hard right, and they slid onto the asphalt. As he accelerated he shouted, "Where did that thing come from? It just exploded in front of us. One minute it was dark, the next minute brighter than daylight."

"Remember what Z said about them popping in and out of another dimension?"

Ryan glanced at her. "You're thinking the spiritual world again?"

Becka looked straight ahead, hoping she was wrong—fearing she was right.

They rounded the bend in the road. Up ahead was the General Store. A handful of people were rushing out, running across the road.

"There's Scotty!" Becka pointed to the front porch of the store, where her brother slouched against the stair railing, his hands in his pockets. Ryan turned the Mustang into the parking lot and skidded to a stop in front of him.

"Where're they going? What happened?" Ryan shouted out the window.

Scott motioned across the road. "Some sort of accident."

Ryan spun around to look, but Becka stared at Scott. Something was wrong with her brother. "You okay?" she called.

He shrugged.

"Scotty, what's wrong?"

"Don't worry about it."

Before Becka could pry any further, they heard the owner running back toward the store. He was red faced and puffing. "Got to call 9-1-1!" he cried. "Some kid flipped his car."

Becka froze. Ryan was already opening his door. "What kind of car?"

"Jeep. The whole thing's balancing on a ledge—could go any second."

Becka leaped out of the car and joined Ryan. They started across the road. She glanced over her shoulder and saw Scott still looking lost. "It's Philip!" she shouted.

He did not move.

"Will you come on?! It's Philip!"

She turned and continued to the other side. When they arrived, they saw what the store owner had described. The Jeep had smashed into a power pole, which had stopped it from flipping over the edge.

The car had slid down the soft bank on its top a dozen or so feet until it came to rest on a narrow outcropping of rock. There it balanced precariously, teetering on the edge of the drop-off. The entire scene was bathed in the eerie blue-and-white sparks of a power line that snapped and crackled on the roadway.

"Oh, man ...," Ryan whispered. Becka shook her head in stunned silence. They moved past the three or four spectators who were keeping their distance from the dancing cable.

"Philip?" Ryan called. "Philip, can you hear me?"

A faint voice answered from inside the Jeep. "Ryan, is that you?" But even as he spoke, the car shifted forward.

"Don't move!" Becka cried.

Ryan carefully negotiated past the sparking wire. Becka followed gingerly.

"Be careful!" an older woman shouted. "Better wait for the EMS." The others agreed.

But Ryan knew they couldn't wait. Not only was there Philip to worry about, there was Krissi. They moved to the edge of the road. A gentle slope of dirt and gravel led ten or fifteen feet farther to the outcropping of rock where the Jeep was balanced. Just past that was the cliff—and a whole lot of darkness.

Ryan called out, "Looks like you're playing teeter-totter on this here cliff."

"I figured it was something like that," Philip shouted. "Listen, I've got to get out of here. I've got to help Krissi."

"One catastrophe at a time, ol' buddy."

"You don't understand." Again the car shifted.

"Philip!" Becka warned.

"Let's see if we can take care of you first," Ryan suggested.

"We've got to hurry, we've got to—" Again the car shifted.

"Philip!"

Philip quit talking and remained still.

Ryan motioned down to the outcropping of granite the Jeep balanced on. There were two, maybe three, extra feet of rock on the right side of the car. Plenty of room for a person to get a foothold and reach out to help Philip.

Becka followed his gaze, then turned on him. "Are you crazy?"

Again the car shifted.

Ryan looked at her. There was her answer. Even if they decided to wait for an EMS, it was doubtful the Jeep would. Already they could hear tiny rocks and bits of granite crumbling and slipping out from under the car. They had to act. Now.

Without another word, Ryan turned and began sliding down the soft slope toward the outcropping of rock. Becka started to follow until he turned to look up at her and demanded, "Where do you think you're going?"

"Same place you are."

He looked at her, trying by sheer intimidation to force her back up the slope. It didn't work.

"Guys?" Philip called. "The side window's popped out. Maybe I can crawl over to it and—"

Again the Jeep tilted forward, only this time it slid an inch or two.

The spectators gasped.

"Philip!" Becka cried.

"I wouldn't do that if I were you," Ryan suggested. He turned to give Becka one last look. She motioned him forward, making it clear that if he didn't take the lead, she would. Reluctantly he turned and continued down the slope. The dirt and gravel slid with them, covering their shoes as they made their way down to the granite outcropping.

Since Ryan had the lead, he was the one to step onto the rock and stoop to look inside at Philip. He grinned. "Hey, bud, got anything for a black eye?"

"Oh, man," Philip groaned. "I didn't mean to do that. I don't know what came over me."

"That's okay. Just don't go getting yourself killed till I get a chance to even the score."

Becka sighed. She hated "machoese." But having a brother, she knew that type of talk was part of the male routine. Either that or one too many Schwarzenegger movies. She could never tell which.

She went to join Ryan. There wasn't enough room for two on the rock, so she dug in and planted herself in the soft dirt beside him. She also grabbed on to a good, solid bush just to be safe.

"Hey, Beck," Philip called from inside, "how's everything going?"

"Could be better."

"I hear you." He shifted, and more rocks slipped from underneath the Jeep. "Any ideas what to do?"

"You can't make it over to this passenger window?" Ryan asked.

"Not without everything giving way."

"What if I were to reach in and grab you? What if I grab you, you hang on, and I pull you through the window?"

"You mean while the Jeep's falling?" Philip tried to laugh, but it came out more like a semi-hysterical giggle. More rocks slid away.

"I don't see any other way." Ryan turned to Becka for confirmation. Her mind was churning a thousand miles an hour, looking for an alternative plan, but he was right. The Jeep's granite perch looked as though it would give way at any moment. There was no other plan.

"And if your hands slip?" Philip asked.

"I guess you'll just have to trust me. Time to have a little faith, ol' buddy."

"This isn't another one of your sermons, is it?"

Ryan grinned. "Could be."

"Could be I should just stay put." Philip coughed and the Jeep creaked precariously. "Then again ..." He swallowed hard and gave a recap. "Okay, let me get this straight. I leap across the cab and grab your hand."

"Check."

"That movement sends the Jeep over the cliff."

"Probably."

"But you hang on and pull me through the window as it's falling."

"You got it."

There was a long pause. Ryan and Becka exchanged glances. It was risky, to say the least. But what else could they do?

Finally, Philip answered. "Okay."

"All right." Ryan repositioned his feet on the granite for the best stance.

Becka reached out and grabbed Ryan's belt with her free hand, clinging to the bush with the other.

"Beck?"

"Yeah, Philip?"

"Would you, uh ... I mean ... would you mind like saying a little prayer?"

Becka was surprised. Then nervous. The last thing in the world she liked to do was to pray out loud. Especially in front of friends. She glanced to the handful of people up on the road. Or in front of crowds.

Still, this was no time for cowardice.

"Sure, Phil," she said, her voice coming out a little hoarse.

More rocks gave way.

"Could you do it, like, soon?"

Becka didn't close her eyes. She looked straight ahead and concentrated on the dirt in front of her. "Dear Lord." She cleared her throat. "Lord, we just ask that you help us do this right. Give Ryan the strength to hang on, and Philip ... give him the faith to let go and jump. In your name, Jesus ... Amen."

Ryan muttered a quiet "Amen." Though she wasn't sure, Becka thought she heard one come from Philip too.

"Well." Philip took a deep breath. "You guys ready?"

Ryan tested his footing one last time and reached his hand into the window. "Let's do it."

"You sure you've forgiven me about that black eye?" Philip said, unable to resist one last chuckle. "Because if you haven't, maybe we should—"

Without further warning, the last of the loose granite slipped away. The Jeep started to slide.

"Philip!" Becka cried.

"Jump!" Ryan shouted. "Jump!"

Philip froze.

"What are you waiting for? Jump!"

The Jeep was sliding away. Without thinking, Ryan lunged into the window.

"Ryan!" Becka screamed as the car's motion pulled him from her grasp. She leaped toward him, grabbing with both hands. She caught his legs and hit the ground. She would not let go. She hung on, pulling him back out of the window as the Jeep continued to slide. She could hear him cry out as the door scraped across his stomach, then banged its way up his ribs, but she hung on until he emerged.

He wasn't alone.

Ryan had grabbed Philip and was hanging on as stubbornly as Becka. His hands were locked on to Philip's wrists in a death grip.

The Jeep continued sliding.

Becka was pulled across the rocky ledge. She still held on to Ryan, who still held on to Philip. Now it was Philip's turn to scream as his upper body scraped through the open window—but his legs still weren't free, and the force of the Jeep's descent pulled all three along the granite toward the precipice.

Becka tried to dig in her feet, her knees, her elbows, anything to slow them down. Ryan did likewise until Philip managed to kick his way out through the window, and he was free—just as the Jeep reached the edge and slipped over, doing a graceful one-and-a-half gainer seventy-five feet into oblivion.

But the trio was still moving. Their momentum on loose stones and gravel made it impossible to stop. All three dug in—flesh and bone against gravel and rock—and cried out in pain. They slowed, then, finally, mercifully, came to a stop. They lay there, bleeding and panting, gasping for air, white billows of breath hovering over their heads. Below, they heard the Jeep explode as it hit bottom.

The noise had barely faded before they heard another sound. One that was much more chilling. A scream. It was distant. Deep in the woods, across the road. And there was no doubt who it was.

They stumbled to their feet. There were plenty of bruises and cuts and scrapes to go around, but there was no time to whine about them.

Another scream.

They scampered up the soft slope to the road, Philip in the lead, Becka and Ryan on his heels.

10

The three ran for all they were worth, crossing the road and starting up a steep, winding driveway. The driveway snaked this way and that for two or three hundred yards. At last they rounded the final turn—and came to a sudden halt.

There was a house in front of them. Well, the skeleton of a house. It was a big, three-story job that was in the process of being built by somebody with lots of bucks. The beams and floors were in, but the walls were only framed, so they could still see through them.

But it wasn't the house that had brought them up short. It was the giant craft hovering fifty feet above them. Philip, Rebecca, and Ryan stood there, staring in disbelief. It was huge. At least the size of a football field. Round, silvery gray with tiny red, green, and yellow lights flashing along the outside. It seemed to hang motionless and absolutely silent.

Ryan was the first to find his voice. "Do you think it's real?"

"What do you mean, 'real'?" Philip asked.

"I mean, is it material or is it ..." His voice dropped off.

"Or is it what?" Philip demanded.

Becka answered, "Spiritual."

Philip looked at her. "You think all this stuff is spiritual?"

Becka continued watching the craft as Ryan explained, "Krissi's automatic writing, her bizarre behavior, her channeling that so-called alien; that's all basic occult junk."

Becka continued, "Remember the demon who pretended to be an angel?" Becka said. "How he kept speaking through Julie and telling you how cool all this was supposed to be?"

Philip nodded, his mind clicking as he put the pieces together. He remembered all too well the demonic showdown up at the Hawthorne mansion just a few weeks before. That had been his and Krissi's first experience with the supernatural—and Krissi's first episode of automatic handwriting. His memories of the demon disguised as an angel were equally clear. It had spoken through Julie, telling them how blessed they were to be chosen for this encounter. Philip might not understand it all, but he was painfully clear on one point: He definitely was not feeling blessed.

He took a deep breath to steady himself. "Well, demon or not, Krissi needs our help." He started toward the house.

Ryan caught his arm. "Philip, if this stuff isn't physical, you can't fight it physically."

"What do you mean?"

"You can't do it with muscle or with that fancy brain of yours. You've got to fight the spiritual with the spiritual. You've got to fight it with faith."

"No sweat," Philip said, forcing a smile. "Besides, I have you two along, right?"

There was another scream. Philip spun around and looked up to see a light shoot from the bottom of the craft. It struck something he couldn't see up on the top floor of the house. There was another scream. Just as desperate, but more hopeless. Philip bolted for the house.

"Philip, wait up!"

He didn't. He couldn't. In fact, he picked up his pace. If Ryan and Becka wanted to help, great. If not, he'd have to do it on his own. He knew all about faith. He'd had it back at the Jeep when he lunged for Ryan's hand, when he wouldn't let go. He'd had faith in Ryan; now he'd have to have faith in himself.

He arrived at the house and stepped though the front framed wall. The dim outline of steps was directly ahead of him. He took them two at a time. There was another scream, followed by pathetic whimpering. His heart pounded harder. She was above him, up on the third level, where the light was shining.

"Hang on, Krissi. Hang on!"

He reached the second floor, then found the next set of stairs. They were a little trickier to climb, since the steps hadn't been nailed down. A few slipped and fell, but he took little notice as he scrambled up to the third and final floor.

When he emerged, he was blinded by the light. But it wasn't shining on him. The beam was directed some thirty feet away, blasting down on a makeshift table—a sheet of plywood stretched between two sawhorses. Six, maybe seven, little creatures huddled around the table. Creatures exactly like the one that had appeared in the cabin doorway. And they were all staring and examining ...

"Krissi!" Philip cried.

She tried to move, to turn and look at him, but something held her down. There were no ropes, no straps. Somehow the light itself held her in place.

He started toward her. Moving across the floor was dangerous since there were only a few loose sheets of plywood laid on the bare joists. But Philip never slowed. He wasn't sure what the creatures were, but they looked small enough for him to take out two or three at a time if he had to. From the way they refused to step aside, it looked as though he might have to.

He was a dozen feet away when one of them raised its hand. A blow struck Philip in the chest. It was as powerful as a karate kick.

He staggered back into a wall brace and leaned there a moment, trying to catch his breath.

Ignoring him, the creatures kept their attention on Krissi.

"No!" Krissi screamed. "No, please ..."

That was all it took. Philip lunged forward, racing toward them.

The first creature looked up and again raised its hand.

This time the blow felt like a Mack truck smashing into him, but instead of throwing Philip into the wall, it lifted and hurled him against a beam in the ceiling. He gasped as the air rushed from his lungs. He tried to move, but something kept pushing him up against the beam. No one held him, nothing touched him—but some invisible force kept pressing his chest, refusing to let him down.

He looked desperately at Krissi. She was deathly pale in the white light. She twisted and screamed as the creatures poked and prodded with various silvery instruments. Her eyes were crazed with fear.

She spotted Philip. "Help me!" she screamed. "Make them stop!"

Using every ounce of his strength, Philip tried to move, but he couldn't. Then, out of the corner of his eye, he spotted Ryan and Becka at the top of the stairs. Becka looked like she was trembling. It could have been from the cold, but Philip didn't think so.

They stood a moment, checking out the situation. Philip wanted to shout at them to hurry, to *do* something—but he couldn't breathe well enough to whisper, let alone shout. Then he saw Becka take a deep breath, and something began to settle over her. He couldn't put his finger on what it was, but ... well, it was a type of boldness. It wasn't something she worked up. There just seemed to be a power that came over her, out of the blue ... naturally, quietly. Philip knew Becka hadn't wanted another confrontation like this, but when she took a step forward, he saw a determination—a confidence—filling her face.

She spoke, her voice full of quiet authority. "In the name of Jesus Christ, I command you to stop this!"

The creatures spun around, startled.

Becka didn't flinch.

The creatures pulled back a few feet, opening up the circle around the table and Krissi.

Philip watched as Ryan stepped forward. "You heard her." His voice, too, was calm, filled with confidence. "By the power and authority of Jesus Christ of Nazareth, we command you to leave her alone!"

The light beaming down on the table began to dim and sputter. At the same time, Philip could feel the pressure against his body start to decrease.

"Now!" Becka demanded. "We order you to release her now."

Immediately the light vanished. So did the hold on Philip. He plummeted to the floor and landed with a thud. For a moment he lay there dazed, but his vision came into focus and he turned to watch Becka and Ryan.

Becka took another step toward the creatures. "Who are you?"

No answer. Just lots of nervous looks and fidgeting.

"Answer me," she said. "I demand for you to show us who you are."

Philip was impressed. He had never seen Rebecca talk or act with such strength and authority. Whatever it was, it had made her completely different than the wilting wallflower he normally saw at school.

Not only was he impressed. So were the creatures.

They were terrified.

"Now!" Becka demanded. "Reveal yourselves now!"

At first, Philip thought his eyes were playing tricks on him, but the gray, triangular heads were no longer gray and triangular. In fact, the creatures' entire bodies were changing, morphing into small, bizarre animal-like things. Some resembled grotesque gargoyles; others, monkey-faced trolls with sharp, gnashing fangs; still others, leather-winged gremlins. Philip recognized them immediately. He'd seen those kinds of things only once before. Back at the mansion, when Becka, Scott, and Ryan had battled demons.

Ryan stepped forward shaking his head. "You guys never give up, do you?"

"Ryan ...," Becka warned.

Ryan nodded, then turned back to the creatures. "So what will it be, boys? Feel like being cast into the lake of fire?" He started toward them.

"Ryan ..."

"Or maybe just a trip into a local herd of swine?" He'd barely gotten the words out when his foot came down on the far edge of the loose sheet of plywood. The sheet dipped, leaving nothing but space under Ryan's feet.

Ryan cried out, clawing at the air frantically, trying to keep his balance. Becka tried to grab his arm, but the other edge of the sheet shot up, catching her in the jaw. Her head snapped back, and she fell to the floor as Ryan dropped through the opening and out of sight. Philip heard his cry, then the sickening thud of his body hitting the second-story floor. Then nothing at all.

"Ryan?" he called. "Are you okay?"

No answer.

He rose and hobbled to the edge of the plywood, where he peered down into the darkness. He couldn't see a thing. "Ry?"

"My ankle ...," came the faint reply. "I think it's broken."

Before he could respond, Philip heard faint movement beside him. He turned to see Becka stirring.

"Beck, you all right?"

Before she could answer, Philip heard another sound.

Little feet. And claws and nails and talons. Scurrying across plywood.

He spun around.

The creatures were coming directly at them! He struggled to his feet. "Becka, look out!"

She was too dazed to move, but she didn't have to worry. The creatures weren't interested in Becka. They were coming at him!

He stepped back, fighting the panic that screamed in his head. He forced all his logic, all his intellect, to the fore. It was okay. He'd seen and heard everything Ryan and Becka had done. Their faith, the power in the way they spoke. He could do that.

He glanced over at Krissi, who now lay motionless.

He had to do it.

Grim resolve filled him again as he looked again at the creatures approaching him. He cleared his throat and, in his most commanding voice, shouted, "I, Philip Andrews, command you—"

"No ...," Becka mumbled, shaking her head.

"It's okay," he answered. "I know what I'm doing." Directing his attention back to the creatures, he shouted, "I command you to stop!"

But they didn't. They were a dozen feet away and closing in fast.

"Stop, I said. I command you to stop!"

They gave no response except for a faint twittering—which sounded suspiciously like laughter.

"Philip," Becka muttered. "You can't—you don't have the authority."

"Stay back!" Philip shouted at them. "I command it!"

Nothing worked. They surrounded him, snapping and clawing at his feet. He tried a different tact. "In the name of Jesus Christ, I command—"

But he never finished. The first one leaped onto his leg. Another followed. He tried to kick them off, but their claws dug deep through his pants and into his calves.

"Augh!" he screamed.

Other creatures joined in, scurrying up his legs and grabbing hold of his waist.

"Beck!" he screamed, fighting and trying to slap them off. "Help me!"

Becka tried to sit up but couldn't. "Stop ...," she choked. But it was unclear whether she was speaking to the creatures or to Philip.

"Beck!"

The frenzied mob had reached his chest, scurrying around and around, pulling themselves onto his shoulders, lashing at his face. Philip staggered. Their paws and talons blocked his vision. He tripped once, twice, then fell to the floor. They swarmed over him relentlessly, tearing at him.

"Help me! Somebody!"

Then another voice spoke out. "In the power and authority of Jesus Christ, I command you to stop!"

The creatures froze.

"Now!"

In a flash, they leaped off Philip and raced for the shadows.

At first Philip didn't recognize the voice, but as he rose to his knees and looked toward the steps, he saw Becka's little brother, Scott.

"Scotty ..." Becka struggled to sit up.

He rushed over to her. "Are you okay?"

She nodded, rubbing her head. "What about you?"

He shrugged. "I—I guess I got a little carried away with that game thing."

"A little?! But you're okay?"

He nodded. "It's not every day you get trashed by a ghoul of the fifteenth degree, but I'm all right now."

A groan from below interrupted them.

Concern flooded Becka's face. "Ryan! He fell ..." She moved to look over the edge. "Ryan? Can you hear me?"

"I'm okay . . . ," came the faint answer.

"Thank heaven."

"We'll be down in a second," Scott called, keeping a careful eye on the moving shadows around them. "We've got a little cleaning up to do here first." Turning to Philip he asked, "You all right?"

Philip nodded, gingerly feeling the scratches on his face.

"Can you get down there and help Ryan out?"

"Sure," he said, then motioned over his shoulder. "But what about those—"

He was interrupted by a choking, gasping sound. He turned—and went ice-cold. It was the most frightening sight he had ever witnessed.

The creatures were racing toward Krissi, who was still on the table. They leaped into the air and dematerialized into clouds of misty vapor . . . a vapor that rushed into Krissi's gasping mouth. One cloud after another after another was pulled in with each ragged breath she took.

"Stop it!" Scott ordered, but he was too late. The last one had already entered her.

Krissi began to shake. Her whole body vibrated on the table. She struggled to turn toward them, her face filled with fear.

Becka rose unsteadily. With Scott's help she moved toward her friend. Philip followed. As they approached, Krissi tried to say something, but no sound came.

"Krissi?" Philip asked cautiously.

He thought she shook her head, but her trembling was so great he couldn't really tell.

Becka and Scott came to a stop a few feet in front of her. Philip knew Krissi wanted—*needed*—to be held, so he continued past them toward the table.

"Wait a sec," Scott said, reaching out and touching his arm. "It's not over yet."

Philip hesitated.

"Krissi?" Becka asked.

The girl's head rotated toward her.

"Do you want those things to leave?"

Anger shot through Philip. "Of course she does! What sort of stupid question is that?"

Becka ignored him and continued looking directly at Krissi. "It has to be your decision, Krissi. Do you want those things to leave?"

Krissi nodded vigorously.

Becka and Scott exchanged glances, then Becka stepped up to the table. She reached out her hand and laid it on Krissi's trembling shoulders. Her words were quiet and simple, but full of a confident faith. "In the name of Jesus Christ of Nazareth ... go."

Krissi's body stiffened. Her head shot back and she let out a violent scream. It seemed to last forever as it echoed through the woods, bouncing back and forth against the trees.

And then she collapsed.

Philip moved in to hold her, and this time Becka and Scott did not stop him. He scooped her body into his arms. It was limp. Whatever had been inside of her was gone. It was over. He buried his face in her hair and fought back the tears.

She stirred against him, and a moment later she was wrapping her arms around his neck. "Oh, Philip," she sobbed. "Philip, it was so awful!"

"It's okay," he soothed in a choked voice. "It's okay. You're safe now."

She clung to him even more tightly. Philip looked over her head at Scott and Becka. He could tell they were beat, but they were smiling. He glanced up to the sky. The hovering craft was gone. So were the lights. Everything was back to normal. He buried his face back in Krissi's hair and hugged her fiercely, overwhelmed by love for her — and gratitude that he had her back.

11

The drive home was long and cramped. Five bruised and battered bodies squeezed together in a Mustang did not make for the most comfortable ride. Of course, the General Store owner had called up the local doctor and had him check them all out. One of the neighbors even offered to let the group spend the night, but no one was too seriously injured and everyone was anxious to get home. So ...

Ryan was in no shape to drive. Something about a cracked rib, a sprained wrist, and a torn ankle ligament made that a little impossible. Philip thought he should stay in the back with Krissi, so that left either Becka or Scott to drive. And since Scott was a couple of years shy of a driver's license, that left Becka.

The Highway Patrol had been called about the Jeep, and Philip had to sign a bunch of papers promising that he and his dad would be back up tomorrow or the next day (something Philip wasn't too thrilled about). But for now they were all heading home.

The episode had been the roughest on Krissi. Not only physically, but emotionally. No one was certain what all she had been through. She didn't want to talk about it, and no one wanted to ask. Not for now. It wouldn't have mattered even if they did. As soon as she hit the backseat and Philip wrapped his arm around her, she dropped off into a deep, sound sleep.

"Will she be okay?" Philip asked.

No one spoke.

"Hello?" he tried again.

Finally Ryan answered from the front seat. "I'm afraid it's not completely over."

"What do you mean?"

Ryan and Becka traded looks. It was her turn to speak. "There's an empty space inside Krissi right now, where this Xandrak guy and his jerks were hanging out."

"You mean the demons?" Philip asked.

Becka nodded. "Unless that space gets filled with something or someone ..." She hesitated. How could she say this diplomatically?

Scott didn't even try. "Then the demons will come back and bring in even more of their buddies."

Philip stared at them in disbelief. "You're kidding. Tell me you're kidding."

Scott shook his head. "It's in the Bible."

Philip sighed heavily. He didn't like that answer. Not one bit. "And by 'someone,' you're talking about Jesus, right?"

"That's right," Ryan answered.

Philip took another breath and slowly let it out. "I tell you, I thought I knew about being a Christian, but there's a lot more to this religious stuff than just showing up at church or asking God for junk."

Ryan nodded. "It's a war. People are fighting for their souls. We're all in it, and we all need help. None of us can do it alone."

"I found that out in a hurry," Philip said, tenderly touching the scratches on his neck and face. "It's been a long time since I've been clobbered like that." A moment passed as he remembered Becka's shining faith—and his own failed efforts. Then he shrugged. "Maybe I'll give religion another fling."

"It's gotta be more than a fling," Ryan said. "Christianity's a way of life, Phil. It's loving God and letting him be your boss. That's what *Lord* means. Christ has to be your boss."

"But other Christians don't do that. They're messing up all the time. Like my mom splitting and leaving me and Dad behind. Talk about a hypocrite."

"We're all hypocrites," Scott said quietly.

Philip turned to him, surprised.

"Think about it. I just wasted the last couple of weeks of my life doing something I knew I wasn't supposed to do."

"And?"

"And it nearly wiped me out. But the cool thing is, when I realized I was wrong, I asked God to forgive me. And he did. I blew it—and I'm forgiven. I mean, if you're really sorry and ask, he'll forgive you of anything. That's the whole point."

Philip glanced about the car. He had a million more questions, but he was too tired to ask. Besides, these guys probably didn't have all the answers. Maybe no one did. Maybe that's where faith came in. The same faith that had saved his life. And Krissi's.

He looked down at her. When she woke, they would talk. He would explain all that had happened, all that he had learned. And maybe, just maybe, the two of them would look deeper into Jesus Christ.

He hoped she'd agree. He leaned back and closed his eyes. He sincerely hoped so.

Three days passed before Becka checked the computer for any messages from Z. And when she did a cold, hard knot formed in her stomach:

Rebecca, Scott: I received an urgent message on the Internet. A young girl in Louisiana is in trouble. She's deeply involved in voodoo and desperately needs your help. You will soon receive airline tickets by mail. Do not be afraid. Your training is complete. Go in his authority. Z

Author's Note

As I developed this series, I had two equal and opposing concerns. First, I didn't want the reader to be too frightened of the devil. Compared to Jesus Christ, Satan is a wimp. The two aren't even in the same league. Although the supernatural evil in these books is based on a certain amount of fact, it's important to understand the awesome protection Jesus Christ offers to all who have committed their lives to him.

This brings me to my second and somewhat opposing concern: Although the powers of darkness are nothing compared to the power of Jesus Christ and the authority he has given his followers, spiritual warfare is not something we casually stroll into. The situations in these novels are extreme to create suspense and drama. But if you should find yourself involved in something even vaguely similar, don't confront it alone. Find an older, more mature Christian (such as a parent, pastor, or youth leader) to talk to. Let them check the situation out to see what is happening, and ask them to help you deal with it.

Yes, we have the victory through Christ, but we should never send in inexperienced soldiers to fight the battle.

Oh, and one final note. When this series was conceived, there were really no bad guys on the Internet. Unfortunately that has changed. Today there are plenty of people out there trying to draw young folks in to dangerous situations through it. Although the characters in this series trust Z, if you should run into a similar situation, be smart. Anyone can *sound* kind and understanding, but their intentions may be entirely different. All that to say, don't take candy from strangers you see … or trust those you don't.

Bill

Bibliography

Bibical references and information used in ***The Haunting*** **came from the following sources:**

Chapter 2

2:04 p.m.

"We are confident, I say, and would prefer to be away from the body and at home with the Lord."

(2 Corinthians 5:8)

"Man is destined to die once, and after that to face judgment."

(Hebrews 9:27a)

Chapter 3

11:54 p.m.

Information on astrology taken from *Hot Topics, Tough Questions* by Bill Myers (Wheaton, Ill.: Victor Books, 1987) 96–97.

Chapter 4

7:10 p.m.

"Jesus had commanded the evil spirit to come out of the man. . . . Jesus asked [the demon], 'What is your name?' 'Legion,' he replied, because many demons had gone into him. And they begged him repeatedly not to order them to go into the Abyss."

(Luke 8:29–31)

"I have given you authority to trample on snakes and scorpions and to overcome all the power of the enemy; nothing will harm you."

(Luke 10:19)

"Whatever you bind on earth will be bound in heaven."

(Matthew 18:18)

"There is no truth in him. When he lies, he speaks his native tongue, for he is a liar and the father of liars."

(John 8:44)

"If two of you on earth agree about anything you ask for, it will be done for you by my Father in heaven."

(Matthew 18:19)

Chapter 11

10:10 p.m.

"I am the way and the truth and the life. No one comes to the Father except through me!"

(John 14:6)

"Resist the devil, and he will flee from you."

(James 4:7)

"The Lord rebuke you!"

(Jude v. 9)

Information used in *The Encounter* came from the following sources:

Chapter 1

Information on UFOs taken from Dr. Hugh Ross, *ETs and UFOs* (Pasadena, Calif.: Reason to Believe, 1990), audiocassette.

Chapter 4

Information on role-playing games and the quote from Gary Gygax (p. 269), the creator of Dungeons & Dragons, taken from Joan Hake Robie, *The Truth about Dungeons & Dragons* (Lancaster, Pa.: Starburst, Inc., 1991), 11, 49, 57, 59.

Chapter 5

Information on UFOs taken from Dr. Hugh Ross, *ETs and UFOs* (Pasadena, Calif.: Reason to Believe, 1990), audiocassette.

Quote from Dr. Jacques Valle (p. 283) taken from Michael Lindemann, *UFOs & the Alien Presence: Six Viewpoints* (Santa Barbara, Calif.: The 2020 Group, 1991), 85. Emphasis on demons added.

Bill Myers
bestselling author
DEADLY LOYALTY
collection
nearly 400,000 FORBIDDEN DOORS books sold

Read a portion of the first chapter of *Deadly Loyalty Collection*, Volume 3 in the Forbidden Doors Series.

1

There was an ominous clunk under the Boeing 737. Rebecca Williams stiffened, then glanced nervously at her younger brother, Scott. He sat on her left next to the window. Although he was her "little" brother, he would pass her in height before long. He had a thin frame like Becka's.

"It's just the landing gear coming down," he said, doing his best to sound like an experienced air traveler.

Becka nodded. She took a deep breath and tried to release her sweaty grip on the armrests. It didn't work. She didn't like flying. Not at all. Come to think of it, Becka didn't like the whole purpose of this trip.

Who did Z, the mysterious adviser on the Internet, think she was, anyway? What was he doing sending her and her brother off to Louisiana to help some girl caught up in voodoo? Granted, they'd had lots of experience battling the supernatural lately. First, there was the Ouija board incident at the Ascension Bookshop.

Becka could never forget how Scott battled that group of satanists! They wanted revenge after Becka exposed Maxwell Hunter, the reincarnation guru. And let's not forget the so-called ghost at Hawthorne mansion, the counterfeit angel, and that last encounter with a phony UFO.

But voodoo in Louisiana? Becka didn't know a thing about voodoo. She barely knew anything about Louisiana.

Fortunately Mom had an aunt who lived in the area, so she'd insisted on coming along with them to visit her. Becka looked forward to seeing her great-aunt once more.

Becka looked to her right, where her mother rested comfortably, her eyes closed. *Good ol' Mom.* Maybe the trip would do her some good. Ever since Dad died she'd been fretting and working nonstop. This trip just might give her the rest she needed.

Clunk ... clunk ... brang!

Then again ...

It was the same sound, only louder. Becka looked to Scott, hoping for more reassurance. "What's that clunking?" she asked.

Scott shrugged. "I don't know, but it's the *brang* that bothers me."

So much for reassurance.

Suddenly the intercom came on. "Ladies and gentlemen, this is your captain speaking. There seems to be a problem with the landing gear ..."

The collective gasp from the passengers did little to help Becka relax.

"I've radioed ahead for emergency measures ..."

Becka felt her mother's hand rest on top of hers. She turned to Mom.

"Don't worry," Mom said. "We'll be all right."

Don't worry?! Yeah, right.

The pilot's voice resumed. "The ground crew is going to spray the runway with foam."

"Foam?" Scott exclaimed. "Does he mean like shaving cream?"

"I'll advise you as the situation develops," the pilot continued. "Please try to remain calm."

CLUNK-CLUNK-BRAAANG!

The sound had grown steadily louder.

Becka looked past Scott out the window. They were flying low over New Orleans and dropping fast. As the plane suddenly banked to the left, she saw the airport and immediately wished she hadn't. Several large tankers sprayed foam on the runway. Fire trucks and ambulances were everywhere.

Now it was the head flight attendant's turn to be on the intercom. "Please make sure your seat belts are fastened securely across your lap. Then bend over as far as you can in the seat, keeping your head down. Hold a pillow to your face with one hand, and wrap your other arm around your knees."

Becka fought the fear down as she glanced at her mother. Mom had her eyes shut. Becka wondered if she was praying. Not a bad idea.

CLUNK-CLUNK-BRAAANG!

Another attendant hurried through the aisle, passing out pillows. She tried to appear calm but failed miserably.

The plane banked back to the right. Becka laid her face down on the pillow in her lap and gave her seat belt another tug.

The intercom buzzed once more with the pilot's voice. "Ladies and gentlemen, we are about to land on the foam ... Please hold on."

CLUNK-CLUNK-BRAAANG!

"Don't be alarmed," he said. "That's just the landing gear ... I'll keep trying it as we come in."

Becka remained hunched over with her face on the pillow. She could feel the plane dropping, and still the landing gear was not coming down. They were going to land with no wheels!

CLUNK-CLUNK-BRAAANG!

CLUNK-CLUNK-BRAAANG!

She glanced at Scott, who stared back at her from his pillow. He tried to force an encouraging grin, but there was no missing the look of concern on his face.

She turned to look at Mom. Her eyes were still closed. Becka hoped that she continued to pray.

CLUNK-CLUNK-BRAAANG!

CLUNK-CLUNK-BRAAANG!

Becka's thoughts shot to Ryan Riordan, her boyfriend back home. If she died, how would he handle the news? And what about her friends—Julie, Krissi, and Philip? How would they handle it? She also thought of Dad—of perhaps seeing him soon. Too soon. It was this final thought that jolted her back to the present and caused her to pray. It wasn't that she didn't want to see Dad again. She just had a few more things to do first.

CLUNK-CLUNK-BRAAANG!

CLUNK-CLUNK-BRAAANG!!

CLUNK-CLUNK-CLUNK-DAARRRRRREEEEEEEE . . .

Something was different!

The plane veered sharply upward. Becka couldn't resist the temptation to sit up and glance out the window.

The pilot spoke once more. "Ladies and gentlemen, the landing gear has engaged. We are out of danger. I repeat. We are out of danger. We will land on a different runway in just a few moments."

"Thank you, Lord," Mom whispered. She sounded relieved as she sat up, then reached over and hugged both of her children. "Thank you . . ."

Becka breathed a sigh of relief as she joined the applause of the other passengers. They were safe. At least for now. But all the same, she couldn't help wondering if this was some sort of omen—a warning of the dangers that were about to begin.

The three o'clock bell at Sorrento High rang. Throngs of kids poured out of the old, weathered building. One fifteen-year-old girl slowed her pace as she headed for the bus. No one talked to her. Her clothes were more ragged than most. They were too shabby to be fashionable and too conservative to be alternative.

Sara Thomas had never fit in. She had never felt like she belonged, no matter where she was. As she approached the school bus and stepped inside, she steeled herself, waiting for the taunts.

None came. Just the usual after-school chatter.

Carefully she took a seat, stealing a glance to the rear of the bus. Ronnie Fitzgerald and John Noey were engrossed in a tattoo magazine.

Maybe they'd forget about her today.

With a swoosh and a thud, the door closed. The bus jerked forward.

Maybe today would be different.

Then again, maybe not. They had traveled less than a mile when it began ...

"Hey, Rags, you shopping at Goodwill or the Salvation Army these days?"

Sara recognized Ronnie's shrill, nasal voice.

"Hey! I'm talking to you."

She didn't turn around.

"I heard Goodwill's got a special on those cruddy, stained sweaters you like so much," John Noey said snidely.

Before she could catch herself, Sara glanced down at the brown chocolate stain on her yellow sweater.

The boys roared.

"Is that from a candy bar or did your dog do a number on it?" Ronnie shouted.

Most of the others on the bus smirked and snickered. A few laughed out loud.

Sara stared out the window as the taunts continued.

As always, she tried to block out the voices. And, as always, she failed. But not for long.

Soon, she thought. *Soon they'll pay. They'll both pay.*

She reached into her purse and clutched the tiny cloth-and-straw doll. Already she was thinking about her revenge.

And already she was starting to smile.

Aunt Myrna's farmhouse was simple but clean. The furniture inside was made mostly of dark wood. The chairs looked like they'd been there a hundred years ... and could easily last another hundred.

After Becka dropped her bags off in the small attic room that she would be using, she headed down to the kitchen, grabbed an apple out of the fruit basket, and strolled out to the front porch. As the screen door slammed, she vaguely heard Aunt Myrna telling Mom something about a farmhand named John Garrett who was supposed to drop by.

It was hot and humid, which reminded her of her childhood days in South America. Several months had passed since Dad's death and their move from Brazil back to California. But the humidity and the smells of the rich vegetation here in Louisiana sent her mind drifting back to the Brazilian rain forests.

Unlike California, everything in Louisiana was lush and wild. Plant life seemed to explode all around. And the water. There was water everywhere—lakes, ponds, and marshes. Although most of the area around the bayou was swamp, even the dry land never really felt dry. Still, it was beautiful.

Even surrounded by beauty, Becka felt nervous. Very nervous. Z had given them so little information. Just that a young girl named Sara Thomas lived in the area and that she was in serious trouble—caught up in some kind of voodoo. Z had also stressed that Becka and Scott were not to be afraid.

"Your training is complete," he had said. "Go in his authority."

His authority. God's authority. Becka had certainly seen God work in the past. There was no denying that. But even now as she looked around, she felt a strange sense of—what? Apprehension? Uncertainty?

During the other adventures, she had always been on her home turf. But being in a strange place, helping somebody she didn't even know ... it all made her nervous. Very nervous.

The late afternoon sun shimmered on the vast sea of sugarcane before her as she sat on the steps. Wind quietly rippled through the cane, making the stalks appear like great scarecrows with arms beckoning her to come closer. Closer. Closer ...

Something grabbed her hand.

Becka let out a gasp and turned to see a small goat eight inches from her face. It gobbled the last of her apple.

"Aunt Myrna!" she shrieked. "There's an animal loose out here!"

"He won't bother you none."

Becka turned, startled at hearing a voice come from the field of sugarcane. She tried to locate the source of the voice while keeping one eye on the goat in case he decided to go for a finger or two.

A young African-American man suddenly walked out of the field. Becka guessed that he was about seventeen. He was tall, lean, and handsome, in a rugged sort of way.

He nodded to the goat. "That's Lukey. He's more pet than farm animal." He entered the yard and stuffed his hands into his pockets. "Try scratching his nose. He likes that."

"Oh, that's okay," Rebecca said quickly. "I'd rather not just now." Then, rising to her feet, she said, "You must be John Garrett. Aunt Myrna said you'd be coming."

The young man nodded. "Miss Myrna said I should be showing you and your brother around the place some."

"So let's get started," Scott said, appearing suddenly in the doorway. "Wow. Cool goat. C'mere, boy." He crossed to the animal. It rubbed its head against his arm. "Hey!" Scott looked up with a broad smile. "He likes me!"

"He likes everybody," John Garrett said, already turning back toward the field. "We better get started if we're going. The foreman's called a meeting of us farmhands. It should be starting pretty soon."

Scott went to walk beside John. Becka fell in behind.

In seconds the two boys were hitting it off. Becka could only marvel. Her brother got along with everybody. In fact, when they'd moved to California, he fit in like he'd always been there. Unfortunately, it wasn't so easy for Becka to make friends. She figured that was partly why she felt so uncomfortable about this trip. She didn't like the idea of barging into a total stranger's life, even if they were supposed to help her.

But that was only part of the reason. There was something else: a feeling. It felt eerie ... like something she couldn't quite explain but couldn't shake off.

"John," she called, trying to sound casual, "do you know anything about voodoo?"

He glanced back at her and laughed. "Not much. 'Cept my grandpa used to speak Gumbo all the time."

"Gumbo?" she asked.

"It's kind of a mesh of African dialects. A lot of the people into voodoo speak it. But you really got to be careful who you talk to about voodoo around these parts."

"Why's that?" Scott asked.

"Lots of folks believe in it, and if you upset them, they'd just as soon drop a curse on you as look at you."

Becka felt a tiny shiver run across her back. "A curse? Does stuff like that really happen?"

"Oh yeah. I heard about this woman who lived down the

road from my father. She made an old *mambo* mad, and the mambo put a curse on her."

"*Mambo?*" Scott echoed with a snort. "Sounds like some kind of dance step."

John shot him a knowing look. "They're like high priestesses. And they're nothing to mess with."

"So what happened to this woman?" Scott asked.

"I heard she suddenly died in horrible pain."

"That's awful!" Becka shuddered. "Did you ever see her?"

John shook his head. "My father's cousin said he did, though. Not only that, I also heard about an old man who refused to pay the *hungan* for helping him get back his wife." At Scott's raised eyebrows John explained. "A hungan is like the male version of a mambo — the high priest. The man who wouldn't pay carried a powerful root with him at all times so the hungan couldn't work magic on him while he was alive. The root was like a good-luck charm. But when he died and they took him to the morgue, his body started shaking all over the place. And when they cut him open, they found he was full of scorpions!"

"Come on — scorpions?" Scott scoffed.

But Becka was not scoffing. In fact she felt more uneasy by the moment. "How about him?" she asked. "Did you see him?"

John shook his head again. "No, that happened before I was born. I know it sounds crazy, but some of this curse stuff might be true."

Scott shook his head, his face filled with skepticism. "I don't know. Sounds pretty fantastic to me. Like something out of a B movie."

"Maybe so," John continued. "But one thing I do know, and that's to never cross Big Sweet. I've heard his magic's powerful."

"Who's Big Sweet?" Scott asked.

"You don't know who Big Sweet is? He's Miss Myrna's foreman. He's head of the harvest crew. Been picking sugarcane all his life. That's why they call him Big Sweet."

"Why's he so dangerous?" Becka asked.

"He's the local hungan. People say his father was a disciple of Marie Leveau. She's called the Queen of Conjure. She was a powerful mambo who used to live in the French Quarter of New Orleans."

"And you're afraid of him?" Becka asked.

"Everybody's afraid of Big Sweet." John turned back to Becka. There was something about his look that caused a cold knot to form deep in her stomach. "Everybody's afraid ... and you'd better be too."

Suddenly a horn bellowed across the fields. John spun toward the sound, looking startled.

"What's that?" Scott asked.

The other boy started moving away from them toward the sound. Becka and Scott exchanged concerned glances. John was clearly very nervous. "That's Big Sweet's horn," he said. "It's his conch shell. The meeting's starting. I gotta go."

"What about showing us the farm?" Scott called as John moved away.

"I can take you into the swamp tomorrow after chores. But I gotta go now."

"Yeah, but— "

"Look, I can't be late. I gotta go." With that he disappeared into the cane.

"John!" Scott called. "Hey, John! Hold on a minute!"

But there was no answer.

Scott turned to Becka. She knew her expression held the same concern she saw in her brother's face. The horn continued to bellow. Finally Becka cleared her throat. "I ... uh ... I guess we'd better head back."

"Yeah. I can't wait to get the lowdown on all this stuff from Z tonight. I'll bet he knows about this Big Sweet guy."

"And Sara Thomas," Becka reminded him.

"Right," Scott said. "But the more we learn about Big Sweet, the faster we'll be able to blow him away."

"Blow him away?" Becka felt herself growing impatient with her brother. "Come on, Scotty. You sound like a Schwarzenegger movie."

"That's me!" Scott threw a few mock karate kicks. "Scott Williams, Demon Terminator."

"Scott, this isn't a joke."

"What's the matter? Afraid Big Sweet may slap a curse on you?"

"Stop it!"

"Afraid he might hatch a lizard in your ear or give you a monkey face? Hmmm, looks like somebody's already done that."

"Scotty!"

"Come on, Beck—lighten up!" Then, looking across the field, his face lit up with an idea. "Let's save ourselves a little time and take a shortcut through the cane."

Becka began to protest, but her brother had already started out. And there was one thing about Scott—when he made up his mind to do something, there was no stopping him. With a heavy sigh, she followed.

The stalks of cane towered over their heads. Becka knew that Scott was right about one thing. By taking this shortcut they'd get back to the house a lot faster. And with all the uneasiness she had been feeling out there, especially now that they were alone ... well, the sooner they got home, the better.

Unfortunately, "sooner" was way too long, now that Scott was in his teasing mode. He kept jumping around and darting between the stalks of cane like some ghoul.

Brothers. What a pain, Becka thought.

"Oogity-boogity! Me Big Sweet. Me cast a big curse on you."

"Knock it off!" Becka muttered between clenched teeth. She was going to bean him if he kept it up.

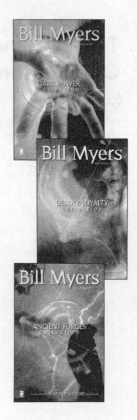

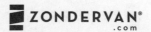

Echoes From the Edge

A New Trilogy from Bestselling Author Bryan Davis!

This fast-paced adventure fantasy trilogy starts with murder and leads teenagers Nathan and Kelly out of their once-familiar world as they struggle to find answers to the tragedy. A mysterious mirror with phantom images, a camera that takes pictures of things they can't see, and a violin that unlocks unrecognizable voices ... each enigma takes the teens further into an alternate universe where nothing is as it seems.

Beyond the Reflection's Edge

Book One

Softcover • ISBN: 978-0-310-71554-2

After sixteen-year-old Nathan Shepherd's parents are murdered during a corporate investigation, he teams up with a friend to solve the case. They discover mirrors that reflect events from the past and future, a camera that photographs people who aren't there, and a violin that echoes unseen voices.

Books 2 and 3 coming soon!

Pick up a copy today at your favorite bookstore!

ZONDERVAN®
.com